Frenched

MELANIE HARLOW

ISBN-13: 978-1496129628

I had resolved to love you no more; I considered I had made a vow, taken a veil, and am as it were dead and buried, yet there rises unexpectedly from the bottom of my heart a passion which triumphs over all these thoughts, and darkens alike my reason and my religion. You reign in such inward retreats of my soul that I know not where to attack you; when I endeavor to break those chains by which I am bound to you I only deceive myself, and all my efforts but serve to bind them faster.

Heloise d'Argenteuil

Chapter One

Top Five Reasons (Out of 100) I Am NEVER Coming Out Of This Blanket Fort

1) 220 hand-engraved invitations.
2) $18,000 hand-pieced Vera Wang gown.
3) 1500 Felicity roses imported from Ecuador.
4) Bridal portrait on the current cover of Wedding Chic magazine.
5) Text message from fiancé calling off dream wedding a week before it happens.

I threw the pen on the floor and propped the pad of paper against my headboard. If anyone managed to get past my locked bedroom door, they could read the list and not pester me, unless they wanted to hear the other ninety-five.

"Mia, please. You have to come out of there." Coco rattled the handle before pounding on the door again.

"No, I don't." I pulled the crisp white sheets over my head and yanked my pillow into the tent with me. Embroidered on the pillowcase in navy thread was TBM, for Tucker and Mia Branch. The monogrammed sheet set had been a wedding shower gift, along with monogrammed towels, a duvet, some throw pillows, a set of luggage, and even a bathrobe. The softest, most comfortable bathrobe in the universe. *Tainted* with Tucker Branch's initials.

"Then you have to let me in."

"Why? Do you have wine?"

"It's nine A.M!"

"And?"

"Mia, please. You don't have to come out. I just want to talk to you. Come on, we'll...make a list or something. You love making lists."

I did love making lists. They calmed me, made me feel like I was in control, on top of things, sticking to a plan. But all over the floor were crumpled and wadded-up lists with titles like Pooping Your Pants in Public and Other Things That Are ALMOST As Humiliating as This But Not Quite and Not 10, Not 50, but 100 Reasons Why Tucker is a Fucker, and I was pretty sure making another one would not make me feel better. "No deal. And who's we? Who else is here? I told you not to let my mother in again."

"No, your mother went back to Chicago. It's just Erin. She's making some coffee."

Coffee sounded pretty good, actually. Maybe not as good as wine, but a close second. I waffled a bit, and Coco sensed my hesitation.

"You can put some Bailey's in it," she coaxed.

Good enough. I threw the sheets off me and slid out of bed, a king-sized monstrosity with a horribly uncomfortable mattress that Tucker bought purely because it was the most expensive one in the store. I told him it was too soft for me, but he's the kind of person who just assumes the most costly brand of anything is always the best. Now I was stuck sleeping in it alone.

Alone, between my expensive TBM-monogrammed sheets on my expensive squishy mattress in an expensive fucking suburban townhouse that I didn't even own. I'd moved out of my cool downtown Detroit loft months ago, and there was a waitlist to get into that building.

FML. That's what I need to monogram on all this shit.

It gave me an idea, which brightened my mood a bit, so after unlocking the door I went into the adjoining bathroom and grabbed my nail scissors from a drawer. I avoided looking at myself in the mirror—I was almost positive I'd showered at least once in the last week, but my curly hair probably looked like I'd stuck my finger in a socket and then been rolled over by a Zamboni. Multiple times.

That's pretty much how I felt, too.

When I emerged, Coco was opening the curtains and cranking open the windows in the bedroom. She wore running shorts and a hoodie, and her long black hair was pulled back in a ponytail.

"Oh my God, Mia. It's so stuffy in here."

"You wanted to come in," I reminded her. I sat on the bed and took one king-sized pillow on my lap. Then I carefully started cutting the monogram from the case.

Coco gasped. "What are you doing? Those are expensive sheets!" She tried to grab the pillow from me, but I held on tight.

"I'm cutting the TBM off this pillowcase. Wait, I guess I could leave the M. Only the Fucker's initials have to go."

Coco sighed and let go, dropping onto the bed beside me. "And this will make you feel better?"

I shrugged as I went back to work. Snip. *Be gone, TB. For fucking ever.* "It might."

"You plan on cutting his name off everything in here?" She glanced around. "It's gonna take a while."

"I've got time. I took a few weeks off, remember? Because I'm supposed to be getting married tonight and going to France tomorrow." The words were so bitter in my mouth I wanted to spit after saying them.

"Well, I can think of a lot more fun things to do than *this* with that time off. Even going to work is better than this." She shook her head and pointed at me. "You're leaving the house today, even if I have to drag you out of here by your hair, caveman style. I can't see you in this depressed funk any longer."

I cocked a brow at her. "Didn't you hear me? It is supposed to be *my wedding day*. Now it's nothing but a gazillion-dollar fiasco."

She looked down her nose at me. "I heard you. And I know. I helped plan your gazillion-dollar fiasco. But it's been a week since Tucker called it off, and you've been holed up in here long enough."

"Yay, you're awake." Erin entered the room with a tray and set it down on the bed. It held three cups of coffee, a pitcher of cream, and a bowl of sugar. One of the cups said Branch Industries on the side and another had a photo of Tucker and me on it, a gift from his little niece, one of the few people in his family I would miss. But Tucker's handsome face made my guts churn.

I gave Erin the stink eye. "Coco said there would be Bailey's."

Erin rolled her eyes but left the room to retrieve the booze.

"It's in the bar cart in the living room!" I called. "Bring the whole bottle!"

"Here. Have some of this, please." Coco handed me a cup with the Devine Events logo on the side, which was the event planning business we ran together.

"I'll wait for the liquor," I told her, going back to my cutting. When the first king-sized pillow was done, I reached for the second. "You know, I don't even like these sheets. I didn't want plain white. I wanted the blue ones with the paisley. A little damn color."

Coco picked up a throw pillow and bunched it under her chin. "Then why'd you register for the white?"

"Because Tucker insisted. He said I could plan the wedding any way I wanted to, but he got to make our interior design choices."

"What's he got against color?" She looked around. Everything in the room was white, navy, or gray.

"Beats me. But the man's favorite color is *pewter*, for fuck's sake. This entire house looks like one giant cloudy-ass day."

The corners of Coco's mouth lifted. "A joke. That's a good sign."

I stopped snipping and met her eyes. "That wasn't a joke."

"Come on, Mia." She took the scissors from my hand and set the mutilated pillowcase aside. "It's time to start getting over this. You know, there's color

6

outside. And wine. And meals. When's the last time you ate something decent?"

I shrugged. "I don't know." The seven days since I'd gotten the Dear Jane text from Tucker were a bit of a blur—I remembered trying desperately to reach him the first day, succeeding on the second when he finally returned my frantic calls (from Vegas, mind you), and a lot of screaming, crying, and phone-throwing after that. Days three, four, and five were a haze of wine and naps and dealing with my mother, and days six and seven were spent wallowing and making lists. And now defacing pillowcases. I glanced at his closet door with a laser beam eye—maybe his precious custom suits would be next.

I was reaching for the scissors again when Erin returned with the Bailey's and poured a shot into each cup. That actually made me smile a little—my girls never let me drink alone.

"OK." She handed Coco the Branch Industries cup and held up the one with the photo on it. "To waking up and starting over."

"Cheers." Coco clinked mugs with Erin. "I was just saying the same thing to her. You have your entire life ahead of you, Mia. And we've already decided this was a blessing in disguise. He didn't deserve you." She touched her cup to mine before taking a sip.

"*You* decided that. I will never feel that this humiliation is anything but punishment."

"Punishment for what?" Erin asked. "What could you possibly need punishing for?"

I groaned. "God, so many things... For ignoring everyone who told me Tucker would never settle down and feeling so fucking superior that I was proving them wrong. For ignoring that little voice in the back of my brain telling me something was off. For refusing to admit to anyone—or even to myself—that everything wasn't perfect between us, and maybe getting married wasn't the right idea."

"Even so, you don't deserve punishment." Erin rubbed my leg. "You're human, Mia. We all make mistakes."

"This was more than just a mistake. I deliberately ignored any sign that I was making the wrong decision. All I could think about was pulling off the dream wedding. And it was nothing but a stupid fantasy." Anger at myself knotted with my wrath for Tucker, pulling my stomach muscles so tight they ached.

"See? That's what I'm saying," Coco soothed. "You knew this was coming, deep down inside. Better to know now before you married him, right?"

I squeezed my eyes shut and lifted the cup to my lips. The bitterness of the French roast laced with the sweetness of Bailey's tasted so good, I took two more big swallows before speaking. "I know. Rationally, I know what you're saying is true, but all I can think about are the thousand little details that were supposed to make this day the biggest, bestest day of my life." I gestured toward my closet door, where a wedding dress still hung, wrapped in its protective bag. "That's my wedding gown over there. Which I paid for myself. Which I should be wearing tonight at five o'clock when four hundred-plus people watch me walk down the aisle on the rooftop of the Ritz. Oh, God—" I gave Coco a panicked look. "Tell me someone called the Ritz."

She rubbed my hand. "Those things were taken care of. And you do so much business with all those vendors, most of them didn't even keep your deposit."

Relief loosened the tension in my shoulders. I'd been so out of it over the past week, I wasn't sure what had been done. I'd had clients cancel a wedding once or twice in my career, but never with only a week to go. "It wasn't *my* deposit. They can keep Tucker's money, for all I care. He won't miss it." I took another glug of coffee. "What about the guests?"

"Done," said Erin. "You've got nothing to worry about except moving forward."

"I'm totally doing that." I lifted up a pillow with a hole in the case. "See?"

Erin paled, not easy for a girl with her fair Irish complexion. "I'm just gonna take that gown out of here, OK honey? Be right back." She set her coffee cup on the tray and grabbed the dress, scurrying from the room with a worried expression.

I watched her go, a vise squeezing my heart. "That dress was *the one,* Coco. I felt it the moment I put it on. Now I'll never wear it again."

"You might," Coco said hopefully. "You never know."

"I won't. I'll die an old maid, cold and alone. I won't even have cats because I'm allergic to them."

She rolled her eyes. "Mia, please. You're twenty-seven."

"But I wanted to be married by twenty-eight, and now that's impossible! I wanted to start a family by thirty, and I'll have to scrap that plan too!"

"Now you just sound ridiculous. Your uterus is not going to shrivel up and die at age thirty."

"Sorry for being ridiculous about my dreams." My chin jutted out. "But that's how I feel."

She rubbed my back. "You want to talk about it some more?"

"What's left to say?"

"I don't know. Are you...are you sad about losing Tucker? Or just about the wedding?"

I swallowed hard. "Both, I guess."

"Do you still love him?"

My first reaction was revulsion, but then his handsome face swam before my eyes. And I could still smell him on the sheets. He always smelled so good, and dressed so impeccably. And he could be thoughtful and generous and fun. We'd had so many plans together, starting tonight. *Tucker, how could you do this to me?* My throat tightened. "No. Yes. I don't know."

"I wish you would have said something about those doubts you had. I feel awful that I didn't sense them. I see you every day. We talked about this wedding nonstop." Her blue eyes were full of guilt.

"It's not your fault. I put on a good show." I shrugged. "People were always saying what a perfect couple we made. I was trying to be that."

"You *looked* perfect," Erin clarified as she returned to the bed. "But no one knows anything about anyone else's relationship for real. Look at my parents—married for twenty years before my mom got sick of his closet alcoholism and mean behavior and left. People were shocked. I can't tell you how many of her friends said to her, 'Your marriage seemed so perfect.'" She shook her head. "They were clueless, even her best friends, because in public he was so charming. She kept it all in because she was embarrassed."

I grimaced and brought my coffee to my lips. "I know *that* feeling."

Coco toyed with her coffee cup. "How was it between the two of you when you were alone? Did things feel right?"

"I guess so. I mean, he's not the most open person in the world. He didn't talk about his feelings a lot, but he did say he loved me. And he was romantic in some ways, always getting me little gifts—or big ones, even—and taking me places and stuff."

"Yeah, he loved showing you off, that was obvious." Erin's tone was harsh. "And showing off how good he was to you."

"But what about when you were *alone* alone?" Coco went on. "Was the sex still good?"

"Not as good as it should have been." I shrugged. "It was OK. He's hot, and he got the job done, I suppose, but there wasn't much variation on the theme."

Erin laughed. "What was the theme?"

"Fast and clean."

Coco choked on her coffee. "What?"

"Yeah," I said, warming to the subject. It actually felt good to finally speak the less-than-perfect truth. "He has two positions he likes, and once we get into one of the Approved Positions, that's how we stay until he's finished—which doesn't take long. He doesn't like moving around because that causes wet spots on the sheets. He has an aversion to bodily fluids."

"Oh my *God*." Erin's jaw hung open. "You must be joking."

"No. And he doesn't like oral sex for the same reason."

"Not even blow jobs?"

I shook my head. "Nope. And forget about the other kind. Oh, and after he's finished, he races to the bathroom to clean himself up. Whether I'm finished or not."

Both of them sat there blinking at me in disbelief. "Holy shit, Mia," Coco said. "I'm pretty sure the universe did you a big favor here. You deserve a way better man than that asshole. I don't care how good looking he is. Or how rich. Any man that jumps out of bed to go clean himself up before making sure his woman is satisfied is a prick."

"Agreed." Erin nodded emphatically. "I wish you had said something about this sooner."

"Why? I wouldn't have listened to reason. I was too busy planning metro Detroit's most glamorous wedding of the year," I said, quoting from the article in Wedding Chic magazine. They'd done a whole profile of me, complete with photo shoot. "Oh, God, that stupid magazine article...all those pictures." I slammed my eyes shut.

"Forget that. No one reads that magazine anyway." Erin put her hand on my arm. "And some other scandal will replace you on Facebook."

I opened my eyes to see Coco glaring at Erin. "It's on Facebook?" They'd confiscated my laptop days ago, probably so I couldn't check social media.

My friends both bit their bottom lips, and Coco glanced to her left, which she always does when she lies. "No, no. She just meant people have sent messages on Facebook hoping you're OK."

"Christ, Coco. You're the worst liar in the world." I set my cup down and flopped onto my back. "It's OK. I'm sure it's all over the Internet that Tucker Branch jilted me a week before the wedding. People love gossip. I'll just have to deal with it."

Silence.

Propping myself on my elbows, I opened one eye and frowned at their nervous expressions. "What?"

"Well," Erin began as Coco's eyeballs flicked to the left again, "it's not so much the gossip as Tucker's post. Uh, posts."

"What posts?"

"He, um, tweeted something about barely escaping a burning building by ditching the ball and chain. And he followed that up with a lot of pics of himself with girls in Vegas."

My stomach lurched. "He didn't."

Coco nodded. "He did."

Dropping my head back onto the pillow again, I flung my arms over my burning face. *Tucker, you bastard. Did you ever really love me? Why did you even propose?*

I thought about the night Tucker had given me the ring, a big, beautiful diamond set in platinum, which he'd had the waiter place into a flute of expensive champagne on our one-year anniversary. At the time I'd loved the spectacle of his getting down on one knee in front of everyone at the restaurant, but I had to admit half of the thrill was because everyone had told me what a playboy he was, that he'd never take me seriously, that he'd break my heart into a million pieces. But he hadn't.

For a solid year we'd had a blast together—whenever we had time, that is. Running Devine Events kept me crazy busy, and he worked a ton of hours as VP of Sales at his family's bolt and screw corporation. Neither of us was particularly clingy or emotionally needy, so we enjoyed each other's company when we could and didn't whine about the times we were apart.

He often said I was the ideal woman for him—beautiful, smart, and low maintenance. Those were his criteria. And I'd thought he was the ideal man—a gorgeous suit-and-tie guy with a master's degree, a trust fund, and a flair for showy romantic gestures in front of an audience. The former drama student in me adored that.

So after downing the champagne, I slipped that ring on my finger and got busy planning a wedding worthy of a princess and playboy heir. I also moved into his townhouse, but even then we didn't make a lot of demands on each other's time.

Maybe we should have.

Maybe you're supposed to want to actually be together more than Tucker and I wanted to. Maybe you should miss each other when you're apart. Maybe the regret you feel after your fiancé calls off your wedding should be more about the man and less about the dress, the roses, and the menu.

(Surf and turf, by the way. Lobster and filet mignon. And the wine…oh good God, the wine.)

I squeezed my eyes shut. "Ugh, I'm so embarrassed. How could I have been so dumb?"

"Come on, Mia," Erin said. "Don't be so hard on yourself." Each of my two best friends took a hand and pulled me up to a seated position. "It was a fantasy, like you said. Anyone would have been caught up in it."

"Well, now it's all just one big fucking waste," I said bitterly. "All that time and money—gone."

They glanced at each other. "You know what we think?" Coco patted my hand.

"What?"

"You should go to France tomorrow."

"What! By myself?"

"Yes." Erin got off the bed and disappeared into my walk-in closet. Before I could ask her what she was doing, Coco started in.

"You've been working nonstop, Mia, and planning your own wedding every spare second. Now you need a vacation, alone. You need time to reflect and think and just get over this."

I blinked at her in disbelief. "And going to Paris alone is going to help me do that? When it was supposed to be my *honeymoon*?"

Frenched

"Don't think of it as a honeymoon." Erin appeared with my big old suitcase, the only one that was not monogrammed with TBM. The bright red one that I'd taken on all our girl trips—just the sight of it made me perk up a little. "Think of it as Tucker's parting gift to you—an all-expenses-paid luxury send-off!"

"I can't. That wasn't the plan."

"Fuck the plan for once, Mia!" Coco bounced off the bed and gestured dramatically. "Just do it! Think of *Paris*—think of all the things on your list you've always wanted to see! Those things are still there, and they'll look the same even without Tucker at your side. In fact, they'll look better."

It was true, I did have a Paris list. I had several, actually. One for dining, one for drinking, one for shopping, one for museums and cathedrals, one for outdoor attractions, one for romance…the idea soured in my mind. "No. It was going to be my honeymoon, goddammit. All I'd do is sit around drinking wine and brooding that this was supposed to be the most romantic week of my life and instead I'm there alone."

"But think of how good that wine will be!" Erin smiled so brightly I almost laughed. "You're just going to do the same thing if you sit around here for the week. Why not do it in view of the Eiffel tower?"

"The Louvre!" Coco added, clapping her hands.

"The Pont Neuf!"

"Notre Dame!"

"The Arc de Triomphe!"

"OK, OK, please." I put up my hands to stop the ad campaign. "Please don't start singing The Marseillaise. I get it. France is awesome. Yay France. I'm just not up for it. And you know how I am about flying."

"I'll give you a sleeping pill. You're going." Erin put the suitcase on the bed and unzipped it. "Now let's pack your bags. This trip is paid for, and if you don't go, then Coco and I are going, and we might love it so much we'll decide we're a lesbian couple and stay there without you."

"You're so not her type," I said. But I allowed her to pull me to my feet. "Coco goes for tall, dark, and tattooed. That little heart above your ass doesn't count."

Erin smiled sweetly. "But it's *Paris.* Anything can happen there."

"And I just thought of another benefit," Coco added. "Your mother will be a whole country away. You destroyed your phone and we stole your computer, so she won't even be able to get a hold of you."

I chewed my lip. That was a benefit—my mother's anxiety drove me nuts even when she didn't have to deal with the fact that her daughter's wedding was just canceled.

Frenched

"Go to Paris, Mia." Coco's eyes pleaded with me. "You've been talking about it since you were a kid."

"If you're miserable, you can hop on a flight home—my mom will change your ticket for nothing," promised Erin, whose mother worked for Delta. "But at least you can say you've been there."

I hesitated. Could I do it, really?

"If you don't, I'm telling your mother to come back to Detroit because you need her."

I shot Coco a murderous look. "OK, OK, I'll go. To the most romantic city on earth. Alone."

They squealed and clapped their hands. "Good girl," Coco said. "Now let's get you packed, and we're putting in all the sexy little outfits you had planned—I *know* there's an outfits list here somewhere."

"I'll bet French men don't jump out of bed to clean up right after sex," added Erin.

"Please. I'd be happy just to stray from the Approved Positions." I stretched a little and actually felt a flutter of excitement in my stomach, which was odd because I am not a person who can fly by the seat of her pants and enjoy it. I am a planner, a list-maker, a think-it-through-in-advance kind of girl. But for once, I was going to do something spontaneous.

Maybe I'd even enjoy it.

Chapter Two

This was a horrible idea.

As the airplane shuddered and swayed from side to side, I closed my eyes and clutched my roiling stomach.

3 Things I Always Wanted to Do in Paris, But I Died Getting There

1) Sip champagne in view of the Eiffel Tower.
2) Shop at the Clignancourt flea market.
3) Make out in the rain without worrying about an umbrella.

I opened my eyes and frowned. Even if I managed to make it to Paris alive, I'd have to scratch the whole kissing-sans-umbrella bit off the list since this was no longer a romantic vacation. The rainy liplock fantasy was actually very unlike me, since I always plan ahead and don't tend to get caught in inclement weather without proper raingear. But there's just something so romantic about being swept away by a kiss in the middle of a downpour, so swept away that you don't even care you're getting wet—in fact, that only makes it better.

Once, one time, when we were first dating, Tucker and I were hiking near Tahquamenon Falls when it began to drizzle, and we made out for about thirty seconds, but the whole experience was sort of ruined by the way he kept wincing and glancing skyward at the darkening clouds. He could be kind of fanatical about his hair. Truth be told, I couldn't stop thinking about my hair either, because I'd just blown it out that morning, and it's such a chore. So I was sort of glad when Tucker said, "I'm getting wet, babe. Did you bring an umbrella?"

Of course I'd brought an umbrella. I always bring an umbrella.

The plane lurched again and I clenched the armrests with both hands. "Oh!"

The woman next to me patted my white knuckles on the armrest between us. "It's just some turbulence. We'll be through it in a few minutes."

Or we'll all suffer death by unnatural impact with the Atlantic Ocean. That could happen too.

But I just nodded, unable to speak.

Oh God, why did I think I could do this alone?

Somewhere in my purse was the sleeping pill Erin had given me, but I was paralyzed with fear and couldn't seem to let go of my armrests.

"See? All smooth now."

I looked over at the woman with the soothing voice. She was about my mom's age, maybe a little older, with a neat gray cap of hair, beautiful skin, and a stylish blue scarf wrapped around her neck.

She's sitting in Tucker's seat.

Shoving that unwelcome thought from my head, I smiled weakly. "Nervous flyer."

She nodded. "I have a friend like that too. Never flies anywhere without a stiff drink first to calm her nerves."

"That sounds good."

"Let's get you one then. What's the point of sitting in first class if you can't get a little tipsy before dinner?" She smiled, revealing beautiful white teeth.

She signaled the flight attendant, who brought us champagne in glass flutes a few minutes later. Trying not to gulp, I imbibed the fizzy golden liquid quickly, and my glass was refilled just as fast. Gradually, a warm buzz replaced the clammy anxiety.

"First time to Paris?"

I nodded. "Yes. It was...a gift. The trip was a gift." I couldn't bring myself to tell her about Tucker. "I'm just a little unsure of myself, traveling alone."

Frenched

"What a wonderful gift! I'm Anneke, by the way."

"Mia."

"Nice to meet you, Mia. And don't be scared; I travel alone quite often. I think every woman should take a trip just for herself, by herself, at least once in her lifetime. Just be careful and smart and enjoy yourself." Her smile widened. "Paris is magical."

"Good." I swallowed some more champagne. "I could use a little magic."

#

Arriving with a hangover was so not on the Paris list.

Neither was an argument with my mother.

She picked up the phone on the first ring and shrieked hello. "Mia? Is that you? What's wrong? Are you OK?" She thought my decision to travel to Europe by myself was ludicrous and she was positive I was going to be attacked, kidnapped, and sold into sex slavery.

I held the phone away from my ear. "I'm fine, Mom. You said to call when I arrived, and I did."

"You don't sound fine at all."

"I'm just tired, OK? I'm tired and hungry and I have to unpack." And cry. There was definitely crying ahead. Maybe throwing things.

"How's the room?"

I looked around the gorgeously appointed Junior Deluxe Suite at the Plaza Athenee. Tucker knew how to travel in style, I'll say that much. The king-sized bed was laden with pillows, the seating area was spacious and elegant with its Louis XIV style furniture, and the view into the quiet inner courtyard was charming. Goddamn birds were chirping right outside the window.

In French, no less. C'est magni-fucking-fique.

"The room's amazing. But Mom, I have to go, OK? I'm exhausted."

"OK, darling. But don't take a nap, remember, otherwise your body won't adjust to the time difference and you'll be miserable for days. I learned that lesson the hard way. And I don't think you should go wandering the streets alone at night so maybe do some sight-seeing now. Or go get a massage at the spa or something. You sound so tense."

My head threatened to burst. I couldn't even speak. Stop talking, Mother.

She sighed. "This was a bad idea. You're not well. I wish you'd have let me come with you. Maybe I should meet you in Paris. We can do some shopping, or—"

Frenched

I found my voice, fast. "NO! No, Mom. I'm fine. Seriously."

"Well, I just don't feel right about this."

I forced myself to sound cheerful. "Listen, the sun is shining, my suite is beautiful, and I can even see the Eiffel Tower out my window," I lied. "I'm dying to get out in the air. I'm going to unpack a few things and take a stroll."

"You're sure?"

"I'm sure. And I need the alone time, OK? So I'm not going to be calling you every five minutes."

"Don't be silly, dear. Once a day is fine."

I gritted my teeth. "Fine. Once a day."

"I'm just worried about you, Mia. You've never traveled this far alone before. You've always had me or the girls or Tucker with you. And you're not in your right frame of mind, either. Women make poor decisions when they're stressed and heartbroken. Did you pack those pills I gave you?"

"I have them, Mom." No sense telling her I planned on self-medicating with wine, not Prozac. "I'll talk to you tomorrow."

"All right. Love you."

"Love you too.

Finally, we said goodbye and I flopped in a heap on the bed. I'd promised Coco and Erin I'd call one of them and let them know I'd arrived without mishap but I didn't think I could hold back tears if I heard their voices. Jet lag and loneliness overwhelmed me, and my eyes filled. This was not the way I'd planned to start off my trip, with a pounding headache and a sinking feeling that coming here by myself was a mistake. I was too tired to unpack my bags, too cranky to pull out my Paris guidebooks and get excited, and too miserable to write in the travel journal Coco and Erin had given me.

Everywhere I looked there were reminders that this was supposed to be a romantic trip for two: the twin closets, the bottle of champagne and two glasses on the desk, the vase of beautiful peach roses on the coffee table. My chest tightened at the sight of those flowers as I recalled the 1500 Felicity roses that had been sacrificed for my nonexistent wedding.

Even the incredible white marble bathroom depressed me with its fluffy his and hers robes and side-by-side sinks in the vanity. I returned to the bed, crawled in, and lay my cheek on a striped satin pillow. My eyelids felt heavier than my suitcase. I wanted a nap, and goddammit, I was going to take a nap, no matter what my mother said about jet lag. As I drifted off to sleep, I made a list.

Things and People That Can Fuck Off

1) Jet Lag, for obvious reasons.
2) Anneke, for suggesting champagne on the flight.

3) Air France, for turbulence that made me drink suggested champagne.
4) My mother, for telling me to take drugs instead of a nap.
5) Tucker. For everything. Repeatedly.

#

After a four-hour nap, I felt revived, my head clearer. I splashed some water on my face, drank a giant bottle of Vittel, and heaved my suitcase on a stand in order to unpack it.

Living out of a suitcase is impossible for me, even if it's just for a week or so. I can't stand the way everything gets unfolded and jumbled up inside, and it's too hard to keep clean and dirty clothes separated. Plus, unpacking and organizing gives me a ridiculous kick. I love it so much that Coco sometimes says I should have been a professional closet organizer, but who wants to spend their career in people's closets?

I plugged my iPod into the dock on the desk and scrolled to my Paris playlist. As Frank Sinatra crooned April in Paris, I actually hummed along while I unzipped my garment bag and hung dresses, blouses and two skirts. From my suitcase pouches I pulled out sneakers, flats, and two pairs of heels, and set them in the closet. I placed lingerie, pajamas, jeans, tops, and socks in drawers, scowling only once at the sexy black Aubade bra and panties I'd purchased for this trip. They'd cost me roughly the same as a car payment but I'd wanted to surprise Tucker, who appreciated luxury items. Vowing to put them on at least once during the next ten days, even if I just pranced around my hotel room in them by myself, I tucked them in alongside my usual cotton underwear and basic bras.

By the time I pulled my toiletries from my bag and began setting them up in the gorgeous white marble bathroom, my steps were light and bouncey, the way they are when something makes me truly happy.

The last thing I did was take out my guidebooks and set them up on the desk. Coco and Erin hadn't let me have my iPad back, but they had let me print the daily itineraries I'd created and take a few books with me. I spread them out and stared at them before sweeping them all back into my suitcase and stowing it in the closet. Fuck it, I'm going to wander tonight, like Anneke said. I'm going to change my clothes, walk out the door, and just see where my feet take me.

But first I had to check my outfit calendar to see what I'd planned to wear this evening.

One step at a time, right?

Chapter Three

My first evening alone in Paris started out fine. Since I hadn't eaten and was getting hungry, I thought about ordering room service but then decided to brave eating alone in a restaurant—something I'd never done before. Wearing a sweet little strapless flowered dress with a denim jacket and flats, I slung my bag over my shoulder with only my wallet, bottle of water, a street map of Paris, and my camera inside. I had no plan whatsoever and surprised myself by adoring the little kick of freedom it gave me.

Heading down Avenue Montaigne with a spring in my step, I gravitated toward the Eiffel Tower, crossing over the Seine on the Pont de l'Alma and trying not to grin like an idiot while *I'm crossing over the Seine!* ran through my mind. I felt like shouting it. On the other side, I followed the river toward the tower, and even if I'd wanted to hide my smile, I couldn't do it.

It was just so incredible! The actual *Eiffel Tower*, right there, huge and monstrous and beautiful, looming above me bigger and bigger as I got closer. No matter how impressive it looks in photographs or movies, nothing compares to actually seeing it in person, watching the sun set behind it. I felt a quick tug of regret that I was seeing it by myself, but only because I knew that later on, no words would ever be enough to describe how gorgeous the light was, how small I felt beneath the arches, how my heart raced when I thought, *I'm really in Paris.*

I wanted to climb to the top, but my stomach was growling so fiercely that I couldn't ignore it. Unwilling to spend any more time indoors, I found a sandwich stand, ordered ham and cheese on half a baguette, and ate it as I walked back toward the tower.

When I was done, I took a few pictures from the ground before climbing the seven hundred steps to the second floor and taking a lift up to the top. I exited the elevator wild with anticipation and went straight for the railing. When I looked out, I couldn't help gasping. The guidebooks hadn't lied—the view of Paris at twilight was breathtaking. And even if I was on my own in the most romantic city in the world, it was still full of beauty and history and culture. I'd take it all in, as much as I could in one week, and I wouldn't have to worry about what anyone else wanted to do at any moment. There would be no Tucker to rush me through museums because he doesn't like art, or roll his eyes at seeing yet *another* cathedral, or yawn his way through an opera. The entire city was at my feet, and it had plenty to offer. To hell with romance!

Grinning at my new positive attitude, I looked to my left just in time to see a gorgeous young couple take a selfie of themselves kissing with the view behind them. My lips drooped as I turned away.

No, don't turn away. Their love did not come at the expense of your own.

A few deep breaths later, I was fine. I even smiled at them.

See? You can do this.

To celebrate making peace with my first adventure as an Independent Woman, I went to the champagne bar, ordered a glass, and made a silent toast. *To being in Paris, a dream come true.*

My throat was still tingling from the bubbles when I heard a gasps and murmurs in the crowd behind me. I turned around and saw a young man down on one knee in front of a beautiful girl, whose fingertips were pressed to her lips. Wide-eyed, I watched as the man took a ring box from his coat pocket and opened it up.

Oh my God. This can't be happening.

I glugged my champagne, taking in the scene with bug-eyed disbelief. I mean, really? Just when I decided Paris didn't have to be all about the romance, a proposal takes place ten feet away from me? I couldn't hear what he said, but I saw her nod happily as he slid the ring on her finger. "Yes!" she cried, and the entire crowd burst into applause and wild cheers as the woman leaned down and kissed her new fiancée.

Smiling half-heartedly, I set my glass down and slipped through the crowd toward the lift, a lump lodged in my throat where the bubbles had lingered just moments before.

I tried to perk myself up with a stroll along the Seine, but my Independent Woman positivity had fizzled.

Everywhere I looked I saw couples in love.

Fucking *everywhere.*

Holding hands on the bridges, sneaking a kiss on cozy street corners, whispering to one another in whatever languages they spoke, exchanging secret smiles, ducking into bars and restaurants, laughing at all the unattached losers in the city—at least that's what it felt like to me.

I shuffled aimlessly along the river, which looked brooding and gloomy now that the light had faded. Eventually I meandered down Boulevard St. Germain and into what I guessed was the Latin Quarter. The sights, sounds, and smells of the bustling streets should have cheered me up, but the area was full of young people, and somehow my gaze still went to every clinging couple.

Damn you, Tucker. That should have been us.

Frenched

With every step, anger ran hotter through my veins. A little voice in my head told me I was being stupid, I didn't really want Tucker here, and I probably looked like an ill-tempered toddler, stomping down the street with my arms crossed and a scowl on my face, but I didn't care. I was mad at Tucker for jilting me, mad at myself for letting it get to that point, mad at Coco and Erin for making me come here alone, mad at all the couples I'd seen, mad at France, mad at love.

I was also lost. Uncrossing my arms, I stopped walking and looked around, but I saw no major landmarks or street signs. It was dark, and though I hated the thought of pulling out my map and marking myself as a pathetic tourist, what else could I do? Panic tightened my chest, and I forced myself to take a few deep breaths and calm down before the scenarios my mother had worried about infiltrated my brain.

OK, that's it. I need wine.

I walked one more block and, as luck would have it, found myself passing a building with English words painted on it: The Beaver Bar & Grill. Upon closer inspection of its signage, I discovered it was a Canadian sports bar. Pausing a moment to consider, I decided I wasn't mad at Canada, beavers, or sports, so I went in and glanced around.

It was a small place, not noisy or crowded, just a few people sitting along a long wooden bar on the left and a group or two at tables in the rear. Eyeing all the patrons carefully, I looked for couples kissing or whispering or groping each other, anything that might signal an engagement was imminent, but didn't see much love in the air. Most people seemed to be drinking tall glasses of beer and watching a hockey game on a large television in the back or the one over the bar.

"You looking for someone?"

Surprised that I'd been addressed in English, I glanced to my left, where the bartender stood drying a beer glass and watching me with an amused smile. In maybe his late twenties, he had a head full of messy longish curls and a prominent jaw covered with dark scruff.

"I'm sorry, what?"

"You had a very determined expression on your face. Are you looking for someone?" He raised his brows as he repeated the question, and I detected only the barest trace of an accent.

"How did you know I spoke English?"

One side of his mouth hooked up. "I know an American when I see one."

For some reason the comment bugged me. What was so obviously American about me? I wasn't wearing a Nike t-shirt or white sneakers or a baseball cap. I parked my hands on my hips and blew hair out of my face. "I could be Canadian."

"Nah." He shook his head and set the glass down.

"What makes you so sure?"

"A Canadian would've just answered the question."

Bristling a little, I dropped my hands and squared my shoulders. "No, I am not looking for anyone."

"Oh. The way you were scavenging the crowd with those big eyes, I thought maybe you were here to catch your boyfriend with somebody else."

"I do not have a *boyfriend*!"

He held up his hands. "Sorry. Or girlfriend, whatever. I just meant you looked like you knew what you came in for, but it wasn't a good time."

"For your information, that is *exactly* what I came in for." I marched over to the closest barstool and sat down with a huff. "And no, I don't have a girlfriend either. I'm alone. *Alone*," I repeated even louder, drawing stares from the few patrons sitting at the bar. One got up and moved to the next stool down, farther away from me. "Is that OK with you?"

"Love, it's all OK with me. Why don't you tell me what you want to drink?"

"Don't use that word."

"What word?"

"Love," I spat.

"Sorry, I just haven't learned your name yet."

"That's not what I meant. I don't care what you call me, I just don't want to hear any more about love tonight, or see it, or smell it in the goddamn air."

He nodded. "That bad, huh?"

"Yes. That's what I was doing when I came in, making sure there were no obvious couples in love in here. They're fucking everywhere in this city. You can't even walk down the street without seeing people hanging all over each other, kissing and hugging and being fucking happy together. It's like a crime to walk down the street alone."

"There's plenty of people alone here."

"Not that I've seen."

He shrugged. "Well, Paris is a romantic place."

"Paris can kiss my ass."

"Why don't I get you a drink, um…"

"Mia."

"I'm Lucas." He offered his hand across the bar, and I shook it. "So what's your pleasure, Mia?" He smiled and called a greeting in French to some people entering the bar behind me.

"A plane ticket back to Detroit. I want to go home."

"Well. Can't help you there, but I bet you can grab a flight tomorrow. And since it's your last night in Paris, let me pour you a glass of wine."

"It's my *first* night in Paris," I said miserably. "*And* my last."

His brown eyes went wide. "In that case, the wine's on me. Hang on."

Moving to the far end of the bar, he pulled a wine bottle off a shelf and poured a glass. I watched as he filled a few drink orders for other people, and noticed he spoke French with everyone but me. Although my ear wasn't expert by any means, he sounded like a native speaker. And yet he also spoke English with a pretty good American accent. I had to admit I was a little curious about him.

Propping my chin in my hand, I looked him over more carefully. He wasn't tall or built like Tucker, but he was slender and possibly muscular in a less obvious way. He had a trim waist and a cute butt, shown off nicely in gray pants worn more fitted than Tucker wore his. Too bad he was such a mess above the shoulders, though—that scraggly hair probably hadn't been washed in days, and even though he had nice full lips, you could barely see them with all the scruff on his face. I thought he could be handsome if he'd invest in a razor and a good haircut.

My taste in guys is clean-shaven and neatly coiffed with a pretty face, which was Tucker Branch to a T. He was as vain as any woman I knew, worked out daily and spent hours in front of a mirror, but it never bothered me. His careful attention to his appearance meant he cared what I thought; he wanted to look good for me. As the memory of his hard, cut body underneath his gorgeous custom suits infiltrated my brain, I experienced a pang of regret. *God, he's just so good-looking. Those blue eyes. The sculpted abs. The smell of his neck when he'd cover my body with his.*

"Here you go." Lucas set down a glass of red wine, generously poured. I liked how the outside corners of his brown eyes got a little crinkly when he smiled, but he was no Tucker Branch. *I'll bet he doesn't smell as good either.* But Coco might have liked Lucas; he was more her type. I wondered if he had any tattoos.

"Thanks." I offered a small, tight-lipped smile, and he winced.

"Jesus Christ, Mia. It can't be that bad."

"Oh, yes it can."

He leaned forward onto his elbows. "Try me."

I took a deep breath. "OK. But wine first." Lifting the glass to my lips, I took a hefty drink. It was delicious—big and earthy and velvety on my tongue. "This is incredible," I told him before taking another sip.

His smile deepened. "I'm glad you like it."

After a few more swallows, I set the glass on the bar with a clink, but I didn't let it go. I stared at my fingers on the stem as I admitted, "This trip to Paris was supposed to be my honeymoon. But my fiancé called off the wedding."

Without a word, he walked to the end of the bar, grabbed the wine bottle from the shelf and poured more into my glass, replacing what I'd drunk.

I looked up at him gratefully. "Thanks. It's been rough."

"I'm sorry. Was it a total shock?"

I sighed. "Yes and no. If I'd been honest with myself, I think I would've realized that things weren't

38

perfect. But I was so caught up in planning the perfect wedding that I didn't want to admit the marriage might be a mistake."

Lucas nodded, leaning on the bar again. "Did he give you a reason? I'm sorry, I don't mean to pry."

"It's OK." I paused to drink some more wine before going on. "It's nothing earth-shattering, really. He said he loved me, but that he wasn't ready to get married yet."

"And you were?"

"Sure. I mean, I'm twenty-seven, almost twenty-eight. I've always planned on being married by that age, and, you know…" I lifted my shoulders. "We were in love. We were the perfect couple."

"Clearly."

I narrowed my eyes. Was he making fun of me? "All I meant was I thought we were a good match at the time. I could totally see our life together."

"You had that all planned out too, huh?"

I didn't care how good the wine was, Lucas was starting to get on my nerves. While I wondered how to respond, several customers needed his attention and then more people came in the door, keeping him busy for the next twenty minutes. I didn't mind, though—his last couple remarks had pissed me off. And I had bigger problems than a rude bartender, like what to do with my miserable self for the rest of the week.

Trying to be positive again, I made a list.

Things I Like About the Trip So Far

1) Seeing the Eiffel Tower
2) This glass of wine.

And then I stopped, because I couldn't even think of a third item for the list. Earlier I'd told my mother that I needed the alone time, but now I wasn't sure I could handle it. But what could I do? Go home tomorrow and admit to Coco and Erin that I wasn't as strong as they thought I was?

How depressing.

After another gulp of wine, I considered giving in to my mother and letting her fly over here and join me—maybe having someone to see the city with would help me feel less alone. Just as quickly as it came to me, I tossed out that idea, knowing that I could not tolerate my mother's nervous nagging for a solid week. If Coco or Erin could fly over I would stay, but I knew that was impossible. Coco was running Devine Events on her own while I was gone, and Erin was a teacher. There was no way she could drop everything and come to Paris. But who else was there? My dad?

I considered it as I rolled the last sip around in my mouth. My dad lived outside Detroit too, and he and I got along great, but he was remarried with young children. For that reason alone, I couldn't see him taking off for a week, even if he could get time off from his law practice, which wasn't likely at such short notice. But knowing my dad, who didn't say anything to me when I told him about Tucker, just held me and let me sob, he'd rearrange anything he could to in order to get here and be with me. I couldn't do that to him.

An Imagine Dragons song that Tucker and I had both liked came over the speakers, and I slumped lower on my barstool. *That's it—I'm just gonna go home. This is too painful.* And it wasn't like I'd be out any money. Tucker had called Coco, who let it go to voicemail but played me the message, telling her that he wanted me to take the trip and I could use the credit card he'd given me for any expenses while I was here. He really must have been feeling guilty, because he also said I could stay in the townhouse as long as I needed to. He'd be in Vegas for another week and then he'd stay somewhere else until I moved out.

God, moving out…

Tears filled my eyes and I hunted in my bag for a tissue. Lucas returned and wordlessly refilled my glass before being called over to the register by a waitress in a tight t-shirt. I wiped my eyes and blew my nose, embarrassed to be blubbering in front of strangers in public.

But at least I had wine.

I drank the second glass even faster than the first, but I was still surprised at the buzz I had when it was empty. Maybe French wine had a higher alcohol content or something? I knew nothing about wine; mostly I just knew how to describe what I liked best—big, full reds like this one where the fruit isn't overwhelming and there's a hint of something earthy or smoky. *Maybe I'll take a wine course when I get back. Knowing more about wine would be helpful for work.* And Coco had always wanted me to take that gourmet cooking class with her. I could do that as well. In fact, all the time I'd spent planning my wedding, I could now spend doing new things, meeting new people.

Feeling better now that the decision had been made, I dug my credit card out of my wallet and signaled Lucas that I was ready to go.

Chapter Four

He smiled at me as he approached, and it was so friendly and apologetic, I forgot that I was annoyed with him.

"Give me one second." He filled a tall glass with beer from the tap. "Don't go anywhere."

Where the hell would I go? I still had no idea how to get back to the hotel from here—I'd have to ask him. A few more minutes passed before Lucas got a break, but by then another bartender had shown up to work.

"Sorry about that." Lucas dried his hands on a towel and came back to my end of the bar. "Can I pour you another glass?"

I bit my lip. "I probably shouldn't. It's really good, though. What is it?"

"It's a wine from the Rhône Valley, where I'm from."

43

"I wondered if you were French. You speak English so well, you could almost pass for American."

"French mom, American dad," he explained. "I was born here but raised in both places."

"Where in the U.S did you live?" Maybe it was the wine, but I was curious about him.

"In upstate New York mostly, but I live in the city now."

I smiled. "I love New York City. But I hate flying, and New York's a long drive from Detroit."

"You hate flying, yet you want to get on another plane first thing in the morning?"

"I have to."

"No, you don't."

Shaking my head, I insisted, "Yes, I do. You don't understand."

"Sure I do. Your fiancé called off the wedding and you're angry and sad or whatever because you're getting close to your marriage deadline or whatever, but that doesn't mean you can't have a good time here. You came all this way, even though you hate to fly. There must have been a reason."

Oh, yeah. *That's* why I was annoyed with him.

Aggravated anew, I sat taller on my seat. "The *reason* was that I've always wanted to see Paris. It's been a dream of mine since I was a kid. I had every day planned out, I knew exactly what we would do, the things we would see. And I thought I could handle it on my own, but now that I'm here, I can't, OK? I can't handle all the love and romance and fucking happiness all around me when I was supposed to be here on my honeymoon! It isn't fair!" My voice was rising and several people glanced my way, especially since I thumped my hand on the bar with my last word. But how dare he ruin my buzz and the tenuous peace I'd made with myself about going home!

He shrugged. "Lots of things in life aren't fair. Doesn't matter what city you're in."

I rolled my eyes as all the attitude progress I'd made during my second glass of wine came undone. "Spare me the platitudes. I've heard a boatload of them in the week since I was unceremoniously dumped—via text message, mind you—seven days before my goddamn wedding."

Lucas regarded me carefully. "You've got a problem."

Brilliant, this asshole. "Yes. My problem is that I'm on my honeymoon, *alone*."

"That's not your problem."

My jaw fell open. Who the hell was he to tell me what my problem was? He went on before I could protest.

"Your problem is that you thought things were going to be one way and they're not. You're not even telling me you miss the guy who was supposed to be here with you. You just don't want to be here alone because that wasn't the plan."

"That is not what I said!"

He laughed. "That's exactly what you said."

"Well…" I flapped my hands. "That's not what I meant. I'm flustered. And drunk."

"So you *do* miss him? Because I don't see a heartbroken girl here in front of me. I see someone who's angry that her relationship ended badly mostly because it ruined an *idea* she had about the perfect life. And she flew all the way here, but even Paris isn't enough to distract her from the fact she didn't get exactly what she wanted when she wanted it."

"It was more than an idea! It was *real*. At least, it felt real…most of the time." My spine curled as the fight left my body. Even my voice weakened. "But what do I know?"

He spoke softer too. "Want to know what I think?"

"No."

He held up his hands. "Fair enough."

I put my credit card on the bar. "I want to pay my bill and leave."

"The wine is on the house."

"Because you feel sorry for me?" I snapped. *God, Mia, just shut up.* Why I was letting this guy get to me, I had no idea. Wasn't I in this bar because I felt sorry for myself?

He hesitated before answering. "Yes. Originally, I felt sorry for you because some asshole treated you wrong. But now that I know a little more, I think he did you a big favor. Now I feel sorry for you

46

because you're going to let one bad day ruin a dream that you've had for such a long time. You know, if you leave tomorrow, I bet you never come back. I bet you'll always think of Paris as a miserable, lonely place."

I opened my mouth to argue and then closed it. Was he right? Was I letting one bad day speak louder than a lifetime of dreaming about Paris?

"But I'd also bet you're stronger than you think."

I met his eyes, and they were serious. Was he right? I'd known coming here wouldn't be easy, but I'd gotten on that plane. Cocking my head, I asked, "Were you a psych major or something?"

He grinned. "Double major—music and psychology. Graduate degree in psych. Look, I know we just met, and I do tend to analyze people and open my big mouth when I should probably just keep my opinion to myself. But when you walked in here alone and looked around, I thought, *There is a woman who knows what she wants.* That confidence is sexy."

"But I'm not confident." The words came out like a whimper as I stared down at my left hand, where my ring used to be. I wondered where it was now—I'd thrown it in the toilet, but Coco had rescued it.

"Yes, you are. You're just a little scared right now."

Exhaling, I looked up at him through my lashes. "You argue with everything I say. It's really annoying."

"Sorry. Let me make it up to you."

"How?"

He thought for a moment. "Well, let's make a deal. You agree to give Paris one more day, and I'll agree to spend the day being your tour guide—no psycho-analysis, I promise. If you're still miserable even when you have a friend by your side, you can grab a flight home the next day. I'll even call the airline for you."

"A friend, huh?"

"You think about it." He moved down the bar to fill drink orders, and I checked out his ass again. It really was cute. And though he wasn't my first choice for a travel companion—I'd rank him somewhere above my mother and below Coco and Erin—the offer was sort of sweet, and I figured he'd make a pretty good guide, being native and all. I could give it one more day.

When he returned, I held up two fingers. "I have two conditions."

He folded his arms across his chest. "Name them."

"You have to quit arguing with everything I say about myself. You don't even know me."

"Yes, I do."

I drew in a huge angry breath, but he burst out laughing. "Sorry." He flashed his palms at me. "But you're cute when you're mad, you know. It's going to be hard for me to resist poking at you just a little."

My mouth hung open. Was he flirting with me? I was half furious, half flattered. On one hand, he'd irritated me to no end tonight with his smart-ass, know-it-all attitude, but on the other…My God, how long had it been since someone had flirted with me this way?

The other bartender called for help, and Lucas held up one finger over his shoulder to put him off a moment. "So? What's the second condition?"

"There must be wine."

He grinned. "Deal." I put out my hand and we shook on it, and then suddenly he pulled me toward him over the bar, kissed each of my cheeks, and then the first one again. "Nice to meet you, Mia. Welcome to Paris."

#

Despite Lucas's opinion, I did not feel confident enough to take the Metro for the first time at night, so he put me in a cab and gave the driver directions to the hotel. Lucas raised an eyebrow at my fancy digs but didn't make any smart comments. We agreed he'd meet me there in the lobby at ten the next morning—he argued for noon, but I insisted on earlier.

"I have to work until two," he complained.

"Better get right home afterward, then. We've got a lot of ground to cover tomorrow if you're going to sell Paris to me in just one day."

He groaned and opened the cab door, and I flashed him a victory smile. I'd sort of been expecting at least a hug or something, but he didn't go in for one, so I didn't either. Sliding into the back seat, I lifted a hand in farewell as he shut the door and did the same.

It was oddly disappointing.

#

The next morning I woke at eight, showered, and donned the smaller of the two robes that hung in the bathroom. Humming along with Kate Nash's "Paris", one of my favorite songs on the Paris playlist, I let my curls air-dry as I sipped a delicious pot of room-service coffee, nibbled on strawberries and *pain au chocolat*, and sifted through my clothes for just the right outfit. According to the English-language newspaper that had been waiting at my door, the day would be overcast but not rainy, and the temperature mild.

Hmmmm. Tapping a finger on my lips, I considered my wardrobe. I wanted to look nice but not like I was trying hard—because I wasn't—but I needed to be comfortable too. My flats had been OK for walking yesterday, but I thought I might go with sneakers today. I paired them with my favorite jeans, rolled up, and a plain white tank top. In case I got chilly, I tossed a soft little sweater in watermelon pink over my shoulders.

Once I was dressed, I put on some mascara and fussed a little with my hair, but really, there wasn't much I could do once it was dry. Kerastase made products I loved, but sometimes my curls had a mind of their own. Today, thankfully, they were behaving properly.

I finished my coffee and was brushing my teeth when the front desk called up letting me know I had a guest in the lobby. I rinsed, spit, and put on my favorite lip balm before slinging my bag over my shoulder and rushing out the door.

On the elevator ride down, my stomach was actually jumping—what the hell? I put a hand over it and reminded myself not to expect too much out of this day. Lucas was a nice guy and all, maybe even a little attractive, but there was no guarantee I was going to enjoy his company for hours on end, nor he mine. In fact, this day could be totally awkward if we didn't have anything in common. I'd have to think of an excuse to cut out early if that was the case.

After exiting the elevator, I walked into the elegant lobby and scanned the crowd.

"Looking for someone?" The voice came from behind me, and I turned to find Lucas standing there, hands in his pockets.

I smiled. "This time, I am."

He returned the smile before leaning in and kissing me, once on each cheek. Was it my imagination, or was he cuter this morning than he'd been at the bar last night? Was something different? I took a quick inventory—no, the scruff was still there and the hair was still kind of a mess. Jesus, did the man own a comb?

But his outfit wasn't bad. The gray pants from last night were making a repeat performance, but on top he wore a white shirt and a cardigan sweater. It was cute in a sort of nerdy-chic way.

We exited the hotel and Lucas gestured left. "This way."

"Where are we going?" I fell in step beside him.

"For coffee."

A sound of frustration escaped me. "I've already had coffee! I want to *see* something!"

"Relax, princess. We're going to stroll up the Champs-Élysées like proper tourists and then sit at a cafe and have coffee in view of the Arc de Triomphe. You'll be able to cross two famous sights off your list."

"How you do know I have a list?"

He grinned sideways at me. "Just a guess."

Pursing my lips, I smacked him on the shoulder. "You said no analyzing today."

His eyes lit up. "Oh my God, you've got a list for everything, don't you? I bet you even have one that says 'Tuesday Morning: blue jeans, pink sweater, gray sneakers.'" He raised his voice to a high feminine pitch to mimic me. "Outfit change at four forty-five into cocktail dress and black heels."

"Stop it. I do not." I lifted my chin and kept walking, refusing to look at him lest my expression give me away. How fucking annoying that his stupid analyses of me were so spot-on.

Lucas laughed. "I was kidding, but you do, don't you? You *do* have an outfit list!"

"So what if I do? What's wrong with being organized and planning ahead? I'm good at that." I'd always thought of my well-preparedness as an asset, so why were my cheeks so hot?

"Nothing's wrong with it at all, princess." He took my elbow to pull me up a side street, and I tugged it from his grasp.

"Stop calling me that. I'm not a princess."

"Says the girl staying at the Plaza Athenee."

"I'm not paying for it, remember? The ex-fiance?"

Lucas paused. "Oh, yeah. I forgot about him."

"I wish I could forget about him."

"You can. You will." He tossed his arm over my shoulder and squeezed for just a moment, surprising me. "I'm sorry I teased you."

We walked slowly up the Champs, stopping occasionally so I could ooh and ahh over the merchandise in store windows lining the avenue. I entered a few shops, but he chose to wait outside each time, never telling me to hurry up or complaining that he hadn't had his coffee yet, like Tucker would have. Tucker didn't get the point of window shopping—if he liked something he saw, he bought it.

I did see some pretty things I'd have liked to get for myself or for my girlfriends, but my credit card couldn't handle the price tags. And although I had Tucker's card and even his permission to use it, I just didn't feel right about it.

"Not even a souvenir t-shirt?" Lucas asked when I came out of yet another store empty-handed.

I shook my head. "Even the t-shirts are a little steep for me."

"Yeah, these places jack up their prices because it's prime real estate. But I know some better shopping areas, less touristy ones. I'll tell you where to go."

"Thanks. I'd like that."

At the end of the avenue stood the Arc de Triomphe, massive and solid and majestic, way bigger than I'd imagined it to be. As we got closer I stopped walking and stared, open-mouthed. "Oh my God, it's so huge!"

"I hear that a lot."

I made a face at him. "Hahaha. Just be quiet and let me enjoy this stuff, OK? That's your only job today."

He saluted me.

"So can we climb it?"

"*You* can climb it."

"Why only me?"

He shrugged. "I'm not fond of heights."

I looked at the Roman arch again. It *was* pretty high at the top. "You've never been up there?"

"I have. The view's incredible."

"Well, I'll go by myself then."

"No problem. I'll wait for you here." We'd reached the end of the block, where a café with a huge red awning and lots of tiny outdoor tables sat kitty corner from the arch. Lucas chose an empty table and sat down. "Aren't you going now?"

"I guess so." But I stood there a moment longer, feeling strangely let down that he wouldn't accompany me. "You sure you won't go with me?"

"I'm sure. Go on." He waved me toward a metro station sign. "The easiest way is to go underground and take the walkway."

I followed his instructions and used my Paris Museum Pass to enter. I actually had two passes—I'd ordered them ahead of time for Tucker and me. As I climbed the hundreds of steps to get to the top of the arch, I thought of maybe giving the other one to Lucas. *I wonder if he likes art.* I knew he must like music since he majored in it along with psych, but other than that and his job, I knew almost nothing about him, not even his last name.

My leg muscles were burning after a few dozen stairs, but it felt good, and the physical exertion lifted my mood. *When I get down, I'll ask more about him, and I'll be open-minded and even pleasant, dammit. I won't compare him unfavorably to Fucker, I'll stop judging his hair, facial or otherwise, and I'll even thank him for spending the day with me.*

Because really, when I thought about it, he could have just sent me on my way last night. For heaven's sake, it's not like I'd been so charming he'd been unable to resist me. I'd been pretty bitchy, actually.

A little breathless from the climb, I reached the top and stepped into the wind, pulling my sweater tighter around me. Carefully, I approached the edge and took in the panoramic view. But rather than the Eiffel Tower or Louvre or La Défense, my eye immediately sought the café where Lucas was waiting for me, and I thought I saw him there, but I couldn't be certain. I pulled out my camera and took a few pictures before heading back down the steps, through the underground walkway, and back up to the café. Lucas was right where I'd left him, an empty coffee cup on the table. He'd been checking his phone, but quickly tucked it into his pocket when he saw me, something else Tucker would never have done. He was glued to that thing.

"So? How was it?" Lucas pulled the chair on the other side of the table out for me.

"It was amazing. It was breathtaking. It was…" I lowered myself into the chair and pumped my fists in the air. "Triumphant."

Lucas laughed and raised his hand for the waiter. "That good, huh?"

"Well, I didn't see anyone kissing or getting engaged, which automatically makes it better than my visit to the Eiffel Tower yesterday."

"Good. Would you like coffee?" he asked as the waiter approached.

"Sure, thanks."

Lucas held up two fingers. "Deux cafés." The waiter picked up the empty cup and retreated, and I leaned forward onto my elbows.

"So, Lucas…wait, what's your last name?"

"Fournier."

"So, Lucas Fournier. You majored in psych and music, you're a bartender, and you're scared of heights. Tell me something else about you."

"I didn't say I was scared of heights."

I blinked. "Yes, you did."

"I said I wasn't *fond* of them. There's a difference."

A smile tugged at one corner of my mouth. "Of course. Pardonnez-moi."

"And I'm not really a bartender. The Beaver belongs to my brother Gilles, and I just fill in there sometimes when I'm in Paris."

"What do you normally do?"

"I teach intro psych at NYU. I'm just here through the summer visiting my mother and doing a little research."

"In psychology?" I asked before taking a sip.

"In music, actually."

"What are you researching?"

"The traditional folk music of Romani guitarists. I'd like to write a book about it."

I tilted my head at the unfamiliar word. "Romani, what's that?"

"Well, a lot of people refer to them as gypsies, but that term sounds a little harsh these days."

"Aha. And do you play guitar as well?"

He smiled. "I do."

Intrigued, I set my cup down. "Can I hear you play?"

"Did you bring a guitar?"

"Not here, silly. Maybe later?"

He raised an eyebrow. "You planning on coming home with me?"

Immediately my cheeks burned. I'd gone from pleasant to pervy in under a minute. "No—I didn't mean—I'm sorry, I just—"

Frenched

Lucas laughed as he reached over and patted my shoulder. "Relax, Mia. I'm only teasing." He pulled some money from his pocket and laid it on the table.

I bit my lip—I didn't want him to think he had to keep paying for things. This wasn't a date. "Thanks. I need to change some money, I guess."

"Does that mean you're staying?" Lucas looked at me with a gleam in his eye.

I wanted to say yes, but I didn't want him to stop trying to sway me. There was something really enjoyable about being the sole focus of his attention. "Still undecided."

"All right, then. I've got work to do. Come on."

Chapter Five

"So nothing romantic, right?" Lucas rubbed his chin as we walked. He'd helped me change some money and now we were headed toward a Metro entrance.

"Right."

"Damn, that's a tall order in Paris, but I think I have an idea."

I followed him down the cement steps, at the bottom of which he took my arm. "Come here. Do you know how to read this?" He led me over to a large map of the routes on the wall.

Quickly I looked it over. I actually love maps and I'm usually really good at reading them. "Each route is has a number and a different color, right? And the little dots are stops?"

"Yes. And the bigger shapes, the white ones, indicate where you can make a transfer to another line. The key is to look at the name of the stop that's on the end of the line in the direction you want to go. For example, here we are..." He pointed over my shoulder to a big white oval on the map. "At Charles de Gaulle – Étoile."

He was standing so close behind me that I could feel his breath in my hair. I wondered if it smelled like coffee and then scolded myself for having such a weird thought. "Right."

"And we want to go here." He slid his finger across the map to a stop labeled Père Lachaise.

"Père Lachaise...like the cemetery?"

"Yes. Dead people and stone monuments. Not romantic, right?"

I laughed, peeking at him over my shoulder. Holy shit, he was close. My temple actually grazed his chin, and he stepped back, clearing his throat.

"So, how do we get there?" he asked. "You tell me."

"Hmmm." Sucking my lips between my teeth, I studied the map, but my navigational skills didn't feel too sharp, for some reason, and I was pretty sure that reason was Lucas's scruffy jaw. It hadn't been as scratchy as I'd imagined. *What the hell, Mia? Focus.* "Uh, we look for the number three and we want to go in the direction of...Gallieni?"

"Well, you could. Except the number three doesn't stop at Charles de Gaulle – Étoile. We'd have to make a transfer."

"Oh." I squinted at the map again, but I could still feel his whiskers on my skin. *Fucking concentrate, goddammit! You don't even like scruff.* "Oh! I see. We get on the…number two and sort of go up and around. That way we don't have to transfer."

"Exactly."

Beaming with pride, I turned around. "So I need a ticket, right?"

"Yes. Over there." Lucas led me to one of the ticket machines and watched as I got started, changing the language to English and moving through each step.

At one particular screen, I hesitated. "How many should I buy?"

"Is it just for one day?"

I kept my eyes on the screen. "I don't know. Maybe two."

"Aha! My plan is working!" he gloated.

I shrugged, refusing to look at him. "It might be. A little."

"Get a book of ten."

I paid by credit card and put nine tickets inside my wallet. Lucas had some kind of pass he swiped, and I fed my ticket into the machine and followed him through the turnstile. At that point he wanted me to lead the way, so I looked at all the signs carefully before choosing which tunnel to take.

When we arrived at the tracks, Lucas held up his hand and I high-fived him. "Way to go, princess. You successfully navigated the metro. I have confidence you can get yourself anywhere in Paris now, even when you're on your own."

"Thank you." I took a small bow, but I felt a twinge of sadness when I imagined myself doing all this alone.

While we waited for the train, Lucas asked me what I did back in Detroit.

"I'm an event planner."

He burst out laughing. "Of course you are."

Indignant, I stuck my hands on my hips. "What's funny about that?"

"Nothing." He stopped guffawing but couldn't wipe the grin off his face. "It's the perfect job for you. I bet you're really good at it."

"I am, thank you very much." I sniffed, slinging my bag higher on my shoulder. "I worked for someone else for a while after college and then started my own business when I was only twenty-five. Well, my best friend and I started it—she had inherited some money and we'd always wanted to do something together. So we went for it."

He looked impressed. "Very cool. How's it going?"

"Very well, actually. We were on the news last year for being two of the top up-and-coming young entrepreneurs in the city. We got a lot of business out of that, weddings mostly, but a bunch of them are pretty big-budget." A flicker of discomfort on Lucas's face made me pause, and for a second I wondered what I'd said wrong until I realized I'd mentioned *weddings*. But surprisingly, neither the word nor the idea bothered me.

Huh.

"And what's the name of your company?"

"Devine Events. Devine is my last name."

He smiled at me again, but it was softer. More admiring than amused. "It suits you."

At that moment the train pulled into the station, roaring along the tracks as a blush warmed my face. I dropped my eyes to the ground. What the hell? Was he flirting with me? Was flirting allowed on this tour? And what's with the way my heart was beating? It felt huge and clumsy in my chest as we boarded the train.

There was only one empty seat, and Lucas gestured for me to sit. He remained standing, and even though the train's movement wasn't smooth, he didn't hold on to anything, just stood in the aisle with his feet planted wide and his arms crossed. Why that turned me on a little, I had no idea, but I felt a stir low in my belly.

Hmm. I guess he's growing on me.

Haha, growing on me.

Turning my cheek so he couldn't see the smile I was trying to hide, I berated myself for the dirty thought. *Stop it, Mia. And don't even look at his crotch right now. Don't do it, don't do it, don't —*

I did it. I couldn't help myself.

Frenched

It wasn't a longing gaze or anything, more like just a passing glance, and it didn't tell me anything, but I was still scared he'd noticed. I switched my focus to my sneakers.

A few stops later, the seat next to me was vacated and Lucas sat down. "So are you a cemetery person? Was Père Lachaise on your list?"

"I don't know if I'd call myself a cemetery person, but I believe it was on the list. Remind me who's buried there?"

"Lots of people. But names you'd know are Jim Morrison, Edith Piaf, Chopin, Oscar Wilde, Balzac, Gertrude Stein…"

I raised my eyebrows. "I'm impressed, Professor Fournier."

He shrugged. "I'm a cemetery person. I think they're beautiful and relaxing. Peaceful."

I considered it. "Yeah, I can see that."

"I just hope it's not crammed with tourists today, although it is the season."

"We ruin your soulful hipster vibe, is that it?"

He thumped my leg and leaned closer to me. "Yes, in fact, you do."

"Well, I'll try to rein in my excitement but no promises."

Our faces were close, nearly nose to nose. My breath got stuck in my lungs as his eyes dropped to my lips for a second. *Jesus, he's going to kiss me. Right here on the train, he's totally going to kiss me!*

But before I could even decide how I felt about it, he leaned back in his seat. "You don't wear lipstick. I noticed that last night."

It took me a second to recover. "What? Oh, no. I don't, not usually."

"I like that. I think lipstick is gross."

"You do?"

"Yeah. It's all sticky and goopy, and it gets all over everything, and I don't know what the hell toxic chemicals it's made of these days, but it *never comes off.*"

I wrinkled my nose. "Yeah, I think there are some hazardous ingredients in a lot of them. I'm a lip balm person myself."

Lucas cocked his head and looked at me askance. "Good to know."

Bang bang bang went my swollen heart against my ribs.

Damn, it was official—he was flirting with me, and I liked it.

"This is us." Lucas nudged me, and I stood when he did, but I did not have his sea legs and immediately fell forward as the train swerved into the station. Lucas caught me easily against his chest. "Whoa. You OK?"

"Yes, sorry. But I think I have to hold on."

"I've got you." He turned me around and held me by the shoulders until the train came to a stop and the doors opened. "Here we go." Once we were on solid ground, he let go of me.

And I kind of wished he hadn't.

#

Much to Lucas's dismay, there were quite a few busloads of tourists at Père Lachaise. We managed to avoid the crowds by skipping the big names and just wandering the dirt and cobblestone paths with no particular destination. I'd asked if there was somewhere I could get a map or a Who's Buried Where kind of guide, but Lucas insisted that we didn't need one. "I come here a lot," he assured me. "Let's just walk, and if you're curious about something, I'll tell you what I know."

"But I love maps. I want a map. I *need* a map," I whined.

"No, you don't."

I gave him a withering look, and he held up his hands. "I know I said I wouldn't argue with you, but let's just try it my way, and if it doesn't work for you, I promise I'll go buy you a map."

It made my palms a little itchy to think of meandering through such a big famous place without a guide, but I figured I could try to endure it for Lucas's sake.

67

And actually, I enjoyed it.

With no particular route to follow or timetable set, I found myself in less of a rush than I usually was when sightseeing, noticing things that I probably wouldn't have if I'd had my nose stuck in a guide.

And Lucas hadn't exaggerated—he was able to tell me a lot of stories about the people buried there, whether they were musicians, actors, writers or politicians. "This one here?" He gestured toward a bronze-gone-green statue of a man reclining on his tomb. "Best story ever."

I paused in front of it. "Really? Who was he?"

"He was a French president who died while getting a blowjob from his mistress. His epitaph in French is, '*Il voulait être César, il ne fut sue Pompée*,' which could mean 'He wanted to be Caesar but ended being Pompey.'" Lucas's eyes glittered. "*Or* it could mean, 'He wanted to be Caesar but ended being pumped.'"

I gasped and clapped a hand over my mouth. "God, that would *never* be allowed on the grave of an American President."

Lucas shook his head. "Probably not."

"You're pretty good with all this history," I said as we continued walking.

"I find it interesting."

I elbowed him. "Especially the parts with blowjobs, I bet." To my surprise, he blushed, and the word *adorable* popped into my head. "I'm serious. It's amazing how much you know about this place."

"I have a good memory is all."

I sighed. "I don't. I have to write everything down or I forget things constantly."

He looked at me in surprise. "Really? I'd have thought you were one of those girls who always remembers everyone's name and where you met and what they were wearing."

"Not if I don't write it down somewhere. There's a reason I like lists so much—I'm not just obsessed with them for fun."

"Fun," he scoffed, nudging me with his shoulder. "Lists are not fun."

I giggled and went to shove him back but he dodged it and threw his arms around me from behind, pinning my arms to my sides so I couldn't move. "Behave, princess." His breath tickled my neck through my hair, sending a weightless joy rushing up inside me.

"What if I don't want to behave?"

Lucas went completely still, and for a moment I thought I might have gone too far. *Change the subject.*

"Hey, what's that?" Up ahead was one of the most elaborate tombs I'd ever seen—it was almost like its own little Gothic chapel without walls. Inside the structure lay two statues in repose right next to each other, their hands steepled in prayer.

Lucas released me. "Ah. Abelard and Heloise. But that's one I don't know if I can tell you about."

"Why not?" Moving closer to it, I stared at the stonework, nearly breathless at its beauty.

"Because it's a very tragic romantic story. I'm not sure it's advisable on this excursion."

"No, tell me. I promise I can handle it."

"OK. But I warned you. Ugh—" He took an elbow in the gut from me before going on. "So Abelard was a twelfth-century teacher and philosopher, and he'd heard about this brilliant young beauty named Heloise. He convinces her uncle to let him tutor her, only they don't get much studying done."

I put a hand on his arm. "Let me guess—more blowjobs."

"You have a dirty mind, princess. But yes, I suppose there were blowjobs. Now don't interrupt."

"Sorry, go on." I put my hands at the top of the iron fence surrounding the tomb and focused on the figures lying there, trying to ignore the way his nearness was starting to make my whole body tingle.

"They carry on a passionate, illicit love affair for a while," Lucas went on, "long enough for Heloise to get pregnant, and it's a big scandal because he's so much older than she is. Anyway, the uncle finds out and tries to separate them, but they marry in secret."

Rapt, I imagined it all as he talked—the late night tutoring sessions that ended in passionate kisses when their desire for one another became too much to bear. The secret trysts—I pictured them lying on some kind of bearskin rug in front of a fireplace, the flames casting golden light on their glistening bodies. The secret wedding ceremony, hurriedly conducted in hushed voices in a tiny chapel. "Go on," I urged, feeling more than a little aroused myself. "Then what happened?"

"Well, it gets a bit gruesome at this point. Abelard fears for their safety because the uncle's kind of a dick and not too happy about the marriage. So he hides Heloise in a convent and goes back to Paris alone, where he's attacked and, uh, castrated." Lucas shivered and adjusted the crotch of his pants.

I gasped. "No!"

"Yes. He's so ashamed he decides he can't face Heloise, and he becomes a monk. She's so devastated she gives up her child, joins a convent, and becomes a nun."

My mouth fell open. "What? They never saw each other again?"

"I don't think so. But they wrote to each other for twenty years. And the love letters survived."

"Love letters, really? Are they romantic?"

"I've never read them, actually. But I think they are. And lovesick crazies from all over the world come and leave letters here, hoping it will bring them good luck, although if you think about it, that makes no sense at all. These two weren't reunited until death."

I sighed again, exasperated. "You were right. You shouldn't have told me that story. Now I'm all…" I fidgeted uncomfortably. *Turned on.* "Discombobulated."

"I think I know what will fix that."

My stomach cartwheeled, and I licked my lips. "What?"

"Wine. And maybe some food."

"Oh. Right."

Wait a minute. Was I actually disappointed that he meant wine instead of something more suggestive? What the hell was wrong with me? It was *wine*, for fuck's sake. My favorite thing.

Tucking my sweater more snugly around me, I smiled at him. "Yes, that sounds perfect. Let's go."

Chapter Six

Lucas chose a table by the window in the brasserie we'd picked, and I took a seat across from him. "I'm famished. What time is it anyway?"

"It's just after two."

"Is it? Wow, time flies when you're having fun." I thanked the waiter who handed me the menu and opened it up.

"*Are* you having fun?"

I looked up and saw Lucas studying me curiously. "Of course I am. Aren't you?"

"Yes. But I don't need to be convinced to stay in Paris. Have you made a decision yet?"

"I'm this close." I held up one hand with my thumb and finger just an inch apart and continued in a whisper. "After some wine, it might be official."

"OK, then, this bottle better be good." He considered the list and looked up at me through thick, dark lashes. "What would you like?"

"Hmmmm. I really loved what you poured for me last night. The one from the Rhône Valley."

"Want to try another Rhône or something different?"

"You pick. I'll just enjoy. Oh, could you order me a salad like the one that's on that lady's plate over there?" I tried to point without being obvious.

Twisting in his chair, Lucas looked behind him. "It's a Salad Niçoise," he said. "Now you can order it."

"But your French is so much better." Lacing my fingers together under my chin, I attempted a winning smile. "Really, I don't speak it well at all. Could you order it, please?"

He shook his head. "What are you going to do when I'm not around to order for you? You should do it. Don't be scared."

The thought of uttering French words in front of Lucas made me sweat a little, but when the waiter came around, I managed to order the salad and even ask for some water. Lucas ordered the wine—at least that's what I assumed all the rapid-fire French was about—and a Salad Niçoise also.

"See? Was that so hard?" he asked when we were alone again.

"I guess not," I admitted, smoothing my napkin onto my lap. I knew he was right about learning to speak for myself, because even if I did stay, I couldn't expect Lucas to spend all his time with me. This was probably just a one-day deal. A hollow pit formed in my stomach, and I realized how sad I would be if I didn't see him again after today. When I looked up, I saw him watching me with a serious expression on his face.

"Mia, would—"

But he was interrupted by the waiter approaching with a pitcher of water and two glasses. Lucas poured water for us, and I waited for him to say whatever it was he'd been about to say, but he didn't.

"You were going to ask me something?" I prompted.

He shook his head and took a drink of water. "No."

"Yes, you were. Right before the water arrived. You said my name."

His brow furrowed, and either he had a good poker face or he really hadn't had anything of importance to say. "I don't remember, I guess."

My chest caved a little, and I picked up my water. *What is this? Why am I getting weird and mopey about Lucas?* Last night I hadn't even liked him that much. So my first impression of him had been off, so what? I found him attractive in spite of the scruff, big deal. So beyond the smartass mouth was a curious mind and a romantic soul, whatever. I hadn't come here to meet a man; I'd come here to forget one. Straightening up in my seat, I vowed to quit allowing serious thoughts to get in the way of a good time.

Our wine arrived, and I watched as the waiter poured the ruby-colored liquid into glasses. My insides got quivery with excitement the way they always do when I'm anticipating a really good glass of wine. I must have bounced a little in my chair or something because Lucas laughed. "Excited?"

"Totally. Can I drink it now or do I have to let it sit for a while so oxygen wafts around above it or something?" I waved a hand in the air over my glass.

"No, you can drink it now."

"Good." I picked up my glass and breathed in the aroma as if I knew what I was doing. "So you know about wine?"

"A little. My family has a small vineyard in Provence."

I lowered the glass. "Are you serious?"

"Yes. In fact, this wine is very similar to one we make. Try it."

"Say no more." The wine was cool on my lips, and I let it linger in my mouth a few seconds before swallowing. "Mmm. Delicious. I wish I knew better how to describe it. Soft? Silky?" I took another sip. "God, it's just *so good*. Sorry I don't have better words."

"Don't apologize. I'm glad you like it."

The waiter brought our salads and Lucas set down his glass in favor of his fork, but I wasn't quite ready to part with mine yet.

"So tell me something about this wine."

"Well, I don't know nearly as much as my brothers, and I'm not much into rules about wine, but the first thing any expert would tell you is that this is the wrong wine to have with these salads."

"Who cares about that? I'm with you—no rules." After one more sip, I swirled it around in the glass. "But what's something about it you can teach me?"

"Well, this wine is a Châteauneuf-du-Pape, which can have up to thirteen different varietals—but don't ask me to name them all."

"How about just one?"

He thought for a second. "Grenache."

I nodded. "Good enough."

As we ate our salads and polished off the bottle of wine, Lucas and I chatted easily about wine, our families, and our childhoods. His mother had been a film actress.

"But she only acted for maybe five, six years before quitting to marry a Count," he said.

"A Count? Really?"

"Really. Old name, old money. That's where the vineyard comes from. She had two sons with him before he admitted he preferred men."

I paused with a bite halfway to my mouth. "No way."

He nodded. "They stayed good friends, though. He's a great guy. He and his partner run the vineyard and my mom is a constant guest there in the summertime." He paused before adding, "With her new husband."

"What? God, that's so French. Is the current husband your dad?"

"Nope. My dad was an American musician on a European tour. He met my mom here, fell in love, and left the band to stay and marry her. When I was about six we moved to the U.S. When I was twelve, she decided their affair had run its course and moved back to France. Now she's married to the tennis pro at her club, who's ten years younger than she is."

"Oh. Well, good for her."

"And for the pro too. He spends his summers sunning himself at the Count's pool and practicing his serve on the Count's court."

"And everyone gets along?"

He shrugged. "Well enough."

"Where's your dad now?"

"He works as a studio musician in New York, but he also teaches college classes on music theory."

I nodded slowly. "Wow. You had quite a childhood. Mine's boring by comparison."

"Try me."

"Well, Mom was a legal secretary, Dad was a lawyer, I was an oopsie. They married but it didn't work out, and I did the back and forth thing until I graduated from high school. Now my dad is married to another attorney and they have three little girls, and my mom is married to a cardiac surgeon. They live in Chicago, which is a good place for her."

"Why's that?"

"Because it's three hundred miles from me."

He smiled. "You don't get along?"

"Well enough, I suppose. But you know what?" I drained the last drop of wine in my glass. "Let's not talk about her. She stresses me out, and I am feeling *amazingly* good about life right now."

He poured the remains of the bottle into our glasses. "Good wine will do that for you."

"It's not just the wine."

Shit, did I say that out loud?

Lucas froze for a moment, eyes locked on mine, the wine bottle still suspended above the table. Finally he set it down. "Oh?"

Heat rushed my face, but I didn't look away. "Yes. Lucas, this is the best day I've had in a long time. In fact, I'd forgotten what it was like to feel this way."

"What way?"

I lifted my shoulders. "Happy. Carefree. Just…excited about what might come next, even though I have no idea what it will be."

"In life or in Paris?"

I smiled. "Both."

Triumph danced in his eyes. "So you're staying."

"I'm staying. But!" I held up one finger. "I still want the rest of my day with you as tour guide."

"I'm all yours."

Are you?

I watched him bring the rim of the glass to his lips and drink, and I imagined the wine slipping into his mouth, between his teeth, sliding over his tongue. The image was so erotic I squeezed my thighs together against the gush of arousal between my legs.

Whoa, Nelly.

Picking up my own glass, I looked out the window and sipped, trying to recall the last time I'd been really good and hot before even being touched. I used to get excited thinking about Tucker's good looks and hard body, but I'd learned pretty quickly he wasn't quite the sexual dynamo his reputation made him out to be. My gut feeling was that he'd had a lot of one-nighters with girls who didn't come back for seconds, and that suited him just fine. It meant he never had to get to know anyone sexually, really spend time learning what they wanted, what they needed, what they liked.

Not that he'd done that with me either.

Frowning, I watched a couple kiss before parting on the sidewalk outside. I'd tried—I'd really tried—to be the kind of woman a man desired in bed. I made it perfectly clear I was willing to try different things—not only willing but interested—and I offered myself in every way, but he just wasn't interested in changing his routine. Because it worked for him, every time.

What an asshole. Why did I ever think he was good enough?

"Hey, you. No frowning."

I looked over at Lucas. "Sorry. I was just thinking."

"What about?"

I finished my wine and set the glass down with a clank. "Sex."

Lucas's eyebrows shot up. "Should I get the check?"

Dissolving into giggles, I dug into my bag for my wallet and took out my credit card. "Yes, but not for that reason. I want to see more Paris today. And I want to pay for lunch."

"No." Lucas pushed my hand away when I tried to lay down the card. "My treat. I chose an expensive bottle of wine."

"So what? I loved it! Please let me pay for lunch. You've been so nice to spend this entire day showing me around."

"I wanted to do that. It was my idea, remember?"

"I know, but—"

"But nothing. Put your card away. You can buy our next bottle of wine, OK?"

I dropped my hand to my lap, nodding once. "I like the way you think, Lucas Fournier."

#

Outside the restaurant, Lucas asked what I wanted to do next.

Make out with you.

The thought slammed into my head with astonishing speed, and I tried to banish it just as quickly. What if he wasn't feeling any chemistry between us?

"Hmmm. Let's see—we've done a monument and a cemetery, so I'll vote for a museum or a cathedral."

Lucas looked skyward, where the sun was trying hard to peek through heavy clouds. "Well, the light's not awesome for stained glass windows but I think it might be even worse tomorrow, so let's do a cathedral."

"Notre-Dame?"

"You got it."

We took the Metro to a stop a few blocks from the Seine, and rather than switch to another line to get closer, we decided to walk. The day had warmed up and gotten a little humid, so I shrugged out of my sweater and tied it around my waist.

"So I have to ask," said Lucas, who'd been pretty quiet since the restaurant. "Why were you thinking about sex before?"

Frenched

Because watching you drink wine made me hot in the pants. I glanced over at him and decided to go with a different reason. "Because Tucker was boring in bed."

"What?"

I held up my hands. "Truth. I used to offer, in an effort to improve what was *not* a very interesting or mutually satisfying part of our relationship, to do more fun things than we were doing, but he had a routine that worked for him and didn't really feel it was necessary to deviate from it."

Lucas stopped walking and stuck a hand out in front of me to halt my steps. "Tell me you're not serious."

I laughed. "I'm serious. He didn't even like blowjobs. Maybe he heard that story about the French President and got scared."

Lucas stared at me for a moment, then slowly shook his head. "Nah. I'm pretty sure he was just an asshole who didn't know what he had. You deserve a lot better."

Was it the compliment or the alcohol that gave me the fleeting urge to reach over, grab him by the cardigan and smash my lips to his? What would he do? He said flirty things to me sometimes, but other times he acted totally platonic and casual, even a little aloof. Was he waiting for me to make the first move?

We stood there in silence for a full ten seconds, during which I couldn't help wondering what he'd be like in bed.

I'll bet he's a million times more generous than Tucker. I'll bet he's fun and hot and willing to take it slow sometimes. Just talking about sex with him felt so easy...and damn if I wasn't turned on again thinking about him that way. My stupid nipples were hard, poking right through the thin material of my bra and cotton tank. I don't have huge breasts or anything, barely a C cup, but my nipples get incredibly hard and they're ultra-sensitive. Naturally, Lucas's eyes were drawn right to them, but then it was obvious what he was looking at and he dropped his gaze to the ground, his cheeks coloring.

I opened my mouth, racking my brain for something clever or flirty to say, but the moment had dragged on too long, and Lucas just gave me a quick smile and started walking again.

Shit.

Next time, I'd be braver. What did I have to lose, anyway?

As we got closer to the river, the towers of Notre Dame came into view, and Lucas began telling me a little bit about the *Île de la Cité*, the small island in the middle of the Seine on which the cathedral stood. I listened with interest as he told me about narrow medieval streets, stone walls, and the construction of Notre-Dame, which took almost two hundred years.

"God, imagine dedicating all that time and labor to something you knew would never be finished in your lifetime," I said. "Or even your children's lifetime. You work your ass off for something and then you never even see it completed."

Lucas shrugged. "I think it was less about the finished product for them and more about their faith. The *reason* they were building it."

It may have been an offhand comment, but it made me think about the huge, ridiculous wedding I'd planned for myself, and how mad I'd been that it didn't come off. *I should have been thinking more about the reason for the marriage, and less about the wedding.* But I'd never felt the kind of devotion to him I should have, nor had strong faith in the relationship. *Thank God we didn't get married.*

Lucas insisted the outside of the Gothic masterpiece was even more magnificent than the inside, so we spent quite a bit of time looking at its exterior—from the bridge we crossed over the Seine, from the square in front of the cathedral, from the garden behind it. I wanted to know the names of all these things but Lucas wouldn't let me open my guidebook.

"What does it matter what the name of the bridge is? You don't need to stick your nose in a book right now, Mia—look at the damn cathedral."

"I don't think you're supposed to call it a *damn* cathedral." I handed him the book. "How about if you read to me while I look?"

Lucas nodded. "That is acceptable."

We found an empty bench and sat down. Leaning back, I studied the church while Lucas read to me about buttresses, barrel vaults, and gargoyles. After a few minutes, though, I stopped being fascinated by characteristics of Gothic cathedrals and starting rhapsodizing about the low, fluid sound of Lucas's voice, the expressive way he read, the charming hint of an accent that sometimes crept beneath his words when he wasn't paying attention. Hiding a smile, I told myself to quit drifting and pay attention—I'd have a hard enough time remembering any of the information—but his reading was so sweet and soothing, I grew a little drowsy.

When he was done, he closed the book and said, "Want to go inside?"

Actually, I kind of just wanted to sit there with him on that bench, maybe lay my head in his lap. Kiss him. Take a nap or admire the scenery. But instead I got to my feet and stretched. "Yes."

After we toured the crypts underneath Notre-Dame and admired the soaring ceilings and gorgeous stained glass windows inside, I asked Lucas to climb the tower with me.

"What? No, Mia. I already told you I don't like heights." He shoved his hands in his pockets. "I'll wait for you outside."

"No." I have no idea what made me act so bold but I actually took his hands out of his pockets and held them between us. "Please, Lucas. We won't stay up there long, and I promise I won't make you go to the edge."

"Why do you need me up there?" His expression was pained. "The view's the same whether you're alone or not."

"I know. And it's not that I won't enjoy it alone. I just really want you to come up there with me."

His shoulders sagged a little as he exhaled, closing his eyes.

"Please, Lucas, for me?" I shook his hands.

He opened his eyes and peered at me warily. "You're gonna make me do this, aren't you."

I nodded. "Yep. So you might as well give in sooner rather than later."

He grimaced. "All right. I'll do it."

Three hundred eighty-seven steep, narrow spiral steps later, we emerged at the top. Lucas was a bit pale and skittish, but I took his hand and tugged him forward. "Come on. Show me where you live."

Reluctantly he moved closer to the edge but remained behind me, speaking into my hair to be heard above the wind. Over my left shoulder, he pointed in the direction of the river. "I have a studio apartment in the sixth, near Saint-Germain-des-Prés. It actually belongs to my mother but I'm the only one who stays there anymore."

"And where is she? At the vineyard?" I was curious about his family, but mostly I was enjoying having him stand so close behind me.

"No, she's visiting friends in Nice right now. Are you cold?"

I glanced back to see him looking down my arm, where gooseflesh had blanketed my skin. "A little. It's breezy up here."

"Want your sweater?" Before I could answer, he tugged the wrap loose from my waist and held it up for me to slip my arms into.

"Thanks. I'd like to see your apartment sometime." He went silent and motionless for a moment, and I wondered if the statement been too suggestive. "I mean, if you have time. No big deal. I'm just curious about apartments. I have to find a new one when I get back, and—"

"Mia, would you like to have dinner with me tonight?"

He wants to have dinner with me! Even my toes tingled. And how cute was the anxious expression on his face, like he was scared I might say no? "Sounds great."

Smiling, I looked out over the city again and thought how lucky it was that I'd chosen to walk into his bar last night instead of just going home. I turned back to him, an impish grin on my face. "I'm really glad I came in The Beaver last night."

He burst out laughing. "You know how bad that sounds, right?"

I nodded happily, and my heartbeat quickened—I loved making him laugh. "That's why I said it that way. But I really do mean it, Lucas. This day would have been a disaster without you. In fact, I probably would have just gone home."

"I'm glad you didn't."

"Will you take a picture with me?"

"I'll take a picture *of* you. You don't need me in it."

"I want you in it. Come on, please ask someone if they'll take one for us. I want to remember this day with you." His expression softened and he tapped the shoulder of a woman nearby. She nodded and smiled, and I handed her my camera.

It seemed sort of awkward and military to stand side by side, arms down, so I moved closer to Lucas, hoping he'd put an arm around me. He didn't, so I moved in front of him.

"You have to stop moving so she can take the picture," he said.

"Quiet. Just try to look happy, so I can lie and tell my friends I charmed a French man."

"OK," said the woman. "*Un, deux, trois*."

I smiled as Lucas whispered in my ear, "You won't have to lie."

89

Chapter Seven

Lucas wanted a chance to clean up before dinner, and jet lag was starting to catch up with me, so I figured I could use a rest. After we exited the tower, he pointed me in the direction of a less pricey shopping area that was between Notre Dame and the Plaza Athénée and gave me specific directions for getting back. Then he gave me a quick hug and said he'd come for me at eight. I crossed the Seine in the opposite direction from him and found the rue de Rivoli without a problem, but instead of shopping I spent the next hour and a half wandering down the street in a complete daze, unable to take my mind off Lucas and the night ahead.

By this time, my wine buzz had worn off and I was getting a little anxious. Was this a date or not? Were things going to get romantic—or at least a little sexy—between us? I was ready to admit that I wanted them to—he was the complete opposite of my usual type, but there was something about him that appealed to me. I wanted to know what it was like to *be* with him…that way. But was he attracted to me like I was to him? Maybe he still just felt sorry for me. Biting my thumbnail, I decided to skip shopping and just walk back to my hotel.

I also needed to give some consideration to my own motives. Yesterday I'd been heartbroken over my aborted nuptials. As recently as last night, I'd compared Tucker's looks to Lucas's, unfavorably. Was I on the rebound already? Just looking for a warm body to show me some proper attention?

Because Hook Up With Scruffy Half-French Musician/Bartender was *so* not on the Paris list.

But did I even have to care if it was just a rebound fling? Would Lucas? We were two consenting adults. We were allowed to have some fun, right?

Finally, I dropped my hand to my side and sighed.

Jesus, Mia, stop thinking so much. No need to overanalyze. If something happens tonight, let it happen, and if it doesn't—no big deal. You met a new friend who gave you the courage to do something on your own you never would have done. Now stop trying to fucking plan everything. Just go with the flow.

When I got up to my room, the message light was blinking on my phone.

Dreading the sound of my mother's nervous tittering, I played the message, but it turned out to be

Coco. A smile took over my face at the sound of her low, smoky voice.

"Hi, honey! Just checking in with you to see how things are going. We're thinking about you all the time and dying to know what you're up to. How's the wine? The food, the shopping, the men? We can't wait to hear all about it and we hope you're misbehaving just enough. Love you, babe."

I thought about calling her back, but decided I'd wait one more day—perhaps I'd have something more exciting to tell her after my maybe-date with Lucas.

There was a second message, which was indeed my mother, fussing nonstop for three entire minutes about my physical and mental well-being. Holding the phone away from my ear, I rolled my eyes and hung it up before she even finished. No way was I calling her back. This day had turned out to be a lot of fun, with the promise of more to come. The last thing I wanted was to let my mother's nerves bring me down.

Flopping facedown into the pillow, I fell sound asleep inside a minute.

#

I woke up in a little puddle of drool with my shoes still on, feet hanging off the bed, totally panicked. Had I overslept? Frantic, I checked the bedside clock, which assured me I had forty-five minutes before Lucas would be here to collect me, so I put on some music and danced around the spacious room, elated about the evening ahead.

After a quick bath, I wrapped myself in a towel and perused my clothing. Since this date wasn't on my outfit calendar either, I had to wing it. Originally I'd planned on wearing a dress and heels tonight, but I wasn't sure that would be right anymore.

After trying on five different outfits, I settled on dressy jeans, a flowy sleeveless blouse with a beaded neck in a soft shade of pink, and a fitted ivory jacket that was slightly cropped. I was tempted to wear my new shoes, strappy nude Jimmy Choos with skyscraper heels, which I'd bought for the trip and had never worn. But I stuck to flats in case we did a lot of walking—Tucker always got cabs when we traveled, but Lucas seemed to like walking or taking the Metro, and I did too. Giving the gorgeous sandals a longing look and a kiss on the sole, I put them back on the closet floor and slipped on my flats.

After I touched up my hair, I added a little smoky eye makeup, but I skipped the lipstick, filling in my lips with dusky pink liner and going over it with balm. Rubbing them together, I made sure they were neither sticky nor goopy, just soft with a hint of color.

Hell, with a little luck, maybe I could cross Kiss on a Train off the Paris list tonight.

See, Lucas? Lists are *fun.*

The final step was a little spritz of perfume, but when I held the bottle in my hand and sniffed it, the scent reminded me of Tucker. In fact, it had been a gift from him.

I set the bottle back on the marble vanity and decided on scented body lotion instead. It was sweet but not overpowering, and I even took off my clothes to rub it all over my body, ignoring the inner voice demanding to know why I felt it was necessary to have my inner thighs smell like roses and jasmine.

Since I'd taken so long to get ready, I was running about ten minutes behind. Racing down the hall and into the elevator, I hoped I wouldn't cause us to miss a reservation or something. I tapped my foot as the car descended, fidgeting anxiously as I willed it to move faster. *Jesus, Mia. Calm down.*

But when the elevator doors opened and I saw him across the lobby, I couldn't keep the smile from my face nor the hot-air balloon feeling from swooshing up inside me.

His hair had been tamed, and his scruff trimmed—maybe not clean, but much closer to it. Without the shaggy curls and the whiskers, I could better appreciate the handsome planes of his face—the cut of his jaw, the prominent cheekbones, the curve of his mouth. He wore dark jeans, a clean white t-shirt and a blazer, and even though I'd always been a suit and tie kind of girl, the sight of him made my insides tighten. Best of all was the look of his face when he saw me—a cross between surprise and delight.

"I was beginning to think you'd left town after all." He smiled before kissing both my cheeks.

"Sorry," I said, slightly out of breath. "I fell asleep when I got back."

"Good. Naps are amazing. And now I can keep you out late."

Was it my imagination or did he squeeze my arm as he said that? Either way, my blood heated up about a thousand degrees, a hot pooling at my center.

We took the Metro to the Latin Quarter and walked to a small Italian restaurant called Marco Polo. We were seated at an outdoor table on the patio, but tall heat lamps and candles on the table made the crisp night air seem warm and cozy.

"Sorry, I didn't even stop to think that maybe you'd like French food tonight?" Lucas leaned across the table with a worried expression on his face.

"No, not at all. This looks amazing. And I can actually kind of understand the menu." It was in French, of course, but the names of familiar Italian dishes jumped out at me.

"Everything is good here. It's my favorite restaurant in Paris."

"Really? What should I have?"

He went over the menu with me, and when I couldn't decide between two dishes, he ordered them both and promised me I could have as many tastes off his plate as I wanted. I chose a bottle of wine, an Italian red, and made him promise to let me pay for it.

"Let's not worry about that," he said. "Talk to me about what else you'd like to do while you're here."

I told him about wanting to visit the flea market, and we got into a lengthy discussion about our mutual love for old things and the stories behind them. As he talked about some of the vintage pieces in his mother's Paris and his New York apartment, I propped my chin in my hand and thought how different he was from Tucker, who preferred modern to antique. Sometimes he didn't mind if a piece *looked* old, as long as it was a pricey reproduction and not the genuine article, which might fall apart, and besides—someone else had used it. He thought that was weird.

"The flea market isn't open tomorrow, but would you like to do something else?" asked Lucas. "I could take you to a few of my favorite vintage stores."

My chin came off my hand. *He wants to see me again tomorrow!* "I'd love to! But are you sure you're not busy? I don't want to monopolize all your time."

"No, I'm not busy tomorrow. I do have to go out of town the next day, but…" His voice trailed off. "Tomorrow is good."

My happiness deflated. *He's leaving in two days?* But I pasted what I hoped was a bright smile on my face. "OK. Tomorrow sounds great."

Frenched

Our wine and first course arrived, and I forced myself not to think about anything other than the present moment and just enjoy the meal. Lucas was right—the food was delicious. Each course was better than the last, and the service was leisurely, allowing us plenty of time to enjoy each other, too. When I finally tasted my veal Marsala, I could not contain the words of ecstasy bubbling from my lips. "Oh my God. *Oh my God*, it's so good."

Lucas grinned. "You say that a lot."

"I can't help it—it's all the food and wine here. Good thing I don't live in Paris, I'd be big as a house."

"It's nice to see you happy. I was worried last night that your first trip to Paris would be your last."

I swallowed the divine bite in my mouth. "I think I'd come back for the veal alone."

"It's good, isn't it? Here, try this." He cut a piece of his steak and lifted it to my lips across the table.

I moaned at the velvet texture, the hint of rosemary and garlic, and especially at the intimate act of taking it off Lucas's fork. *His mouth was on it right before mine*, I thought, chewing rapturously. *We practically kissed already.*

Of course, it wasn't true, but each time he offered me a bite—and I him—I couldn't help but think we were one step closer. And I really wanted to kiss him. It shocked me how much I wanted to kiss him. *Quit staring at his mouth. You're totally obvious!*

Over coffee, we talked about music and his research and how his father had influenced him. We discovered a mutual love for old jazz standards—no surprise there—and he said he had quite a large collection of vintage records at his Paris and New York apartments.

"You can't beat the sound of vinyl," he said, setting his empty cup down. "It's so much better than digital."

"I've never noticed. Maybe you'll show me the difference sometime." *Like when we're listening to records and making out.*

Across the candle-lit table, he smiled at me, turning my insides into hot wax. "I'd like that."

We stared at each other for a long moment, during which my desire for him went from Butterflies in the Belly to Wet in the Panties. I no longer cared what my motivation was for wanting him. I just knew that I did—and I wanted more than kissing too. My nipples grew stiff and tingly and I imagined his perfect mouth on them. Holy shit. My underwear was totally damp with desire, and the seam of my jeans was pressing against my clit in just the right way. When my mind strayed to his hands reaching under the table, I excused myself.

"I'll be right back." I smiled as he stood up too. Such a gentleman. What the hell was I going to do about that?

Frenched

I used the bathroom inside the restaurant—yes, the panties were soaked. In fact, I nearly ditched them, they were so wet—and by the time I got out, Lucas had paid for dinner, including the wine.

"Don't be mad." He held up his hands. "I promise you can pay for the next one."

I punched him playfully on the shoulder. "I'm totally mad. You promised before, too."

"So what would you like to do?" We left the restaurant patio and began walking slowly down the street. "It's pretty early, and there are a few clubs in this area we could check out, maybe see some live music."

I took a deep breath. *You only live once.* "Actually, I thought maybe you could show me your apartment. We could listen to some of your records or something? I mean, if you want to."

He stopped walking and turned to face me, and his expression was an interesting mix of *yes, please* and *holy shit, did she just say that?* "Um, sure. We could do that. Of course I want to. It's just that…" He struggled to finish the thought. It was obvious he was nervous about taking me back to his place, and I understood why.

But at this point I could bear the wait no longer.

I took a step closer to him, angling my head so that my lips were just beneath his. All he had to do was lower his lips two inches, and they'd be on mine. Suspense had me rising on tiptoe.

Please, Lucas. Kiss me.

Finally he lowered his mouth onto mine, and the warmth of his lips sent bolts of lightning straight to my core.

Tentatively, I put a hand to the back of his neck and opened my lips further, and he began to move his mouth over mine in a way that was both tender and suggestive. He kissed each of my lips, taking them gently between his own. Then he slanted his mouth more fully over mine, tilting his head so that the fit out our lips was tighter, the intensity of the kiss deeper. His hand moved to my hip, and my entire body shivered from the powerful pull of longing within me. God, how long had it been since I'd felt that?

So, so long.

Somewhere in the back of my mind, I remembered we were standing on the street, but I couldn't resist bringing my other hand to Lucas's jaw, desire rippling anew at the feel of his stubble on my palm. I even liked the way it felt on my lips and face—a little scratchy and rough, but new and different and exotic.

Lucas broke off the kiss and looked at me with concern in his eyes.

"Mia. I don't want you to think I—"

"Shhh." I put a finger on his lips. "I'm not thinking anything right now except that I want you to kiss me again."

Frenched

He smiled and brought his mouth to mine once more. Shyly, I tasted his lips with my tongue, and I was rewarded with a low moan from the back of his throat as well as the soft stroke of his tongue against mine, just once.

Oh my God. I'm shaking, I want him so badly.

I pulled back slightly. "Let's go."

"Are you sure?"

"Yes." The word was out before he even finished the question. "And I want to tell you something." I put a hand on his chest. It was warm and hard, and damn, I wanted to see it naked. "I do not now, nor will I ever, think you're anything less than a perfect gentleman, OK? I can tell that you're worried about something—maybe moving too quickly or being too forward or maybe it's the whole canceled wedding thing—"

"All of the above."

"—but unless you've got a girlfriend back in New York or a criminal past or a creepy insect collection at your apartment, I really, really, really want to come over."

He chuckled, the corners of his eyes crinkling the way I liked. "No, no, and *definitely* no. I only want to be sure you're comfortable with it."

"I am." I gave him a quick kiss on the lips for being so sweet. "I like you, Lucas. And I know exactly what I'm doing."

That was a huge lie. Enormous. The Arc de Triomphe of lies.

I wanted Lucas like crazy, if my underwear was any indication. But I had no idea what I was doing.

I just knew that I liked it.

Chapter Eight

We didn't talk a lot on the way to his apartment, but he held my hand the entire time, and I had to try really hard not to start skipping. Had it really been just last night I was shuffling down these streets, miserable and alone, hating couples acting just like we were right now? It seemed impossible to believe how my luck had completely reversed.

"This is my street." Lucas turned left, giving my hand a squeeze.

I glanced around, taking in the seven-story buildings of light stone with detailed entrances and decorative iron railings on the windows. At the street level were a few shops and cafes, but mostly it appeared to be a residential street. I saw no other people out and about and only one car passed us as we walked. "Quiet neighborhood."

At least until I start screaming your name.

Jesus, Mia, stop it! What if he's not thinking what you're thinking?

"It is, pretty much," Lucas said, letting go of me to take a key from his pocket. He went up to a large set of black double doors under a stone pediment and stuck his key in the one on the right. Then he paused to look over his shoulder at me, a grin on his face. "But I have double-paned windows, so we can be as loud as we want."

Oh, he's so thinking it.

I slapped him lightly on the back. "You're awfully confident."

He pushed open the door and stood back to let me enter first, a look of exaggerated innocence on his face. "I meant when I play you some records. Didn't you want to look at my vinyl?"

His naked ass was what I wanted to look at, but I thought that might be too forward to say, so I just bit my lip and moved past him into the building.

"I'm on the third floor." He took my hand and we climbed the stairs, my anticipation rising with each step.

He unlocked the apartment door and pushed it open, again allowing me to enter first. I gasped when he switched on some overhead lights.

"Oh my God, it's beautiful!"

The apartment wasn't big, but it was so stylish and well-appointed, I couldn't imagine needing anything more. Straight ahead was a living room, and immediately to the left was a tiny but gleaming kitchen—all white with black granite counters. The floors were polished light wood, with a black and ivory chevron rug in the living room.

Lucas switched on a lamp, and I wandered deeper inside, turning in a full circle to admire the warm colors and classic décor, which was somehow elegant and masculine at the same time. The ceiling and moldings were white, but the walls were painted a warm taupe. Against the wall to the right was a brown velvet antique sofa, above which hung three large framed mirrors.

Two huge, floor-to-ceiling windows faced the street, each bracketed with long chocolate-colored silk drapes held back by thick rope tassels. Taking a breath, I turned to my left and drifted into the bedroom area, which was behind an antique dressing screen.

The double bed had a plain ivory, rectangular headboard that looked like it was upholstered in leather but I wasn't close enough to touch it—yet. With my stomach jumping, I took in the wall behind the bed, which was papered in brown and white geometric shapes. The bold look was softened by a huge square print of a white rose hanging above the bed.

I looked at Lucas. "Your mother has good taste."

"She does." He laid his keys and wallet on a bench in front of the bedroom window. "Although I don't think she's stayed here in years. She and

Sebastien have a townhouse over on the right bank. Mostly she keeps this for me." He closed the drapes before turning back to me, and I gave him a sly look through lowered lashes.

"Mama's boy, huh? Baby of the family?"

Lucas shrugged. "Not really. Maybe she feels guilty for leaving me to move back here when I was so young."

Nodding slowly, I wondered if he harbored any resentment about that. I'd have asked him, except he was coming toward me with a look in his eye that said I Do Not Want To Talk About My Mother Right Now.

"Can I get you anything?" he asked. "A glass of wine?"

"No, thanks." My hands were gripping my bag, and I felt unsure of myself all of a sudden. I'd actually never had a one-night stand or even gone home with someone on a first date. Would this be awkward? Should I pretend I didn't know what I wanted to do? Should I say what I was thinking or try to be coy?

"You don't look OK. You look nervous." He tipped up my chin, his brown eyes soft and serious. "No pressure, Mia. We can just hang out and listen to records and drink wine, if you want. Or I can take you back to your hotel and see you tomorrow."

God, he really was handsome. How had I not seen it from the moment we met? And he was so sweet and funny and interesting, and right now he had way,

way, *way* too many clothes on. My confidence returned.

"Oh, no. You're not getting off that easy." I dropped my purse to the floor and threw my arms around his neck, crushing my mouth to his. He barely had time to wrap his arms around me when I pulled back slightly. "Well, I don't know, maybe it will be that easy."

He laughed, putting his hands beneath my ass and hitching me up so my legs wrapped around his waist. "You are a fucking delight, princess. It's like you know the dirty jokes in my head I'm too scared to make in front of you."

Giggling, I kicked off my flats and crossed my ankles behind him.

"Never be scared to make a dirty joke in front of me. I have a surprisingly filthy mind."

His eyebrows lifted. "Really."

I nodded. "Are you shocked?"

"Yes. But pleased."

Our mouths came together again, hotter and hungrier and holy shit he knew how to kiss. Now that we weren't in a public place, Lucas kissed me in an entirely different way, his full lips opening wide, his tongue sliding between them, thrusting in and out in a way that hinted at what was to come.

Pulling him tighter to me with my legs, I threaded my fingers through those dark curls, luxuriating in the feel of his thick hair in my hands and the gentle scratch of his stubble on my face. Had I really found it unappealing yesterday? Now I couldn't get enough of it, and I was desperate to feel his weight on me, his bare skin on mine, his naked body between my legs.

"I can't believe this," I whispered as his hot mouth traveled down my neck.

"Me either. But I can't say I haven't been thinking about it all day." His words were muffled against my skin and I felt the vibrations of his voice on my throat, sending another current of desire sluicing through me. He moved toward the bed and lowered me onto my back. "Give me one second."

I released my hold on him, and he straightened, ditched his shoes and shrugged out of his coat, which he tossed on the window seat. Now that he wore only the fitted t-shirt, I could better appreciate the lean muscularity of his upper body, which tapered to a trim waist. I slipped my jacket from my shoulders as well and tossed it over his on the bench. Then leaning back on my hands, I stared at his perfect ass as he opened a small armoire against the wall.

Oh my God, he's so fucking hot. And he's been thinking about me like this all day? I felt giddy, like a teenager with a first crush. I needed to get my hands on him—it took all my willpower to stay on the bed.

"Any requests?" he asked.

"Take off your pants."

He grinned at me over his shoulder. "I meant music."

"Oh. Hmmmm." I rested my chin on my shoulder. "Don't you have an American Chick in My Apartment playlist?"

"No, as a matter of fact, I don't."

"Well then...you can choose."

I nodded, and a moment later, music pulsed softly from hidden speakers. Lucas turned around and took off his t-shirt, dropping it to the floor. No lie, I licked my lips, unable to take my eyes off his bare chest, tight abs, and naked back while he went into the other room to turn off the lights.

He returned to the bedside just as my patience was at the breaking point, and he left the lamp on the nightstand burning.

"Come here," he said.

On my knees, I moved to the edge of the bed, my legs quivering. I wanted this, wanted it badly, but it had been so long since I'd been with anyone besides Tucker...I was simultaneously ecstatic and terrified. Lucas cradled my face in his hands and kissed the tip of my nose. I could practically feel the heat radiating from his bare skin, and my hands ached to touch him.

"We only go as far as you want to," he whispered, planting kisses on each cheek, my forehead, my lips, and then bending to rub his lips on my throat.

As far as I wanted to go? My mind exploded with all the far places I wanted to go with Lucas. Extremely far places. Places so remote I'd never even *thought* about visiting them with anyone else before.

"Lucas." I slid my hands up the sizzling skin on his chest. "My blouse hooks behind my neck. Stop talking and undo it."

Once he'd lifted my blouse from my arms and set it aside, he lowered his mouth to my shoulder and reached behind me to undo my strapless bra. Chills cascaded down my arms as cool air swept over my breasts. Finally we were both naked from the waist up, and Lucas wrapped his arms around me and pulled me close, our bare chests pressed together. "You're so beautiful." His voice was reverent and raw at the same time, and his hot torso against mine made my blood go from simmering to molten.

I slid my hands up his shoulders as his mouth slanted over mine. Lucas's touch was warm on my skin, but I shivered when he moved one hand to my stomach and up my chest, brushing his thumb across one nipple. It tingled beneath his touch and I arched my back, desperate for more.

"Oh God, your body," he murmured, dropping his lips to the swell of one breast. He kissed his way to its peak and circled my nipple with his tongue before taking it in his mouth and sucking gently. My mouth dropped open, my breath coming hard. *I have to get my hands on him.*

110

Frenched

Running one hand down the front of his jeans, my core clenched when I felt how hard and thick he was. Slowly I rubbed my hand up and down the solid length of his cock through his pants and imagined what he would feel like inside me. It was enough to make me stop breathing momentarily.

I reached for his zipper.

But before I could get it down, Lucas looped an arm around my back and moved us lengthwise on the bed, bracing his arms at my sides and settling his hips over mine. Then he kissed me again, setting fire to my lips and tongue as I widened my knees and slid my hands down his lower back.

Ohmygod Ohmygod Ohmygod Ohmygod. Just the weight of his hard, tight body between my legs was goddamn glorious. And when he started to move—

Jesus, did I just yelp?

I couldn't help it. Gripping his ass, I pulled him into me, feeling his hard cock right where I needed it, even through two layers of underwear and two pairs of jeans. I gasped, bucking up against him, feeling more than ever like a teenager, about to go off just from this. We still had our pants on, for fuck's sake. *But God, I'm close already! If he just keeps the rhythm steady, keeps his dick right there, yes, yes, yes, yes, right there, maybe moves a little quicker…* I yanked him into me harder and moved my hips faster.

"Mia, Mia." Lucas swept his lips across my cheek to my earlobe, which he took between his teeth for a second. "Slow down, gorgeous. I'm not in a rush."

"I know, but it just feels so good, and it's been so long since I...I don't want it to go away," I whimpered.

He picked his head up and looked at me strangely. "Don't want what to go away?"

"My orgasm."

"Your orgasm goes away?"

I opened my eyes and peeked at him. "Well, let's just say it's only made a rare appearance during actual sex these last couple years. So when I feel one coming on, I—"

"You feel one coming on already?" The pride in his voice was unmistakable.

"Yes, so please don't stop." I kissed his chin, his jaw, his throat. "God, you smell good." Burying my face in his neck, I breathed him in, digging my heels into the back of his thighs.

"Mia." Lucas took my wrists and pinned them next to my ears on the pillow. "Look at me, please."

"That's not going to help me slow down." But I looked up at his handsome face, my heart beating faster still as I took in the full lips, the straight nose, the long lashes.

"Listen. I don't know what kind of assholes you've been with before, but I promise you, your orgasm will not only make an appearance tonight, it will be the star of the show."

My nipples perked up even more. "Really?"

"Really." He slid down my body, trailing kisses from my lips down the center of my chest to my belly button. Then he unbuttoned and unzipped my jeans, rubbing his mouth and chin back and forth just above the lace of my underwear. "In fact, I will venture to say that there may even be an encore or two."

"Oh. My. God." Yanking the pillow from beneath my head, I smushed it over my face before screaming into it. Loud.

The warm breath of Lucas's laughter tickled low on my belly. "I haven't even done anything yet."

"Yes, you have." My words were muffled by the pillow, so I lifted it up slightly and looked down at him. "Yes, you have. You have no idea."

He smiled seductively before peeling my jeans and underwear all the way off, and I said a quick prayer of thanks that I'd kept my pre-wedding wax appointment. For the first time ever, I was totally bare.

"Just lie back and relax, love." He slid my legs apart, planting a kiss on my left inner thigh, then my right. "Tell me if something feels good and scream all you want."

My eyes were already rolling back in my head as I felt the tip of his tongue tracing the seam straight up my center. I clutched at the pillow over my face, clenching and unclenching my fingers as he did it again and again with slow, deliberate strokes. Then he flattened the entire velvet surface of his tongue on my tingling sex, licking me from bottom to top, savoring me as if I were the most delicious thing he'd ever tasted.

No one had ever, *ever* made me feel this beautiful, this cherished, this out of my mind with desire. Tucker had gone down on me a few times, but somehow it had always felt like he was doing me a favor, which made it less enjoyable. I mean, knowing that he was probably more worried about getting a wet spot on the bed than getting me to come took a little something away from the experience. And he was always so tentative—like he was afraid to really go for it.

But Lucas… Jesus Christ, Lucas was a new world.

I moaned into the pillowcase as he swirled the tip of his tongue around my clit, not on it directly, just teasing little circles that had blood rushing through my lower body, the muscles tightening with need. He kept taunting me that way until I couldn't handle the ache any longer and I threw the pillow aside. "Lucas," I begged.

But instead of hitting the target like I wanted him to, he slid one finger inside me, making me suck in my breath. "You taste so good," he said, his voice low, almost a whisper. "Better than wine."

Smiling, I exhaled. "Impossible."

He slid a second finger in next to the first, moving them in some magical way that made my entire body nearly numb with pleasure, while his lips plucked softly at my hot, humming bundle of nerves.

I looked down at him, nearly losing control at the sight of his dark head between my thighs, at the playful but hungry way he devoured me. "Oh my *god*, Lucas. *It feels fucking amazing.*"

"Mmmmm. Good." Then he zeroed in on the bulls-eye, flicking it with the tip of his tongue before licking me with one long, hard stroke, and then another, keeping a steady, driving rhythm with his hand.

"Oh God, yes!" I lifted my hips to meet his thrusting fingers and hot tongue. Every muscle in my lower body tensed as he took me higher and higher. My hands clawed at the bedspread so fiercely I thought my fingernails might go right through it. "Jesus, Lucas! I'm going to come!"

He moaned, the vibration sending me to the crest of the first wave, and I cried out. My head dropped back as he sucked on my clit and twisted his fingers inside me, pushing me over the top. Closing my fists in his hair, I screamed and throbbed and pointed my toes, riding out the longest, most intense orgasm I had ever experienced.

And not once did I worry about a wet spot.

Chapter Nine

"I think I'm dead," I said after my body had finally stopped convulsing. "You'll have to bury me at Père Lachaise next to that president."

"I'll take that as a compliment."

"You should." My eyes were closed, the silver stars still fading. "God, I didn't even know an orgasm like that was possible."

"Good."

I popped up on my elbows and look at him. The fact that his hair was tousled and his mouth was shiny and wet sent fresh lust careening through me. "And now I want another one. So come here. And leave your pants there."

He smiled. "This is one time I'm not going to argue with you, princess."

I watched, biting my bottom lip, as he undressed all the way and pulled back the covers so we could slip between the sheets. Once his warm, naked body was stretched out next to mine, I ran a hand down his chest and stomach and wrapped my fingers around his hot, hard cock. Willing myself to have patience, I went slow at first, planting kisses on his chest, in the crook of his neck, beneath his ear. I sucked his earlobe and pumped my hand up and down his long shaft. "And your body is fucking amazing, and your tongue—don't even get me started on your tongue."

"Good, because I can't keep it off you." He brought a hand to my hip and slid it up to my breast, squeezing it, teasing my nipple with his fingers. Then he took it in his mouth, biting down with a force just the other side of gentle.

Gasping, I squeezed his flesh a little harder, and he began to thrust into my hand, making me hot with impatience. "God, I can't wait to have you inside me."

"Mmm." He slipped his fingers between my legs, where I was already wet and warm and aching for him.

"Lucas," I rasped. Now."

"Shhh." He plunged his fingers into me with a steady rhythm, sucking on one nipple and then the other until I felt the tension pulling low and tight inside me once more, and I knew if I didn't stop him, I'd explode again in less than a minute. And it wasn't that I didn't want to—but I wanted him inside me first.

"Lucas." I fell to my back and shimmied beneath him. "Please."

"Are you sure?"

"Yes."

"Let me get a condom."

"You have ten seconds." I shut my eyes. "Nine. Eight..."

By the time I got to one, he was centering himself at my core, and my entire body shivered with anticipation. I couldn't remember ever having two orgasms in one night, but I believed if anyone could take me there, Lucas could.

"Mia." Bracing his hands near my shoulders, he pushed slowly inside, and I gasped at the way he stretched and filled me, at the way his unhurried pace allowed me to feel every sensation so fully. It felt so different, so *good* to have someone willing to take his time. Someone to care about fulfilling my needs, someone who wanted to please me.

Someone who whispered my name in awe as he held himself deep within me.

Actually, I think I did die. Because this feels like heaven.

I turned my face to the side, fighting the urge to climax three seconds after he started circling his hips, grinding his pelvic bone on the spot that had me buzzing and twitching like a live wire.

I'd never been with a musician before, but Jesus Christ...Lucas's rhythm and timing were fucking phenomenal. Not to mention the way he moved, with perfect control and a muscular, predatory grace.

"Oh my God." Panting, I ran my hands all over his body, his arms and neck and back, his perfect ass, digging my fingernails into his flesh, my body on fire. "I'm trying so hard not to scream in your ear."

"I'll be insulted if you don't."

I laughed, and then cried out as he began to thrust harder and faster. A strangled moan sounded at the back of his throat, and I brought my knees up to take him deeper.

"Oh yes," I whimpered. "Yes, Lucas. Yes. Yes!" With each word, my volume rose, the storm within me raging stronger. "Oh my God! Don't stop! Don't stop! Don't stop!"

And then, the most incredible thing in the world—Lucas's ragged breaths became pants and then primal sounds and then loud, uncontrollable shouts every time he rocked into me, and I realized it was possible we were going to come together, like *at the same time.* Like in a fucking book or a movie!

Suspended just before the peak of my orgasm, I willed my body to wait for him, and the few seconds I lingered there were equal parts agony and rapture, such that I nearly wept with the effort. Finally, I could bear it no longer and sailed over the top, screaming his name as I pulled him into me, my face buried in his neck, my body tightening around his.

And it happened. It fucking happened.

Just as the rhythmic contractions of my body subsided, Lucas buried himself deep inside me and I felt his cock begin to throb. He moaned long and hard, his movement reduced to tiny little thrusts that redoubled the strength of my climax. Wave after wave after wave of unspeakable pleasure coursed through my body, and I imagined it coursing through his too, as if we were sharing the same current of sexual electricity. My mouth hung open in utter shock, and stars—no, entire fucking galaxies—exploded in front of my eyes.

Eventually our bodies stilled and our hearts stopped threatening to burst right out of our chests, but I still couldn't speak. I could barely breathe.

Not only had I just had the best sex of my entire life, including two name-screaming, hair-pulling, sheet-clawing orgasms, but I'd learned something.

The simultaneous O.

Was not. A myth.

#

"Again," I demanded.

"Again? I've done it twice already."

"Again. I can't get enough."

Lucas rolled his eyes but strummed the opening chords to La Vie En Rose once more on his guitar, and I gleefully clapped my hands. We were sitting on the floor in the living room sharing a plate of grapes—they're called *raisins* in French, how weird is that?—and tearing off pieces of a baguette that Lucas said was from yesterday so it was too old to eat, but it tasted fine to me. Better than fine. In fact, I declared it Best. Baguette. Ever.

I was experiencing a bit of Post Second Orgasm Euphoria.

"I want to know what the lyrics mean." I popped another grape in my mouth. "I think you should sing it for me too this time."

Lucas shook his head. "I don't really know the lyrics by heart or I would, although I'm not a very good singer."

I smiled sweetly. "I wouldn't be critical. You have plenty of other talents."

Grinning, Lucas strummed one more chord before muting the strings with his hands. "Wait." Getting to his feet, he laid the guitar on the couch and went into the bedroom. He returned with a laptop, set it on the little table in front of the window, and opened it up.

While he searched for the song, I started to brush the crumbs off the button-down shirt he'd given me to put on, but then I felt guilty since his floors were so clean. Getting to my feet, I picked up the hem of the shirt so they wouldn't spill everywhere and went to the kitchen to drop them into the garbage. Returning to the rug, I picked up the plate, threw grape stems away, and put it in the tiny dishwasher, admiring the sparkling counters and clean sink again. I'd never have guessed when I first saw Lucas at the bar that his apartment would be so neat. His tidiness was such a nice surprise, it inspired a new list.

Well, that and his tongue.

5 Awesome Things About Lucas

1) He always kisses me at least once on each cheek when he says hello.
2) He knows about wine, history, cathedrals, music, and love stories. (Bonus points for deadly historical blowjob as well as for family owning a vineyard.)
3) He opens doors for me and always allows me to enter a room first.
4) His apartment is beautiful and immaculate, even the bathroom.
5) He knows how to give me multiple orgasms and doesn't give a fuck about a wet spot. In fact, he's proud of them.

"Found it."

A moment later, I heard the scratchy sound of an old recording and then the opening strains of the song. A huge grin stretched my lips, and I walked around the counter into the living room just as Lucas straightened up. The sight of him, wearing jeans but no shirt, barefoot, his curls messed and lying any which way, made my stomach flip.

"Dance with me."

He shook his head. "I'm an even worse dancer than singer, I'm afraid."

"I don't care. Please?" I held out my hand, and he grimaced but took it, pulling me into his chest and wrapping his other arm around me. In my bare feet, my eyes were level with his chin, which meant I could comfortably rest my head on his shoulder. "You're so easy," I teased. "All it takes is 'please' to get you to do something."

"You better be nice or I'm not going to tell you what the lyrics mean," he warned.

I kissed his scruffy chin. "Sorry. I'll be nice."

Closing my eyes, I tipped my head onto his shoulder again and listened as he translated the lyrics for me, and the gist of it was that life looks different when you're in love. Better. Prettier. Although just like this afternoon, my mind drifted from *what* he was saying to *how* he said it. How his voice sometimes cracked when he spoke low and soft. How he held me to his chest so closely I could feel his heartbeat. How he swayed to the song's old-fashioned rhythm, turning us in a slow circle in front of the windows.

My cheek warmed on his bare skin, and I felt something start to stir within me. It had to be going on three AM, and I was drowsy and satisfied, yet I couldn't stop myself from kissing his shoulder, his collarbone, his neck.

Lucas stood still as I kissed my way up to his lips, then he took my head in his hands, bringing his mouth to mine. Between us I felt his cock begin to thicken and rise and press against my pelvic bone. My lower body clenched involuntarily.

"Mmmmm, Lucas?" I turned my head and his mouth moved along my jaw and down my neck.

"Yeah?" His breathing had gone ragged.

"I know I've already had my star turn and one encore already, and I don't want to be greedy, but can we do it again?"

Instead of answering, he walked backward and sat on the couch, pulling me down onto his lap. I straddled him, one knee on either side of his hips, and he began unbuttoning my shirt.

"The couch, really?" I couldn't help but be amazed. We'd closed the drapes and all, but Tucker would *never* have done it on an expensive couch, and this one looked like a nice antique. "You're not worried about...getting something on it?"

"Do I seem worried?" He didn't even pick his head up from my chest, where he was already dragging his tongue over one nipple and twisting the other one between his fingers. Fuck, I loved his mouth and hands on me. His breath on my skin.

"No."

"There's your answer."

I smiled, holding his head to my chest as he nibbled and sucked and bit, circling my hips, rubbing against the erection straining against his jeans. *This feels fucking amazing—maybe he'll let me stay on top.*

Yet another thing Tucker did not enjoy, at least never with me.

Lucas brought his lips back to mine, and I gripped the back of the couch, riding him even harder and feeling him push up to meet me. "Let me get up for one second," he whispered.

When he returned, he kicked off his jeans and pulled me right back where I was.

I had to bite my lip to keep from shouting hallelujah.

After helping him roll the condom on, I slowly lowered my body onto his long, solid cock, my breath caught in my throat. Lucas closed his eyes as I sank down, his expression almost pained. He kept his hands on my hips, but he didn't push.

"Oh my God," he breathed. "You feel so fucking good, I don't know if I can even look at you."

I smiled. "Why?"

"Because you're so gorgeous, and your body's so perfect, and you're so tight and wet and oh fuck, don't move yet…"

But I'd gotten all the way down, gasping at how deep I was able to take him, and couldn't resist rocking my hips a little, just to tease him. "Mmm, Lucas."

"Fuck." His cock pulsed once inside me.

"I love the way that feels," I whispered, squeezing him with my core muscles.

"Mia." My name fell from his lips before he kissed me long and hard and deep, his tongue thrusting into my mouth. He threaded his fingers through my hair as I began to raise and lower myself, sliding up and down his shaft. "Oh God. Just wait—don't move," he begged, curling his fists and pulling on my hair.

I didn't want it to end yet either, so after lowering myself all the way down again, I stayed where I was, reveling in the feel of him so deep and thick within me. He reached between us with one hand and rubbed his thumb over my clit, keeping the other fingers furled tight in my hair.

"Oh my God, how do you know exactly how to touch me?" I whimpered. "Did you read some kind of instruction manual somewhere and memorize it?" His thumb moved quicker, and I could feel the orgasm beginning to build.

"Fuck, Lucas." I *had* to move. If I made him come too soon, so be it—I wouldn't be that far behind. Pumping my hips over his, I grabbed his shoulders and held on. He slid his hands around to my ass and gripped me tight, shoving into me so hard his hips came off the couch. I rocked faster and faster, until the burning hot pressure within me built up so much I cried out, desperate for release.

And then, as if it were his climax that burst my pleasure wide open, Lucas groaned and stiffened beneath me right as my own orgasm peaked, and I rode his throbbing cock as uncontrollable spasms slammed through me.

And I actually screamed, "Oh my *God*, I love Paris!"

Chapter Ten

Once Lucas stopped laughing enough so he could breathe, he stood up and walked us into the bedroom with my legs still wrapped around his waist. "So you're glad you stayed, I take it?"

I nodded. "Very."

"Good." He deposited me on the bed, dropping a kiss on my forehead before going into the bathroom, still grinning.

Closing my eyes, I lay back, my arms flung over my head, my legs hanging off the edge of the bed. If I hadn't been so fucking happy, I'd probably have been embarrassed. But I couldn't stop smiling.

A moment later, Lucas came out and flopped down next to me. "You know, I think that's the best thing I've ever heard during sex."

I peeked at him. "I'm glad I can amuse you."

"You do more than that. God, you're incredible."

I rolled to my side, head propped in my hand. "Sure you're not just saying that because you feel sorry for me?"

"Why would I feel sorry for you?"

"Because I was so miserable yesterday. Because I've never had sex this good before. Because I've never had three orgasms in one night—maybe not even in one week."

He shook his head. "Why the hell did you waste so much time with that guy? If you were mine, I'd never keep my hands off you. Or any other body part."

My belly flipped. *If you were mine…* "Yeah, well, he was different. Do you know that I can count on one hand the number of times he…did the thing you did earlier?"

"Go down on you? Are you kidding me? In two years, you can count the times on one hand?" Lucas looked appalled. "He had the sweetest pussy in all creation right next to him all that time and he didn't spend his days and nights buried in it?"

I shook my head, my pulse quickening at his words. "Yep. It was like, my birthday, our anniversary, and maybe like a random fourth of July or something."

He rolled his eyes. "Jesus, Mia. Don't tell me any more. It just gets worse."

"He had only two positions he liked. I called them the Approved Positions." I was laughing now. "But not to his face, of course."

Lucas groaned and grabbed a pillow, which he folded over his head. "I can't hear you."

I grabbed it and held it to my chest. "I'm only trying to emphasize that tonight has been amazing for many reasons." I batted my lashes. "Three in particular."

Lucas smiled too. "Good. There's more where those came from. But you must be exhausted. Do you want to stay over or do you want me to take you back to your hotel?"

I sighed. "Thanks, but I should go back. You don't have to take me. I can get a cab."

"No, I'll take you." He swung his feet to the floor. "And don't even argue with me, princess. Or you won't get reasons four, five, and six tomorrow."

My jaw dropped. "God, I love Paris."

His crooked smile appeared over his shoulder. "You mentioned that."

#

Lucas rode with me in the cab back to the hotel, even though I told him it wasn't necessary. He even asked the driver to wait while he walked me in. We

130

said goodbye at the elevator, and I had to giggle inwardly at his messy hair, disheveled clothing, and kiss-swollen lips. But I knew I looked the same way.

And I didn't care.

He kissed me softly. "I'll see you tomorrow. Get some rest, and call me when you wake up."

"OK." I had his cell phone number written on a scrap of paper in my purse. "See you then. I had a great day. Thanks for—" I lifted my shoulders. How the hell did you thank someone for everything that Lucas had done for me today?

But before I could finish, he put two fingers over my lips. "Stop. It was my pleasure."

The elevator doors opened behind me and I backed in, unable to keep from smiling at Lucas, who stood there with his hands in his pockets as the doors closed. The elevator ascended quickly, matching the swooping feeling inside me when I thought about the night I'd just experienced. I brought a hand to my mouth and laughed out loud.

Good thing I was alone in the elevator.

I walked down the hall to my room in a goofy-grin daze, exhausted but happy. *So* happy.

So happy I couldn't resist skipping a little before I got to my door.

So happy I couldn't stop smiling as I undressed and hung up my wrinkled blouse.

So happy I twirled my way from the bathroom to the bed after removing my makeup and brushing my teeth.

And then I lay there between the cool sheets, sighing blissfully. Tomorrow maybe I'd analyze my feelings or wonder if my behavior had been wise or examine my reasons for sleeping with a man I met yesterday. But for now, I was just going to bask in the glow.

5 Reasons I Fucking Love Paris

1) Lucas
2) Lucas
3) Lucas
4) Lucas
5) Lucas

#

I woke up around ten and picked up the phone on the nightstand, following the instructions to make an international call. It was probably unforgivable to wake Coco at four AM her time to discuss orgasms but I *had* to talk to somebody. I had to hear someone tell me I wasn't crazy or slutty or both.

Although I didn't feel slutty. In general, I'm not judgmental about sex, and even in the light of morning, my behavior with Lucas didn't strike me as promiscuous. We'd been careful. It's just that I didn't have a habit of being so spontaneous, and I'd come to Paris expecting one thing and experiencing the total opposite.

"Hello?"

"Oh. My. God."

"Mia!" Coco's croaky voice held a note of worry. "What time is it? Are you OK?"

"I'm better than OK." A shiver pulsed through my body. "I'm fucking ecstatic."

Coco sucked in her breath. "What? Oh my God, what's going on over there?"

"You're not going to believe this. I can barely believe it."

"Go on."

I licked my lips. "I met someone."

Her squeal was so loud I had to hold the phone away from my ear. "And?"

"And I had three orgasms last night."

Silence.

"Coco?"

"I'm sorry, I was in shock. Did you say three?"

I smiled. "Yes."

"Who *is* this wizard of O's?"

"His name is Lucas. He's a professor in New York, but he's half-French and living here for the summer."

"Omigod. I'm dying. How old is he?"

"I don't know, actually. We didn't really talk about that." Which was kind of funny and also kind of crazy—I'd never, *never* slept with someone without knowing their age. Or their shirt size, middle name, car make and model. "I'd guess he's about our age, though. Maybe a little older."

"What does he look like?"

Ha. She was going to love this. "You won't believe it."

"Why?"

"Because I don't either. He's got messy dark hair and scruff. And he isn't tall."

"What? What do you mean, messy hair?"

I closed my eyes and pictured it, recalled the feel of it in my hands. "Kind of scraggly. Thick and wavy."

"And *scruff*?"

"Scruff," I confirmed. "Oh, and he plays the guitar."

"Next you're going to tell me he has tattoos."

I giggled. "Not that I noticed. Yet."

"Oh. My. God, Mia. Where did you meet him?"

Flipping on to my stomach, I told her all about my disastrous first evening and how I'd randomly wandered into the bar where he was working. "And the weird thing is, he doesn't really even work there. It's his brother's bar or something, and he was just filling in."

Coco gasped. "It's fate."

I shrugged and wound a strand of hair around my finger. Was there such a thing as fate? I wasn't sure. "Anyway, he offered to be my tour guide for a day so I wouldn't have to see Paris alone. I was ready to turn around and come home before that."

"Sounds like it was a hell of a tour."

"It was. I mean, it didn't get sexy until late in the night, but when it did, it *really* did." In fact, I was getting wet now just thinking about it. Damn.

"I just can't believe it! So will you see him again?"

"Uh huh. Part two of the tour." *Which I hope ends the same way Part One did.* Quickly, I counted the days I had left in my head. Five—although hadn't Lucas said he was leaving Paris tomorrow? Shit. Maybe today was all we had left.

Coco sighed. "This is so amazing. Can I tell Erin?"

"Of course!" I tugged at my hair. "She'll probably think I've lost my mind here."

"No, she won't! She'll be thrilled, just like I am. You deserve this, Mia. And don't start overthinking it."

I sighed. "I'm trying not to. Last night I didn't let myself start analyzing it at all. You would have been proud of me."

"But you're starting to second guess things now?"

I tugged harder on my hair. She knew me too well. "It's so unlike me to act this way. And when I think about the circumstances…"

"Why do you have to think about the circumstances? How does it *feel*?"

I closed my eyes, and he was there. I could smell him, hear him, feel him… Warmth blossomed at my center. "It feels good."

"Well then."

"You're sure this isn't stupid? Or slutty?"

"What? No! Damn it, woman, you're young and newly single. This is what you're *supposed* to be doing! Now listen. I want you to be safe, but keep having fun and throw your fucking caution to the wind, you hear me?"

I laughed. "I hear you. And I'll try. Sorry for waking you, I just—I had to hear you tell me I wasn't crazy."

"You're not crazy. And I'm totally jealous. I love you—call me again, OK?"

"I will. I love you too. Bye."

I hung up the phone and stretched, feeling a soreness in my limbs and abs that hadn't been there yesterday morning, and it widened the secret smile on my face. When I got out of bed and walked to the bathroom, I realized I was tender in places that had not hurt for years. YEARS. Maybe not ever.

Under the hot spray of the shower, I washed my hair and lathered my body with shower gel, and as I ran my hands over my slippery skin, I recalled Lucas's hands on me. And his lips. And his tongue.

And I nearly had to give myself number four because I got so turned on. *No, don't do it.* I paused with my hand sweeping down my stomach. *Wait for him.*

But as I rinsed the shampoo from my hair, a cautious little voice inside me began to ask questions.

Was having sex with Lucas again a bad idea? Was I just setting myself up for more heartbreak? After all, he was leaving town the next day, and I was only in Paris for a short time longer. And what about after that? Would I ever see him again? Suddenly I felt like I'd swallowed a tennis ball.

Stop it right now. You are not planning a wedding with this guy. You are fucking him. You're friends. And that's perfectly OK. You do not have to think about the future, or even tomorrow. You have today and you can make it count.

Swaying back and forth beneath the water, I wondered if I could really do that—not worry about anything except being in the present moment.

You managed it well enough last night.

True. And I'd been rewarded with the best sex of my life, three stellar orgasms, and the promise of another fantastic day with a smart, sexy guy. What more could I ask for?

By the time I rinsed all the soap off, I was totally confident I could enjoy the day—and night—ahead without letting worrisome thoughts about the future get in the way of a good time. After all, Lucas didn't seem concerned, so why should I?

And Coco was right. I'd been through a lot, and I deserved a couple days of pure, unabashed pleasure.

With the memory of Lucas's eyes and voice and smell and fingers and tongue and cock overwhelming my senses, I put my hand back between my legs.

Somehow, I knew he would approve.

Chapter Eleven

Lucas came for me at noon, greeting me with his customary kisses on the cheek. This time I kissed his cheeks too, and the touch of my lips on his stubbly skin ignited me. My belly whooshed like a torch catching fire.

Down, girl.

"Good morning." I wondered if it would be gauche to suggest we skip sightseeing and get straight to the sex.

"Morning." He brushed a curl back from my forehead. "How did you sleep?"

"Like a baby. You?"

"Same." He leaned in to whisper in my ear. "Except that I woke up thinking about you and I had a raging hard-on. I had to take care of it myself. I wished you'd stayed over."

My heart thumped hard as I imagined him jerking himself off thinking about me. Fuck, that was actually really hot. *I should have packed extra underwear in my bag. These are already wet.* "I woke up thinking about you, too," I whispered. "And I'm sore as all get-out."

"Really?" He looked pleased with himself. "I could take you back up to your room and give you a massage. Would that help?"

I shook my head. "Tempting, but it wouldn't help, because I'm pretty sure that massage would lead to other things."

"You're right. We better get going. The longer I stand here looking at you, the more my mind wanders to those other things." He gestured toward the door. "Paris awaits, princess, and I know how you feel about Paris."

I was about to say *fuck Paris, let's just get right to the other things* when I remembered that this would be my last chance to see the city with him as my guide, and I really did love hearing him talk about the places he took me. "OK. What will we do today?"

With his hand at the small of my back, he walked me through the lobby and out of the hotel. "Well, I thought maybe we'd wander over to Le Marais first. There's a lot of cool stuff over there, and the shops I wanted to take you to are in that direction as well."

"Sounds perfect."

Frenched

We took the Metro over to the Marais neighborhoods, and on the train I thought about sex. Lucas held my hand as we walked down quaint streets and through charming village squares, and I thought about sex. We admired medieval and Renaissance architecture, ate sandwiches sitting on the grass in the Place des Vosges, and toured the Victor Hugo museum. I thought about sex the entire time.

I tried hard not to show it, but it was difficult, since every time I looked at Lucas my insides fluttered, or my lower body clenched up, or butterflies swirled in my belly en masse. No matter where my eyes would alight—his hair, his hands, his lips, and yes, OK *fine*, the crotch of his pants—I was assailed with memories of last night.

Jesus, Mia. You're a fiend. Get a grip.

But I couldn't help it. Sex had never played a particularly important role in my relationship with Tucker, at least not as far as I was concerned. But today it was all I could think about. And I knew that when I went home, I'd never go back to the way I was before, sublimating my own sexual desires to appease a man. *I can't believe I did that for so long. I never knew what I was missing.*

Throughout the early afternoon, I wondered if Lucas was thinking about last night as much as I was. We talked a lot about different things—I learned he was twenty-eight, had only the two half-brothers and no sisters, was allergic to shellfish, and did not, in fact, have any tattoos—but neither of us mentioned sex once we left my hotel.

After leaving the Hugo museum, we decided we'd gone long enough without wine, so we ducked into a little bistro on rue St. Paul. Lucas ordered a bottle while I used the bathroom, and when I returned to our table by the window, he looked so delicious in the natural light I decided to be blunt.

I sat down and propped my chin on my hand. "So I have to ask you. How many times have you thought about sex today?"

"Over a million. Easy." He didn't even blink.

I burst out laughing. "Well, I'm glad it's not only me." Lowering my voice to a hush, I said, "I was beginning to think I was some kind of perv for thinking about oral sex in Victor Hugo's apartment."

He leaned across the table. "Don't worry. That's positively tame compared to the things I thought about."

My stomach jumped. "Like what?"

"Not telling. I'll just have to surprise you. Or scare you, one of the two." He brought his lips to mine for a warm, melty kiss that turned my insides to liquid.

"Do both. I might like being a little frightened."

He put his mouth to my ear. "You have no idea what you're saying to me. I'm so hard right now."

"Want me to come sit on your lap?"

He groaned and sat back. "Don't tease me. I can't handle it."

142

Frenched

Actually I probably *would* have gone around the table to sit on his lap, but our wine arrived and after the waiter poured us each a glass, Lucas lifted his up.

"What are we toasting?" I lifted mine as well.

"Oral sex and Victor Hugo?"

I cocked my head. "Doesn't seem quite right."

"Hmm. Couch sex and Edith Piaf?"

I cocked it the other way. "Closer."

"How about…unexpected sex that turns out to be better than you imagined it even though you imagined it *all day long*, including when you were at a cemetery *and* in a church?"

I nodded and pointed a finger at him. "Bingo." We clinked glasses and drank to that.

#

While we were in the café, it sprinkled a little, but by the time we finished our wine, the drizzle had stopped and the sun was starting to filter through the clouds. Lucas said the stores he wanted to take me to were close by, so we headed in their direction.

The day had warmed up—or maybe it was the conversation and the wine—but I felt a little hot, so I slipped the loose white button-down I had on off my shoulders and tied it around my waist. I'd layered it over a pretty, feminine lace-trimmed camisole, which I wore without a bra. If my nipples poked through today, I wouldn't care if Lucas noticed. In fact, I wanted him to.

"So what are you looking for?" he asked as we walked. "Clothing? Books? Jewelry? I'll assume no furniture."

"Well, I do have to find a new place to live when I get home. Maybe I can furnish it with antiques from Paris." I grinned at him. "How much could shipping be?"

"I'm guessing a lot." He was quiet a minute. "Did you live with him already?"

I was surprised he asked, since he'd said he didn't want to hear any more about Tucker. "Yes."

Lucas shoved his hands in his pockets. "Where will you go?"

"I haven't really thought about it yet. And you know what?" I tugged a hand from his pocket and held on to it. "I don't even want to. See?" Galloping a little, I shook his arm. "You're a good influence on me—I'm only thinking about right here, right now, and not even worrying about anything else. Because right now I'm totally happy."

He smiled at me and squeezed my hand. "Good."

We spent the next couple hours wandering in and out of the shops in the Village Saint-Paul. I bought a pair of vintage earrings in an art deco style for Coco and picked out a beautiful blue cashmere scarf for Erin. While I was debating whether or not to purchase the scarf in a different color for my mother, Lucas tapped my shoulder.

"Hey, I'm just going to run across the street, OK? There's a store I want to look in."

I set the scarf down. "I can come with you."

"No, you're not allowed to come with me." He took me by the shoulders and turned me back toward the table of scarves. "I'll meet you outside in ten minutes."

"Okayyyyyy." I glanced over my shoulder but he was already out the door. What the hell? Was he buying me something? Too curious to resist, I went to the front window of the store I was in and looked across the street, half expecting to see a sex toy shop.

It was a bookstore.

Get your mind out of le gutter, Mia.

Giving in to guilt, I bought the two scarves, folded them up in my bag, and went out to meet Lucas on the sidewalk. The afternoon was still overcast, but even the soft gray light seemed pretty, and I closed my eyes, enjoying the feel of the cool breeze on my face and arms.

In a moment I heard Lucas's voice. "I got you something."

I opened my eyes to see him standing there with a plain brown paper package. "You did? Why?"

He shrugged. "I'd been thinking about it since yesterday. Open it."

Half of me wanted to berate him for buying me a gift and the other half was too excited to keep my hands from tearing open the bag. Inside was a paperback book with a medieval painting of a man and woman on the cover. I read the title and gasped.

"The Love Letters of Abelard and Heloise!" I clasped it over my heart, which had skipped several beats. "I don't believe it!"

"Do you like it?" His expression was endearingly hopeful.

"Are you kidding? I love it! Oh my God, Lucas!" I threw my arms around him, and the force nearly knocked him backward. He laughed as he steadied us both, his hands on my hips.

"Good. I wasn't sure they would have it, but I'm glad they did."

Reluctantly, I released him. "Are the letters in French?"

"Well, originally they were in Latin, but they've been translated. This is an English bookstore." He gestured behind me.

"Oh, Lucas, I love it. I can't wait to read them." My eyes were a little misty, and I struggled to swallow. "Thank you."

"You're welcome. I hope you're not mad—they're romantic and all."

I slapped his stomach with the book before dropping it into my bag. "I'm over being mad. I'm all about the romance of Paris now."

"Good to know." He took the brown paper bag from me, wadded it up, and tossed it in a nearby trash container. "In that case, how would you like to see my favorite romantic place in the entire city?"

I flashed him a coy smile. "Is it your apartment?"

He laughed. "No. But it's not far."

"Good. Because I might need a little rest after all this excitement."

"Well," he said, putting his arm around my shoulder as we walked, "you're definitely invited back to my apartment later, but I can't promise you'll get any rest there."

I tipped my head onto his arm. "God, I love Paris."

But what I nearly said was *God, I love you.*
How crazy was that?

#

On the Metro ride over to the Rodin museum, which was where Lucas was taking me, I asked him if he'd ever had a serious girlfriend.

He looked at me sideways. "Why do you ask?"

I shrugged. "Just curious, I guess. You mentioned this place is your favorite romantic spot in Paris, so I assumed…"

"Oh. Well, yes I had a serious girlfriend for a while, but no, I never took her to the Musée Rodin. She's in New York."

A quick stab of jealousy made me press further. "How long were you together?"

"About three years, off and on."

It surprised me, for some reason. "Wow, that's a long time."

"I guess."

"Why'd you break up?"

"We wanted different things."

"Ah." I got the feeling his short answers were an indication he wasn't that into talking about his ex-girlfriend, and probably I shouldn't have asked, but I couldn't resist one last question. "What was her name?"

"Jessica. You want to know her birth date and shoe size too?"

I smacked him on the leg. "Come on. I'm only curious. After all, you know a lot about me and Tucker."

He grimaced. "Much more than I want to, thank you very much. Now no more talking about the past. It's right here, right now, remember?"

"Yes." But I couldn't help wondering about Jessica, the lucky girl on the receiving end of his generous affections for so long a time. What did she look like? How long ago were they together? Why did they really break up? I wondered if she was still in New York and if he ever saw her. The jealousy returned, gripping me hard for a moment, and I had to take a deep breath and hold it until the ill feeling went away.

Here and now. Here and now. Here and now.

I took a few more deep breaths, and Lucas put his arm around me, draping his hand over my shoulder. His fingers grazed the skin just above the top of my cami, really it was the top part of my breast, and my nipples immediately responded. I didn't have to wonder long if Lucas noticed.

He tipped his head to mine buried his face in my hair. "You're killing me in that little top. I'm not going to be able to walk off this train."

I smiled. And I sincerely hoped the Rodin museum wasn't very big. Nothing against nineteenth century art or anything, but I was working on a new list.

Things I Want To Do With Lucas

1) Test my blow job skills (and learn some new ones).
2) Take a shower (see what he looks like wet).

3) Let him do whatever thing he mentioned before that might scare me (whips and chains?)

4) Hear him talk dirty to me (a huge secret turn on)

5) Make him scream my name like I scream his (i.e., loud enough to wake the neighborhood, perhaps the 6th arrondissement, maybe even the whole Latin Quarter)

Not too much to ask, was it?

Chapter Twelve

The museum wasn't very big, but that wasn't why I loved it.

As we wandered through, I could see why Lucas was so enchanted with it. Located in an eighteenth century mansion, each room was a wonder of light and shadow and elegance. The fancy baroque details of the house—the tall arched windows, the parquet floors, the detailed plaster and woodwork on the walls and ceilings, the gilt on the curvy antique furniture—all of it offered the perfect contrast to the raw muscular beauty of Rodin's human figures.

Admittedly, part of my enjoyment was being there with Lucas, who held my hand and spoke quietly to me about Rodin's artistic style and why it appealed to him.

"I like the way he didn't make everything beautiful, you know?" We stood in front of a naked figure of a woman who appeared to be clutching herself in shame. "And I love the fragments, especially the hands. Look at this one here."

He took my by the shoulders and turned me around, and I gasped as we approached a huge sculpture in front of a window. It was two hands, the wrists emerging from the block base, palms and fingers arched toward each other but barely touching. Soft light filtering through the panes created delicate shadows on the hands and in the airy space between them, and I wanted to try to capture it in a photograph, although I knew a picture would never do it justice. "They're so beautiful. Are they praying?"

"No. It's two right hands, see?"

I stopped hunting for my camera and looked closer. "It *is* two right hands. I didn't even notice that." For a moment I stopped to consider how it was possible for two right hands to join that way. "What do you think they're doing?"

Lucas stood right behind me and whispered in my ear. "Well, I have a dirty mind, especially today, but if you ask me, those hands belong to two people having sex. There's a tension there, like they're just about to clasp, that makes me think…" He stood so close, I could feel his breath on my shoulder, his chest on my back, his hips right behind mine. My whole body was intensely aware of him. He brought his right hand up, palm toward me, just in front of my right shoulder. "See?"

Biting my lip, I brought my right hand up to meet his, mirroring the sculpture in front of us. My mind whirled with thoughts of him naked, pressed up tight against my bare back.

Standing up.

Against a wall.

Plunging into me.

Maybe even in the shower.

All wet.

I felt the rise of an erection against my tailbone.

My clit tingled. My core muscles clenched

Fuck.

Woozy with desire, I had to close my eyes for a second. "Jesus, Lucas."

He laughed softly, dropping his hand. "Told you I had a dirty mind. Now you better walk in front of me for a few minutes. I don't want to scare anybody with what's in my pants right now."

Smiling at him over my shoulder, I pulled my camera from my bag and took a picture of the sculpture. It might not capture the artistry or the light, but dammit, I wanted a memento of the time Lucas nearly gave me an orgasm in the middle of the Musée Rodin.

There were plenty of other works of art in that museum that were unbelievably sensual and romantic, but as we strolled outside into the garden, it was the image of the hands I couldn't get out of my head.

Or maybe it was the feel of Lucas's stiff cock on my ass.

I was so hot and bothered, I wasn't sure I would last much longer. As we paused in front of The Thinker, probably Rodin's most famous work ever, I felt guilty that all I could Think about was fucking Lucas in the shower. I cleared my throat, prepared to banish niceties to the Gates of Hell, which was another of Rodin's masterpieces I couldn't concentrate on.

What, it's full of naked writhing bodies!

But before I could suggest we go back to his apartment, get naked and writhe, he asked me if I'd like the see the gardens, and I felt too ashamed to say no. *Come on, Mia. You can give it ten more minutes.*

"Sure. I'd love that," I said.

As we walked toward the large fountain at the back, I wondered again if it was only me having a hard time remaining patient. Lucas kept making jokes about his dirty mind and tented pants, but I was beginning to think my imagination was the filthier of the two.

Then a moment later we reached the edge of the gardens, and Lucas pulled me between two rows of hedges, where a narrow gravel path made a little secret passageway. "I've been waiting to do this all day and I can't wait any longer." He turned me into his arms and kissed me, slanting his mouth over mine and plunging his tongue between my lips like he was starving for me.

I threw my arms around him, pushing my chest against his, desperate to feel his hard muscle on my soft curves. He dropped a hand to my waist and slid it up to one breast, over my camisole. I shivered.

"Mmmmm," I moaned. "That feels so good. I love your hands on me."

That's when the first few splats of rain hit my head. Both of us glanced up and noticed the huge dark clouds moving in. Thunder rumbled softly.

"Perfect timing." Lucas kissed me quickly. "I'm ready to go."

"Me too." We started walking back toward the house when it began to pour, the rain coming down in steady sheets. "Hold on, I have an umbrella." I stopped to dig through my bag.

But it wasn't in there.

Frantically, I rummaged through the contents of my bag, but there was no umbrella to be found.

"Shit, I forgot my umbrella."

And then I began to laugh.

Closing up my bag so the gifts inside wouldn't get wet, I laughed hysterically and twirled in a circle.

"Lucas, I fucking forgot to pack an umbrella! Do you know what this means?"

"Um, we're both going to get very wet?" He had to think I was crazy, but he didn't hurry us out of the rain, even as thunder echoed above us again. Instead he just stood there watching me dance, waiting for me to explain my soggy euphoria.

"That's OK! In fact, it's fucking awesome!" Overwhelmed with joy, I rushed at him, took his chin in my hands and kissed him hard on the mouth.

He laughed. "Does rain turn you on or something?"

"No. Well, it does now, but it never did before. See, I've always had this fantasy about kissing in the rain, but I'm always so well-prepared, I've actually never been caught in the rain on a date without an umbrella." I jumped up and down, my wet hair flapping in my face. "The fact that I left the hotel without one today means that I was so distracted by other things—good things—that I didn't even think to plan ahead for shitty weather! I don't even think I checked it today!"

I'm not sure Lucas appreciated the monumental nature of the statement, but he grinned and pulled me close, kissing me as if he'd never get enough, as if nothing else in the world mattered. Not the people giving us strange looks as they rushed for cover. Not the rain soaking our hair and clothing and streaming down our faces. Not the fact that we'd only

157

met two days before and had less than a day left together.

Or maybe it was as if *only* the last reason mattered.

He kissed me as we waited for the Metro, his arms wrapped around me from behind, his lips soft on my neck. He kissed me on the train, where it was so crowded we had to stand, our damp bodies pressed together at the front of the car, our mouths so close we couldn't resist bringing them lightly together. He kissed me hard in the stairwell of his building, grabbing me as I tried to race up the steps and pinning me to the wall between the second and third stories, my hair dripping on his arms.

"You're all wet. I like you that way," he said, his mouth searing a path down my throat.

We were both panting, hands groping, our sodden clothing too heavy on our bodies. "I'm wet everywhere," I whispered.

With a groan he tore his mouth from me and pulled me up the final flight of stairs so fast my feet barely found purchase on the cement. The ten seconds it took him to unlock and throw open his apartment door felt like an eternity, and the moment we were inside, I dropped my bag, he slammed the door, and we went at each other like feral wolves.

Tongues and teeth gnashing, we tore off every shred of each other's clothing, a cyclone of four hands, frantic breaths, and hammering hearts that mocked the storm raging outside. Rain pounded against the windowpanes as Lucas shoved me back against the door. Dropping to his knees, he forced my heels apart and plunged his tongue between my legs, hooking his arms under my thighs. Gasping, I put my hands in his hair as he tongued me relentlessly, swirling hard circles over my clit before closing his mouth over it, sucking greedily. Then he brought one hand to my belly, flattening his palm over my abdomen and rubbing me with his thumb while his tongue drove inside me again and again.

Oh God oh God oh God, it's happening too fast. I moaned and cursed and clenched my fists in his wet hair, feeling the vortex build low in my stomach and my legs weaken. "Fuck, Lucas, I can't stand, I can't stand."

His mouth traveled up my body, warm and wet on my stomach, my ribs, my chest. He took one nipple into his mouth and sucked hard, while filling his hand with the other breast. I writhed against the door, flattening my palms back against it as I arched into him. It was too much and not enough. My body yearned for everything he could give me with an urgency I'd never felt before. I felt almost violent in my need to have him.

I reached low between us, taking his solid cock in my grasp, sheathing it with both hands. He gasped, growing harder and thicker and driving me mad with the need to feel my lips on him, to lick him up and down, to taste him. By no means was I an experienced giver of fellatio, but I'd done enough research in the attempt to liven things up with Tucker that I had a few ideas.

Yes, this means I googled *blow job advice from guys*.

Several times.

I was totally prepared to test out the top tips, but what really knocked me out was how fucking ecstatic I was about it. Before, I'd kind of approached it like an actual project, but I was jumping out of my skin to go down on Lucas.

Falling to my knees at his feet, I pressed my lips to his upper thigh, and dragged my tongue across his lower abs, keeping his erection firmly in my grip.

Then I looked up at him, with the head of his cock poised just before my open lips.

His mouth was open, his eyes on fire.

Without looking away, I touched my bottom lip to the velvety tip and shook my head slightly from side to side.

"Christ, Mia." His chest rose and fell with labored breaths.

I took him in between my lips, one hard inch at a time, and he tipped forward, hands bracing against the door. Thunder growled in the distance, blending with Lucas's low groan of pleasure as I slid him in deeper, stopping only when he hit the back of my throat. Moaning softly, I kept him there and gave him several slow, tight pulls with one hand.

"Oh my God. Fuck yes." Lucas inhaled and exhaled loudly as I eased my lips up and down his cock and then circled my tongue around the underside of the tip. "*Fuck yes*, you're unbelievable."

I looked up before taking him all the way in again, jerking him into my mouth a little quicker, and my heart pounded at the way he couldn't take his eyes off me, the way he breathed so heavy, the way he spoke.

"God, Mia, you're so fucking beautiful. I love watching you."

It was even hotter than I'd imagined, pleasing him this way. And I loved it as much as he did—my skin burned and heat pulsed through my body. I couldn't remember ever feeling so unabashed, so free to do anything I wanted, so confident that what I was doing felt good. I reached between his legs, teasing and playing and touching him everywhere, watching and listening to see what he liked best.

It was hard to tell.

Everything I did, every inch of his body I explored, made him tremble and curse and moan. "You fucking gorgeous woman, I can't believe the things you do to me. You make me crazy."

I raked my nails down one of his thighs, then slid my palm around to grab his ass. He began to thrust into my mouth, never taking his eyes off the sight of his cock plunging between my lips and exhaling quickly with each drive of his hips. I was so turned on, I reached down to touch myself without event thinking about it—something I never would have done before.

Lucas sucked in his breath. "Yes, God yes. Touch yourself. Let me watch you."

Shamelessly, I rubbed myself where his tongue had been before, dipping my fingers inside my dripping body and feeling how wet he made me.

"Good girl. Now let me taste you again." He reached down and took my arm, lifting my hand to his lips and sucking my fingers.

His cock twitched in my mouth.

"Oh fuck. That's it. Come here." He dragged me to my feet and picked me up beneath my arms, setting me down hard on the kitchen counter. "Now don't fucking move."

He strode from the kitchen into the bedroom and returned just seconds later rolling on the condom.

"Spread your legs."

My belly flipped wildly at his command, and I widened my knees. Reaching around my back, he used one hand to pull me toward the edge of the counter and the other to guide his entrance into me.

"Mm, you're so wet." He kept one hand on my tailbone as he slid in deep, eyes closed. "So tight, so hot."

"Yes," I murmured, snaking my hands around his waist. "It feels so good, Lucas. Don't stop."

"Never," he said, opening his eyes and pushing into me with deep, hard strokes. "I want to be inside you all night."

Our mouths crashed together, a hot tangle of tongues and panting breaths before I grabbed his shoulders and arched back, tilting my hips to feel him in just the right spot. Within minutes, I felt the tremors close in, and I wrapped my legs around his thighs.

As soon as I felt his teeth on my nipple, the orgasm ripped through me, and I cried out, one long, continuous sound of pure pleasure as my body seized up—my hands squeezing his shoulders, my heels digging into his leg muscles, my insides clenched around his pounding cock.

I wanted to pick my head up and watch him come but I couldn't. Instead I fell flat on my back across the counter, my fingers curled over the edge.

"Fuck. Oh my God, look at you." Lucas flattened a hand over one breast and kept the other one locked on my hip, slamming into me harder and faster until his body went rigid and still, pulsing inside me.

Right fucking there on the *kitchen counter*.

I don't think I need to tell you that this was new territory for me.

As was the kitchen floor a short while later (me on top).

And the living room rug not long after that (we took turns).

Eventually we made it into the bedroom, where we collapsed on the bed in a heap of sweaty, exhausted limbs, sore muscles, and really, *really* fucked up hair.

And all I could think was, *How soon can we do it again?*

Chapter Thirteen

We fell asleep, and when I woke up, I watched Lucas for a few minutes. His bedroom window was open slightly, allowing a cool breeze to blow through, and I could still hear the rain, although the thunder had ceased. I rolled onto my belly and set my chin in my hand, breathing in rainy-cool air and the scent of sex on our bodies.

Lucas's skin was a little olive in tone, not very hairy except on his legs, and unmarred from what I could see, except for a small scar on his stomach. The inch-long slash sat just below his bottom left rib. I was tempted to run my finger over it, but I didn't want to wake him.

He lay on his back, one arm tossed above his head, the other across his belly. *I take it back. His armpits are little hairy too.* I stifled a giggle. But his chest was

165

nice and smooth, his nipples the color of wine—couldn't stop the smile now—and his stomach a delicious meal of muscles and lines and that happy little trail that made my mouth water. The sheet was pulled up to his hips, or I'd have had more to enjoy.

"You're awake." Lucas's eyes were open, his voice scratchy. "And you're staring at me."

I laughed. "Sorry. Nothing creepy, I promise. Just enjoying the view."

He closed his eyes and smiled. "Carry on."

Giving him a swat on the chest, I let my head fall onto my upper arm and stretched out next to him. "Mmmm. That was amazing."

"The sex or the nap?"

"Both." I wasn't really a napper—I usually felt guilty about them, like there was always something I could be doing. But waking up next to Lucas on a rainy evening felt even better than crossing something off a list.

"Agreed. But now I'm starving," he said, scratching his stomach.

"Are you? Yeah, I guess we sort of skipped dinner. Poor baby. You had to work so hard without enough energy."

He looked at me. "You. Are not. Work."

I smiled shyly, and he reached out, pulling me close so my body aligned with his and my head rested on his chest.

"But," he continued. "I do need some energy if we're going to keep this up—which I hope we do—so we should probably get something to eat. It must be nine o'clock."

My heart beat hard against his side. Could he feel it? "OK."

But neither of us moved, and in a moment our breathing synced in a way that had me warm and drowsy again. I wrapped an arm around his stomach and Lucas's hand traced spirals on my shoulder. When his stomach growled, it startled me.

"Your body has spoken," I said, sitting up. "Shall we eat?"

"Definitely. What do you feel like?"

I shrugged. "Surprise me."

A grin tugged at the corners of his mouth. "What?"

It split wide open on his face. "Your hair is awesome right now."

Groaning, I wrapped my head in my hands. "I know. So is yours."

"I figured." He swept a hand through his and sat up as well. "I guess I should comb it."

I dropped my arms and feigned shock. "You own a comb?"

He tackled me, throwing me onto my back and hovering above me, my wrists pinned to the bed. His curly mop of hair fell forward, but rather than make me laugh, it had me chewing my bottom lip again, imagining his head between my thighs. What the hell was I going to do when I had to go home? What if I never had this again? Lucas lingered above me a moment, studying me, and both our chests started to expand more rapidly. I felt his engorged cock on my thigh, hard and ready.

"God, you're beautiful," he said.

"I thought you were hungry."

"My stomach can wait," he said, lowering his mouth to my neck. "My dick is more demanding. It wants you now."

Desire oozed between my legs as he sucked my earlobe and began to slide his body over mine.

"Lucas."

"Yeah." His breath was warm in my ear.

"Let's take a shower."

#

4 Insanely Glorious Things
I Realized In The Shower With Lucas
(& 1 Terrifying One)

1) Lucas is Dangerous When Wet. Because when I saw him with his hair soaked and slicked back, it only emphasized the cut of his cheekbones, the arch of his brows, the

angle of his jaw, and I nearly hyperventilated with the need to put my mouth EVERYWHERE.

2) Having someone else wash your hair and soap your body feels more decadent than indulging in molten chocolate cake —especially when that person is naked, sexy as hell, and massages your scalp in a way that makes your toes curl.

3) Kissing in the rain is fun, but making out with Lucas in his shower is fucking outstanding—hot water streaming down our bodies, steam rising all around us, enveloping us in a hot little cloud of lust. It's enough to make you do things you never thought you'd do (See item #4).

4) Having Lucas inside me without any barrier between us is a physical rapture beyond words—actually the rapture is beyond physical. Which brings me to item #5.

5) I think I might have feelings for Lucas. Big ones.

The shower spray was hot on my back, but I was even hotter on Lucas's front. My legs were twined around his hips and he held me aloft with his hands under my ass. Our mouths were connected so tightly not one drop of water permeated the kiss, and I was sucking his tongue into my mouth, wishing I could have more of him inside me.

But we had no condom in the shower.

His cock was trapped between us, sliding between my slippery folds as he moved me against him. He was hard and thick and long, and all I could think of was having him slide into me, just the way we were.

"Lucas, I want you inside me," I said breathlessly. "I'm on the pill."

He pulled his head back and looked at me, water dripping from his dark locks. "We can't."

"You're right, sorry." And he was right. God, what the hell was I thinking? I went back to kissing him, grinding against him, panting with want.

A few seconds later he said, "Well, maybe we can."

"We can?"

"Maybe just for a minute. I mean, if you want to. I won't come."

How the hell could he say that? I knew I couldn't make that kind of promise. And I knew being on the pill shouldn't give us permission to be reckless—it wasn't foolproof. Sex without a condom wasn't smart behavior when you'd only known someone for two days—and yet I wanted to feel him *so badly*. And he was leaving tomorrow. "OK. I just want to feel you that way. Even if it's only for a minute."

170

Frenched

He kissed me before hitching me a little higher, and I used my leg muscles to hold myself up while he positioned himself beneath me. Steam rose around us, lending the moment a dreamlike quality. *It's like it's not even real.* When I felt him at my center, I released my viselike hold on his waist and slid down his hard length, my eyes locked on his.

Oh my God.

I thought it, but he actually said it.

Then he closed his eyes. "You feel so good. Too fucking good."

My body fought the urge to move, to ride him, to feel him thrusting into me.

Fought it for five whole seconds.

"Oh God." I grabbed the back of his neck and circled my hips, squeezing my muscles around him.

"Fuck, Mia." He turned and put my back against the cool white tiles, giving in to his own urge to drive into me, slow at first, then deep and hard. I answered every thrust of his hips with my own, rubbing myself against him in a way that had my body racing toward climax.

The *feeling* of his bare cock inside me was arousing enough, but it was the *thought* that did me in—the notion that the most sensitive, most intimate, most private part of him was inside that part of me, unguarded.

I came hard, biting down on his shoulder and clamping my legs around him, unable even to breathe.

The moment I relaxed my hold on him, Lucas frantically set me down and pulled out. Without even hesitating, I dropped to my knees and took him in my mouth, employing all the little tricks he'd liked before, skipping the slow, teasing phase and going straight for porn star goddess.

"Oh my God, Mia, oh my God, oh fuck, I'm gonna come, so if you don't—"

I silenced him by looking up and meeting his eyes, and he lost control two seconds after that, throbbing and streaming into my mouth as he braced himself against the wall behind me.

When it was over, he reached down and pulled me to my feet, wrapping his arms around me and resting his forehead on my shoulder. "Jesus. Mia."

And his voice cracked. Right over my name.

And that little sound, more than anything else, had me closing my eyes, holding him close, and thinking the terrifying thing.

I'm so in love with him.

#

Which was ridiculous. I wasn't in love with him. I couldn't be. I'd just met the guy two days ago.

I was in love with the way he made me feel during sex, the way he worshipped my body, and let

172

me worship his. We had really incredible sexual chemistry, that was all. And he was a cool person. I'd never had a fuck friend before, so it was only natural that there would be some confusion in my brain about what it all meant.

It means you can enjoy yourself with him without worrying about a relationship. It means you can have amazing, guilt-free sex because there are no expectations. It means no one cares if this is just a rebound fuck fling, so enjoy it while it lasts and then go home and move on with your real life.

Yes. I could do that. I could totally do that. Couldn't I?

Chapter Fourteen

It had stopped raining, and Lucas wanted to take me to dinner in Montmartre. "The food's not amazing, but I want you to hear something."

"I'm up for anything," I said, pulling on my jeans. "Although I wish I had new clothes. These are a little bit damp."

"This place is totally casual, I promise." He came up behind me and kissed my shoulder. "And I love the little top you have on, anyway."

"Thanks. But what I *really* wish I had are my hair products. Yours are sadly lacking." I slipped my feet into my flats. Ugh, those were soaked too.

"Sorry. Would it help if I told you I think you're gorgeous no matter how crazy your hair gets?" Lucas pulled a clean shirt from his closet and began to button it up. It gave me a warm little bloom of pleasure in my belly to watch him dress…it seemed personal and intimate. Like we'd known each other for much longer than we had.

I smiled. "Some. But would it be too much to ask to run by the Plaza?"

"Nothing you ask of me is too much."

My heart stopped beating to balloon in my chest, and then galloped furiously ahead, as if to make up for the lost time.

Quit saying things like that. I'm getting confused.

I thanked him and picked up my jacket, looking away on purpose. It was dangerous to let emotion into this. *I'll have to work harder to control it, keep reminding myself what we are, and more importantly, what we are not.*

To save time, we took a cab to the Plaza, and I invited Lucas to come up to my room while I changed.

"Wow. Pretty fancy," he said, taking in the opulent suite.

I felt embarrassed for some reason, and I didn't want him to think I was spoiled and always traveled this way. "It's way more than I need, really. I'd have been happy with something smaller, but this was already paid for."

"I remember." Lucas eyed the roses and the bed before wandering into the sitting area. Lowering himself onto the couch, he glanced at the newspaper I'd left on the coffee table this morning.

I stripped off my jacket and kicked my shoes into the closet. "I'll just be a minute or two."

"Take your time."

Although I couldn't see him from where I stood, his voice sounded a little funny to me. Was it because of the reference to Tucker? *I shouldn't have brought him up here. He's probably uncomfortable being in a suite my ex-fiance booked for our honeymoon.* But what could I do besides hurry up?

I hung my damp clothing up in the closet to dry out, threw my underwear in my laundry bag, and went to the dresser to choose something dry.

When I opened the top drawer, the Aubade lingerie peeked out at me. I was tempted to put it on, but I didn't want Lucas to see me do it. It would be better if he discovered it underneath clothes, or somehow came home to find me wearing it.

Came home to find you wearing it! Have you lost your mind?

We were not a couple. There was no home. I'd best remember that.

Scowling a little, I pushed the beautiful bra and panties aside and took out something more basic. From the lower drawers I picked out a clean pair of jeans and dug around for a new top. Hmm, what would Lucas like to see me in? He said he'd liked the little cami I'd had on today, but I was guessing that was mostly because it showed some skin. I didn't have another cami like that, but I did have a black off-the-shoulder top I thought he'd like. I kept my strapless bra on and shimmied into a pair of skinny black pants and the top. My flats were too wet to wear again, so I decided to go for heels—black and strappy with little gold studs. If I had to walk a lot, so be it. *Sometimes, beautiful hurts.*

In the bathroom, I threw my hair up in a messy bun and touched up my face.

"OK, ready," I said, coming out of the bathroom. From the closet I grabbed my little black clutch and switched a few things to it.

"Really? God, you're quick." Lucas came around the corner from the sitting area. "And fuck, you're hot."

Smiling, I faced him. "Thank you."

"I can't believe how fast you get ready to go, and you look this good." His eyes swept over my hair, my bare shoulder, my fitted pants.

"I'm usually pretty fast, unless I blow out my hair. That takes a lot of time. Otherwise…" I threw up my arms. "What you see is what you get."

"Lucky for me." He snaked an arm around my waist and pulled me in for a kiss. "Hey, you're tall."

I laughed. "I have heels on tonight."

He looked down and groaned. "Mia, you're *killing* me. Come on, let's go before I lose all control." Glancing over his shoulder, he went on, "And it's a nice room and all, but being here with you feels a little weird."

I patted his cheek. "I totally understand. You don't have to come here again."

We took the Metro to the base of Montmartre and climbed up hundreds of steep, narrow steps lined with cool old lampposts and iron railings. My feet didn't hurt nearly as much as I thought they would in my heels, probably because I was so taken with the scenery. The winding cobblestone streets and sweeping views were probably charming and picturesque during the day, but tonight, with mist hanging in the air, the ground dark and shiny from the rain, and the lamp lights glowing through the fog, Montmartre seemed straight out of an old-fashioned noir film.

Taking my hand, Lucas led me to a restaurant off the main square and right away I heard the reason he'd brought me here. The sound of guitars filtered out through the open doors, and I squeezed his hand as he led me to a small square table near the back of the large, half-filled room.

When we were seated, I studied the three musicians playing with interest. They sat in a semi-circle, and I'm not sure what I expected a gypsy to look like, but it wasn't three portly middle-aged guys in jeans and plaid shirts with electric guitars plugged into amplifiers behind them. In front of them was a small table with a stack of CD's, a little basket of cash, and three glasses of beer. They looked like any regular shmoes busking for tips on the street corner.

But the music.

I'd never heard anything like it before, the way the two rhythm guitars kept up a percussive, driving rhythm with constant strumming on every beat. "My God, their wrists must kill them," I said to Lucas.

He smiled. "They're used to it."

The lead guitarist, the one in the middle, had fingers that flew so quickly over the strings his hands appeared blurry. I'd never seen anything like it.

"Can you play that fast?" I asked.

"Ha. I wish."

I elbowed him. "I bet you can."

"Listen, I'm all right. But these guys are the real deal. That guy there?" He pointed to the musician in the center. "As good as any jazz guitarist I've met in New York."

We drank wine and ate steak frites and salads and listened to the music, Lucas occasionally answering my questions about the name of a song or the style of the music. It was so much fun I almost forgot about sex.

Almost.

But sometimes I'd look over at Lucas and catch him watching me, and he'd give me a slow smile that meant *you know what I'm thinking*. And once he leaned over and whispered in my ear, "I can't stop thinking about the shower," causing my face to get hot and that swooping rush in my core.

At the set break, I was surprised when the lead guitarist wandered over and shook Lucas's hand. They conversed in French, of course, so I had no idea what they were saying, but I smiled and offered my hand when Lucas introduced me. The guitarist's name was Stefan; he had black hair, dark eyes, and a warm, gap-toothed smile. After he shook my hand, he said something to Lucas that made him laugh before heading over to the bar.

"What did he say?" I demanded.

"He said he's never seen me in here with a girl before and figures I must really want to impress you if I brought you to hear him play."

"Oh." I hid my satisfied smile in my wine glass.

"So did it work?" Lucas sat back and regarded me with playful eyes.

"Yes." I *was* impressed, but mostly I was happy to hear that Lucas had never brought a girl here before.

On his way back to the front, Stefan stopped and put a hand on Lucas's shoulder. He asked a question, and at first Lucas shook his head, but after some prodding, appeared to waver. He looked at me. "Stefan is asking me to sit in."

I clapped my hands. "Do it! Please?"

"OK. But don't compare me to this guy." Lucas tapped Stefan on the shoulder.

"He is very good guitarist," Stefan said to me in heavily accented English.

"I believe it." But I was nervous for Lucas, watching him sit in Stefan's chair and loop the strap of the guitar over his head. He chatted with the rhythm guitarists for a moment, counted off the song in French, and they began strumming that chung-chung-chung-chung pattern with alarming speed. My insides knotted up. *Ugh, I hope he isn't going to try to show off with something he can't do.*

I shouldn't have worried. Lucas played with graceful dexterity, his fingers whisking confidently over the strings, embellishing the melody of the tune without filling up all the space with showy runs or a million extra notes.

I was mesmerized.

My favorite part was how happy he looked the entire time, whether smiling at me or at the other guitarists or just watching his hands on the guitar. God, he was so fucking cute. And talented and smart and sweet.

What the hell? There had to be something wrong with him.

He lives in France. That's what's wrong with him.
Only sometimes.
Yeah, like right now. And he's leaving Paris tomorrow.

At the recollection that our time together was running out, my stomach twisted painfully. I pushed back against the unease building in my gut and tried to stay in the moment.

Right here, right now.

But when the song ended, Lucas said something to the other guitarists and counted off another tune. And as soon as he played the opening notes of La Vie En Rose, I sucked in my breath.

In fact, I don't think I breathed through the entire song. He didn't sing or anything, but he played the melody so beautifully that it brought tears to my eyes. The room, which had buzzed with noise before, was hushed and still as he played, and when the song finished, everyone there applauded. Lucas lifted the guitar strap over his head, gave it back to Stefan with a nod of thanks, and returned to me at the table.

"Well? What'd you think?"

I had to swallow hard before speaking. "That was beautiful. Thank you for playing the song for me. It…meant a lot."

"You're welcome. I'll always think of you now when I hear it."

My mouth opened, but I didn't know what to say. We stared at each other, and I realized something had changed between us—he'd acknowledged, in a way, that our time together was limited, that goodbye was near. And honestly, he didn't look too happy about it either.

He sat down and cleared his throat. "Did you get enough to eat? Do you want another glass of wine?"

"No. I mean, yes, I got enough to eat, but no more wine, I guess." For the first time, I felt tongue-tied around Lucas. I didn't want the night to end, but I didn't feel right inviting myself back to his apartment. And I couldn't invite him back to my room either.

Shit. Is this it? I looked over one shoulder toward the door in an effort to conceal the tears forming in my eyes.

"Well…I guess we can go, then. Let me just pay the bill."

"No." I put my hand over it on the table and dragged it toward me. "This one's mine. It's the least I can do for all the time you've spent with me."

"Spent? Are you done with me now?" He seemed genuinely surprised.

I shrugged. "Well, you're leaving, right? Didn't you say last night that you had to go out of town tomorrow?"

"Oh, that's right. Fuck. Tomorrow's Thursday?" He tugged at a strand of hair that had escaped my bun. "You made me forget what day it was."

I had to laugh. "Good."

"I do have to leave Paris tomorrow. I have to go to Vaucluse for my brother's engagement party. My family is all meeting there."

"At the Count's house?"

"Yeah."

I forced a smile. "That'll be fun."

"Yeah." But he looked glum about it, his brow furrowed.

The music started again and I paid the bill with my credit card. Lucas thanked me for dinner and dropped some cash in Stefan's basket before taking my hand and leading me out of the restaurant. Neither of us spoke as we started the walk down the hill.

And then halfway down one of the lamp-lit staircases, Lucas stopped. I walked two steps further and turned to look up at him. "What's wrong?"

He stuck his hands in his pockets. "You should come with me tomorrow."

"What?"

"Come with me to Vaucluse."

My heart was beating way too hard. "Lucas, I can't—"

"Yes, you can." He came down to my step. "I want you to."

"But—"

He took his hands from his pockets and placed them on my upper arms. "And I'm not ready to say goodbye to you."

He kissed me before I could say anything else, silencing with his lips any words of dissent I might have offered. Because there were so many I could think of—*we just met two days ago, who the hell will you say I am, your family will think I'm nuts running off with a guy I just met, and… and I'm scared. I'm feeling too much here. What the hell is this between us?*

184

But when he ran his hands up my shoulders and took my face in his palms, I wanted to melt into a puddle. *He's not ready to say goodbye either.*

"Say you'll come," he whispered on my lips. "You'll love it—it's so beautiful there, and there'll be lots of wine."

I smiled. "I'm sure it'll be beautiful, Lucas. But what about your family? Won't they be mad when you show up with—"

He shook his head before I even finished the question. "They'll be thrilled. Henri and Jean-Paul love to entertain, and my brother and his fiancée said I could bring someone. I just didn't have anyone I wanted to bring before now."

"What about your mom?" For some reason, the thought of meeting his movie star mother made me shiver.

Lucas noticed the chill, and folded me into his arms. "She'll be glad to meet you, I promise. Come on—I climbed the tower for you, I danced with you, I played your song…"

I sighed, too comfortable in Lucas's embrace. Way, way too comfortable. I wrapped my arms around his warm lower back. "I want to…"

"What's holding you back?"

Biting my lip a moment, I decided to be honest. "I guess I'm just wondering about what all this means. I mean, we just met. My wedding was just called off, and—"

He pulled back, holding me at arm's length and shaking me gently. "Stop thinking so much, Mia. It means we have fun together, that's all. It means I'm really, really glad we met and I like being with you. Let's just go to Vaucluse and have a good time, OK? No analyzing it, no deeper meaning, no worrying. Who knows, maybe after three days there, you'll be desperate to fly back to Detroit to escape me and my family."

I smiled. "Somehow I doubt that."

"Then it's settled. You're coming." He squeezed my shoulders. "We'll leave tomorrow after breakfast."

I closed my eyes, wondering if this was a mistake but completely unable to stop myself from nodding. "OK."

"So now the question is, what would you like to do tonight? Are you tired? Do you want me to take you back to your hotel? Do you want to come back to my apartment? You'll need to pack, but you could do it tomorrow."

"Whoa. Brain spinning." *God, what am I doing?*

"Sorry. You're probably not used to just being spontaneous about these things. Especially a trip." He took my hand again and we continued walking down the stairs.

"Ha. You got that right. Before this week, I'd say there wasn't a spontaneous bone in my body."

"I'll put a spontaneous bone in your body."

I shot him a scornful look, although his comment turned me on. "Very funny. Where is Vaucluse anyway?"

"It's in Provence. And don't worry, everything is casual there. You might want to bring a dress for the party Saturday night, but don't—"

"Lucas!" I grabbed his arm. "I didn't even think about that! God, I'm totally unprepared for a trip to Provence! I don't have the right clothes at all."

He rolled his eyes. "Mia, if you want to go home and make a new outfit calendar right now, that's your prerogative. But." He pulled me to him again and slipped a hand underneath my loose top, then slid his fingers beneath the strap of my bra. "I can think of many other things I'd rather do tonight. Want to sleep over?"

I closed my eyes. "Yes. Because I do, in fact, have the perfect outfit for that."

#

"I cannot believe how many times I've had sex in the last twenty-four hours." Clad in a soft t-shirt and a pair of boxers from Lucas's drawers, I took the new toothbrush he'd found for me out of the package and rinsed it. "It is nearly inconceivable."

"Is that good or bad? Here." Lucas squirted some toothpaste on my toothbrush and then his own.

"It's good," I said. "So, so good."

"Glad to hear it."

We brushed, rinsed and spit standing side by side at his bathroom sink and Lucas stood my toothbrush next to his in the holder. *This is too much, too private and cozy. I feel too close to him.* But I tried to play it off.

"Maybe it's a good thing that we'll have to slow down when we go to your family's place," I said, getting into bed. "I'm beginning to think I'm a fiend."

We'd done it twice since we got home from dinner—on the couch again (at my request) and on his bedroom floor. I was amazed at Lucas's ability to recover and do it again so soon.

"What do you mean, slow down? I'm not slowing down." Lucas gave me a horrified look and snapped off the bedside light.

I watched him slide under the covers next to me in the moonlight. "We have to." I propped my head in one hand. "We can't be bonking like bunnies at the Count's *castle* or whatever." I threw my other hand in the air. "It's uncouth!"

Lucas laughed. "Come here. I promise," he said as I snuggled into him, "that the house is very big, and the grounds are enormous. We'll find a way to be alone. There will be no slowing down."

I kissed him before rolling over, putting my back to his front, and he curled an arm around my waist. It felt absurdly comfortable and almost foreign to me. Tucker wasn't really a cuddler. Or a go-again-right-after kind of guy. And due to his aversion to bodily fluids, we'd almost never done it without a condom.

Even then, it had never felt like it had with Lucas in the shower.

Ever.

I wanted to do it again. I chewed my lower lip.

Well, you can't do it again. It makes you think crazy things.

But was this crazy? Maybe normal people did this all the time and I just never knew it. I mean, I'd heard of vacation sex with near strangers, summer loves that you never heard from again, torrid one-night-stands…I'd just never indulged in them. I wondered if Lucas had.

I sucked both lips between my teeth to prevent myself from asking. Did I really want to know? I was torn—what if I wasn't special?

Don't ask, don't ask, don't ask.

But I asked. Of course I did.

"Lucas?"

"Hmm?" His voice was already sleepy.

"Have you ever done this before?"

"Done what before?"

"Had a…" I struggled to label it. "A nonstop fuck fling for days on end."

He laughed. "Nope. I mean, I can't say I've never gone home with someone, but the nonstop thing is new for me."

"Me too." Relief washed over me like rain—I wasn't just one of a string of girls to scream his name in this apartment. Repeatedly.

Then I was quiet for a minute, actually trying to count up the number of orgasms I'd had with Lucas. Holy shit, was it going on ten? That was more than I'd had with Tucker all year, probably.

And we'd *never* had one together. Suddenly I wanted Lucas to know that. To feel special.

"Lucas?"

"Yeah?"

A smile crept onto my lips. "I thought the simultaneous orgasm was just a myth."

"Then we're even."

I blinked. "How so?"

"I thought the gorgeous girl giving me that insane blowjob in the kitchen was a figment of my imagination. Then she did it again in the shower, so I'm beginning to think she might actually be real."

I smiled, letting my tired eyes close. "She's real."

But was she? Lying there in his arms, I wondered if that was true. Was this girl here really me? Or was I acting out some sort of fantasy version of myself, indulging every whim, acting on every impulse? Was this all a reaction to being told ten days ago that my life wasn't what I thought it was? That I couldn't be who I thought I'd be? Maybe I was using this fantasy to avoid facing the truth—I had to start over.

Or was there more to it? Had this girl been inside me the whole time, smothered by the idea of what I thought I should be? Silenced by the fear of admitting I might be making a mistake? Revealing I wasn't perfect? Wasn't I relieved in part that Tucker had called off the wedding? Certainly this girl here in Paris felt more *me* than I'd felt in a long time.

But this still wasn't real life.

Frowning, I snuggled deeper into the crescent of Lucas's body. I didn't care if it wasn't real life.

It felt too fucking good to care.

Chapter Fifteen

After a breakfast of coffee, fruit, and crepes—which Lucas cooked—I went back to the hotel to pack a bag for the trip to Vaucluse. I'd convinced Lucas I could navigate my way back by Metro on my own, and even though I had to study the map for several minutes, I felt quite pleased with myself when I emerged onto the street from the Franklin D. Roosevelt station.

I didn't even feel any shame walking into the hotel in an outfit that was obviously Last Night's. My heels barely touched the ground as I floated through the lobby, humming a tune. It had only been about twelve hours since I'd been there, but it felt like much longer. And my room was just as spacious and beautiful as ever, but it didn't feel as welcoming or charming to me as Lucas's small apartment.

The message light was blinking on my phone, and I grimaced, imagining five of them from my mother, haranguing me for not calling her daily like I said I would.

Sure enough, the first three messages were from her, listing the usual litany of horrible things that could happen to a young woman traveling alone. She demanded I call her back, and she knew I'd spoken to Coco because she'd called her, too. "If you made time for her, you can take five minutes and phone me as well," she snipped. "I'm your mother. I'm only worried about you."

"OK, OK," I grumbled, slipping my heels off. "I'll call you back."

The next message was from Erin, who had also spoken to Coco but just wanted to hear the details from me. "I can't get over it—it's so cool!" she bubbled. "I want the full scoop, so call me when you can. Love you!"

And the last message…was Tucker.

"Hey, Mia."

Long pause, during which my stomach plunged five stories and went kersplat on the Avenue Montaigne.

"I just wanted to call you and…make sure you're OK. Make sure you have everything you need at the hotel." Big sigh. "I'm feeling…bad about the way things ended. I mean, Christ, I don't even know if they *are* ended. Completely, anyway."

Another long pause. I brought a hand to my mouth. Was he fucking serious?

He exhaled again. "I'm thinking about you, that's all. And I was hoping to hear your voice. I don't know where you could be at six in the morning…maybe you're sleeping. Or maybe you got up early and went for a walk. I wonder how you liked finally seeing the Eiffel Tower after dreaming about it for so long. I wish I could have seen your face light up. I remember how we talked about shopping in the Fauborg, having a drink at The Ritz…I wonder if you've done it all already. Don't hate me, but…I wish I were there."

My hand was shaking, the receiver jittering against my ear.

"So anyway. You don't have to call me back. But maybe we can talk when you get home. I…I need to apologize. For lots of things. Well, that's it, I guess. I hope you're enjoying yourself. I'm thinking about you."

Now he wanted to be here? *Now* he was thinking about me? Was this a joke? My entire arm shook as I replaced the receiver, and I sat there staring at it for several minutes, my guts churning. So many things to process… He was hoping to hear my voice. He hoped I was enjoying myself. He needed to apologize. He wasn't sure things were ended.

And he wondered where I could be at six in the morning.

Frenched

In bed with someone who appreciates me, asshole!

I went into the bathroom. I wasn't totally certain I wouldn't throw up. I wished there was such a thing as mental vomiting, because hearing Tucker's voice saying those things had made me so furious, I wanted to purge the experience from my head.

How dare he? How dare he ruin my perfect day by calling and reminding me of the things we were supposed to do together here? *Now* he thought it sounded like a good time? *Fuck you, Tucker.*

Why should I see him or talk to him, ever again? Did I really have to listen to him apologize for humiliating me? He'd done me a favor! My entire body was tensed, my fists clenched, my teeth grinding, my breath shallow.

"Fuck you, Tucker," I said aloud to myself in the mirror. "You didn't want to marry me. You didn't want to be here with me. And you're not. You're not." I forced my breathing to slow. "You're. Not. Here."

OK. Better.

Turning away from my reflection, I stripped off my clothes and got into the shower. As soon as the water hit my back, I was reminded of being in Lucas's arms, steam rising around us. His tongue in my mouth. His hands in my hair. His body against mine. His cock inside me, so deep.

My shoulders and spine relaxed, and I breathed deeply, taking warm vapor into my lungs and releasing it. I flexed my hands, remembering how they felt running through Lucas's messy curls and sliding across his back. I turned toward the spray, opened my mouth, and let the hot water stream to the back of my throat.

Eliciting another memory.

I smiled.

What's past is past. What matters is now.

And right now, I didn't have to think about Tucker, about whether I'd see him ever again, about whether I had to listen to an apology, about what this trip was originally supposed to be.

Because it was a million times better.

#

Lucas met me in the lobby two hours later, a folded garment bag on his shoulder, and together we took the Metro to Gare de Lyon. From there we boarded a TGV train to Avignon; Lucas had purchased two side-by-side seats in first class, and we spent the entire three-hour trip telling childhood stories and asking each other about firsts.

"First kiss."

Lucas didn't hesitate. "Jennifer Henkel. Ninth grade. My basement."

I cocked my head, surprised. "You didn't even *kiss* a girl until ninth grade?"

"Well, it took me until that age to be as tall as them." He grimaced, adding, "And I copped a feel and made a mess in my pants."

I burst out laughing, and he shuddered.

"Stop. The memory still stings. How about you?"

"Brent Adams." I wiped tears from my eyes. "Sixth grade. Horribly embarrassing game of Spin the Bottle. No feels."

"Probably better that way."

"Definitely. OK…first time. You know." I raised my eyebrows suggestively.

"Um, junior year. Hold on, I have to remember her name."

"What?" I slapped his arm. "You can't even remember the name of the first girl you slept with? The girl whose virginity you stole?"

"I didn't say she was a virgin, I said I was." He snapped his fingers. "Samantha Shields!"

"And? How was it?" I tried to picture Lucas ten years ago—what was he like then? Would he have liked me in high school? Would we have been friends, or more than that?

He smiled. "Well, I thought it was great, but I'm not sure she felt the same way. I had no idea what I was doing, and it was very, very fast. I'm not even sure I got my pants all the way off."

I giggled. "Poor girl." But at the mention of taking his pants off, my blood ran a little hotter. "Well, you've learned a lot since then."

He closed his eyes a moment. "God, I hope so. OK, now you. First time."

"College. I had a serious boyfriend my freshman year."

He pursed his lips. "Name, please?"

"Aidan."

"And?"

I shrugged. "It was, you know, sweet. He kept stopping to ask if it was OK. And it was OK. But it wasn't until my *second* college boyfriend that I realized what was possible."

Lucas leaned closer. "You mean he gave you your first orgasm?" he whispered dramatically.

I leaned in too. "Yes."

He pouted. "Damn. Here I was hoping I was the first to chart that territory."

"Well, there have definitely been a few firsts with you, like I said. But no, sorry." I patted his leg. "Someone beat you to that. Although not with his, you know…" I glanced down at Lucas's crotch, which warmed my insides even further.

"No?"

"No. But Matthew was good with his hands. And he liked to talk dirty to me. I thought that was hot."

198

Lucas's eyes widened a little and he tilted his head. "You don't say."

I grinned mischievously. "Now you know my secret."

"It's a good secret to know."

The thought of Lucas talking dirty to me combined with the way his eyes were starting to look a little hungry had me crossing my legs and squeezing them together. I had on a skirt and my thighs felt sticky. "You know, I'm wishing this train wasn't so crowded right now."

"Me too, princess." He put an arm around me and whispered in my ear. "But it's just another half hour or so. When we get to Avignon, we'll rent a car, and maybe we'll take the long way to the villa. I'll fuck you with my hands, my tongue, *and* my cock in the back seat. And it won't be sweet."

Oh, God. My core muscles pulsed with heat—if I shifted in my chair the right way, I was pretty sure I could come if Lucas kept talking like that. I closed my eyes and whimpered.

Lucas continued to speak low in my ear. "Told you there would be no slowing down. In fact, you just added a whole new level to this."

A whole new level. Fuck.

I crossed my legs the other way.

"Are you wet, princess?"

"Yes," I said softly.

"I'm so hard right now."

Of course I had to look. "Jesus, Lucas. You're killing me." My voice was barely a whisper, and I closed my eyes again. How depraved was it to have sex in a train bathroom?

He laughed a low, gravelly sound that made my body hum. "Good."

#

It was a glorious day in Provence, warm and sunny with just a few perfect puffy clouds. Charming villages, wide open blue sky, verdant orchards, gorgeous fields of lavender—I'd never felt so ungrateful to Mother Nature as I did sitting in that rented Toyota SUV, watching it all fly by outside the windows.

It was Lucas's fault.

As soon as we were out of the city and on the open road, he'd reached over and slipped his hand under the hem of my bright yellow skirt and ran it up my thigh.

I'd widened my knees, desperate for him to touch me, nearly exploding the moment his fingers crept beneath my wet panties. "Lucas. That feels so good."

He steered with one hand and drove me crazy with the other, sometimes teasing with light, whispery

200

brushes and sometimes pushing me right to the edge with a deep, plunging stroke. "Fuck, Mia. You're soaking wet. I want to lick it off you." His voice was gruff.

I rocked and moaned in the seat, riding his hand without apology, hoping he was still planning to pull over and give me everything he'd promised.

God, when had I gotten so greedy?

I fucking loved it.

"Lucas," I murmured. "I want you. Can we—"

Suddenly, he swerved off the highway onto an old dirt road cutting through a grove of trees. "Backseat. Now," he ordered.

With my heart pumping hard, I climbed over the seat as he brought the SUV to a stop in a hidden, shady spot well off the main road. He got out of the front and into the back, and the look in his eyes had me panting and reaching for his belt.

"Not so fast, princess," he said. "There's something I want to do first." With that he hooked his arms around my thighs and yanked me down on my back. Then he slid my panties down and off one leg, leaving them dangling from one ankle like a little white flag of surrender.

Kneeling on the floor, he threw my legs over his shoulders and buried his head beneath my skirt.

I cried out at the first upward sweep of his tongue, flattening one sweaty hand on the window and one on the back seat.

"Fuck, you taste so good." He licked me slow and sweet. "Like fucking candy. Like the center of those chocolate eggs at Easter time. Remember those?" He switched to fast little flicks and swirls over my clit and I pounded on the window.

"Are you kidding me? I can't fucking *think* when you're doing this, Lucas, I can hardly breathe. Oh, God. Oh my *God!*" Thrashing my head from side to side, I felt my muscles contract as he shoved his tongue inside me, tilting my hips up with his hands.

"I can't take it, it's too good," I cried, feeling the heat bloom between my legs. "Lucas!"

He reached around with one hand and rubbed my clit hard and fast, and I screamed his name again as I went plank-stiff beneath him, my orgasm beating a rhythm on his tongue.

A second after it stopped, Lucas undid his jeans and shoved them down just enough to free his towering cock. He jerked my legs sideways on the seat, tore open a condom packet with his teeth and rolled it on.

A flash of disappointment hit me—I wanted him skin to skin.

What the fuck, Mia? Are you crazy?
Yes!

Two seconds later he was on me, driving into my wet, hot center with a fury that had me gasping for air, his shoulder smothering my mouth.

I clutched at his shirt, wanting to tear it off him, pop the buttons, rip the seams. I wanted him urgently, desperately, violently.

"Yes," I moaned, loving the brutal way our bodies slapped together. "God, I love it like that."

"You like it rough?" He could barely speak he was pounding into me so hard. "You want me to fuck you harder?"

I whimpered a little at the thought, wondering how it was even possible, but a second later, my eyes rolled back in my head as he lifted his chest off me, braced himself on the front and back seats and hammered into me with even more force. I bucked up beneath him, feeling the second orgasm coming.

"I fucking love it when you move that way, like you can't get enough of my cock," he growled, the words broken up by his powerful thrusts.

I can't, I wanted to tell him. *I can't get enough.* But I was too far gone to talk. My head fell to one side, my mouth open in the silent ecstasy and agony of teetering on the brink.

He slowed down, killing me with a measured, steady rhythm. "Touch your tits for me. Let me watch."

I lifted my shirt and brought my hands to my breasts, pinching my hard, tingling nipples through my lacey bra.

"Yeah, just like that." He moaned and increased his pace again, taking me dangerously close to the edge. "Fuck, you're so perfect. I love watching you, it makes me want to come so hard… oh my God…"

"Yes," I breathed. "Oh, God, yes. Right there. Right there." *Push me over, Lucas. Come with me.*

Words abandoned, he took us both over, each of us crying out with every wave of pleasure pounding through us.

Lucas collapsed on top of me, and I brought my hands to his head, my fingers weaving through the hair I now adored. We breathed heavily, our chests straining at our clothing.

When I found my voice, it was weak and scratchy.

"Car sex. Crossed. Off. The list."

I felt Lucas's chuckle. "How about villa sex? That on the list?"

"It is now."

Chapter Sixteen

We drove the rest of the way to the villa with the windows rolled down, music blaring. Lucas and I had discovered a mutual affinity for vintage Michael Jackson, and though it may have been a bit incongruous to zip through the Provençale countryside with the scent of sunflowers and lavender rushing into the car and the sound of Off the Wall blasting out, it didn't bother us.

Nothing bothered me.

"God, Lucas, I'm so happy right now." I stuck my hand out the window and let the warm air push against it. "Thank you so much for inviting me to come with you."

"You're welcome. I'm glad you came."

I looked over at him.

"What?"

"I'm waiting for the dirty joke after 'glad you came.'"

He wore a grin that matched mine. "No jokes. I'm serious."

I leaned over to kiss his cheek before tilting my head on the window frame, closing my eyes and feeling the wind on my face. *God, I really am happy. I could get used to this.*

No. You can't. It's temporary.

My inner voice was beginning to bug me almost as much as my mother. It was as if they didn't want me to relax and enjoy myself. I'd finally called my mom just before leaving Paris, and she'd pecked at me for several minutes straight but did manage at the end of the diatribe to inquire how I actually was. I told her I was fine, much better than I'd been in a long time, and reassured her that I was perfectly safe and happy.

She almost sounded disappointed. "Well, don't let your guard down. People see a foreign woman traveling alone and figure she's an easy target."

"Got it, Mom." I clenched and unclenched my free hand.

"All right, then, dear. Call again before you leave, OK? What day do you return?"

My body wilted. I didn't want to think about leaving. "Uh, Tuesday."

"And Coco is picking you up at the airport?"

"Erin, I think." Should I tell her about leaving Paris for Provence? I didn't want to, but what if she called the hotel and they told her I hadn't been seen for a couple days? I'd spoken with Erin, giving her all the juicy details, and I'd mentioned going to Vaucluse until Saturday. Maybe that was good enough. She was excited for me, although it was tempered with a bit of worry.

"God, that sounds amazing, Mia. But…but are you sure you should go out of town with him? I mean, I know you guys are setting Paris on fire, but …"

"I'm totally fine, Erin. Trust me."

"You're sure you're safe?"

"Positive."

And I was. I did feel safe with Lucas.

At least physically.

Emotionally, I was a little less sure.

I glanced over at him again, and my stomach flipped at random things—his hand on the wheel, the V of his thighs on the seat, the hair tousling his face in the wind. Then there was everything that couldn't be seen—the easy laughter, the sharp memory, the musical talent, the sound of his voice telling me about cathedrals, medieval love stories, Rodin's sculpture.

And whispering things. Dirty things that set me on fire.

I felt a bolt of arousal between my legs and fidgeted in my seat. *Whoa. You've had enough for a while, so just relax. Bad enough you had to turn your skirt around to dry off the wet spot on the back.*

I brought a hand to my mouth.

Lucas glanced at me. "What's funny?"

"Nothing. Everything. I've come a long way is all."

He took my hand and kissed the back of it. "Yes, you have."

#

Lucas hadn't told me much about the villa itself, but even if he had, words wouldn't have done it justice. We turned off the main highway and onto a country road that looped through fields and orchards, and I hadn't seen a farmhouse in a while when Lucas slowed the car in front of a set of iron gates. On either side, a low stone wall rimmed the edge of the property.

I sat up taller in my seat. "Is this the vineyard?"

"No, the vineyard is on the other side of the house. These are just gardens."

"Gardens? My *grandma* has a garden, Lucas. This is a fairy tale. It's unbelievable!"

Lucas smiled at me before punching a code into the entry system keypad on the driver's side of the wall, and the gates spread.

I craned my neck out the window as we drove up a narrow gravel road flanked on each side by tall skinny bushes that came to a point at the top. They were planted so close together it was hard to see through them, and the house wasn't visible at the end of the drive. My insides trembled with nerves and excitement as we rounded a bend and the villa came into view.

I gasped. "Oh my God!"

I'd never seen anything like it in real life. Ivy climbed light-colored stone walls, and it stood two and a half stories tall, light blue shutters framing the windows and faded orange tiles on the roof. I could tell it had been expanded, but even the new parts had been carefully constructed to match the original. "How old is it?"

"Eighteenth century, the oldest part, anyway." Lucas pulled the Toyota around a circular drive, which was lined with boxy shrubs and huge terra cotta flowerpots. "Henri added the newer parts over the last thirty years, I'd say, plus put in a swimming pool and tennis court. His partner, Jean-Paul, is a gardening fanatic, so he's added some additional gardens and restored some of the old fountains on the property."

Opening the door, I climbed halfway out of the car and stood on the passenger side running board, looking over the roof at the grounds, which seemed to go on forever. I took a deep breath, filling my lungs with a verdant scent that defied description. "God, Lucas. The air here!" I pounded the roof of the car. "I can't get over it."

"It's the lavender fields. And Jean-Paul has a pretty big herb garden too." He opened the back of the

Toyota and pulled out our bags. "After we get settled, I'll take you on a tour of the property."

I hopped off the car and shut the door. "Maybe you shouldn't. I don't think I'll ever want to leave."

Lucas smiled at me. "You'd miss the hustle of Detroit sooner or later."

I lifted my brows. "Um, have you been to Detroit?"

He shook his head.

"I didn't think so. I love it for its heart and resilience, but it doesn't look like this." I swept a hand through the lush air. "And it sure as hell doesn't smell like this."

"Lucas!"

At the sound of someone calling his name, Lucas slammed the back door and turned toward the house. My stomach immediately knotted itself as a silver-haired man with tan skin and eyes so icy blue I could see them from where I stood strode across the gravel drive. He smiled at me before embracing Lucas, kissing him three times on the cheeks.

"Jean-Paul, this is my friend Mia, the American I told you about on the phone."

Jean-Paul took my hand. "Bonjour, Mia. Bienvenue." He kissed each of my cheeks once and smiled with perfect white teeth. He was really very handsome for his age, which I guessed was somewhere in his sixties.

I smiled back. "Thank you."

Frenched

"Everyone here already?" Lucas asked.

"Yes, your family arrived yesterday. We weren't sure what time your train would arrive, so lunch was sort of here and there, but we'll all have dinner together tonight at nine." Jean-Paul spoke very good English, almost without an accent.

"Is Henri cooking?" Lucas asked, slinging his bag over one shoulder and picking up my suitcase.

"Bite your tongue. As if I'd let him in my kitchen."

"Jean-Paul does all the cooking here," Lucas explained to me. "He's amazing, worked for years at gourmet restaurants in Paris."

"And New York for a while too." Jean-Paul looked at me. "Are you from New York, Mia? Lucas didn't say where you met."

"No, Detroit, actually. We…we met in Paris." I followed them up the steps to the house and through the blue-painted door, realizing it might be weird to admit I'd just met Lucas this week and was happily gallivanting about France with him. *Sometimes sans panties.*

"Well, glad you could visit us here." Jean-Paul shut the door behind us as I took in the gorgeous interior with open-mouthed awe. Beyond the entrance, a huge gray stone fireplace dominated a large room, and the stone floors made the room feel cool and airy, but the sumptuous fabrics and tapestries hanging on the walls gave the space warmth and color. "Lucas,

211

your brother and Lisette are using the guest house for all their friends, so I have you and Mia upstairs here. Is that OK?"

"Of course. Which room?"

"Very end of the hall in the west wing."

"Perfect, Jean-Paul. Thanks. I'll show Mia the house and then I was going to take her on a little tour of the grounds. Would you like to join us?"

The older man put up his hands and shook his head. "No, no. It's a beautiful day, but I've got things to do here to prepare for the party tomorrow night." He rolled his eyes. "The caterer is driving me mad."

"Speaking of things that drive you mad, where is my mother?"

Jean-Paul grinned. "She's out by the pool, I believe. Everyone is out there somewhere." He shooed us toward a large stone staircase. "Go on. Unpack so you can enjoy the day."

#

The view from our room was a feast of color, texture, and light. Twisting olive trees. Bright purple and emerald fields of lavender. The turquoise glow of a long rectangular pool surrounded by multi-leveled stone patios. Lush gardens full of pink and yellow blossoms surrounding an old fountain. Over to the right, a tennis court with two male players on it, and off to the left, beyond the pool, the guest house and other buildings, some new, some old and crumbling.

All breathtaking.

In the distance, I could see row after row of vines, striping the land with vibrant green and earthy gold.

"God, I'm in love."

"With the view or with me?"

Omigod! What the fuck? What the actual fuck?

Heart hammering, I kept looking out the window, but I was dying to turn around and see his face—was he teasing me? Was he serious? How should I handle this? *FUCK!* I was totally caught off guard. My eyeballs roved from side to side while I racked my brain for a response that wouldn't terrify or offend him.

Flirty. Flirty could work.

Tossing a coy look over my shoulder, I said, "What do you think?"

The corners of his mouth rose slightly as he lifted his bag onto a chair and focused on unzipping it. "I'm only teasing. I know you meant the view." He took out a pair of pants, a pale blue shirt, and a dark blue blazer. Then he cleared his throat. "Do you have anything that needs to be hung up?"

God, how could he just blow by that moment like it was nothing? My pulse was roaring inside my head. I couldn't breathe right. And something about his response seemed off to me—it was the way he didn't meet my eyes. Had he really only been teasing? Or was he wondering about the way I felt?

Damn it, Lucas. If you want to know what I'm feeling, just ask me!

Not that I was sure of how I felt. My emotions were all tangled up inside me, and I was scared to examine them more closely.

"Mia?" Lucas looked at me quizzically, and I remembered he'd asked me a question about hanging up clothes.

"Oh. Yes, thanks for reminding me." I'd packed my little carry-on suitcase with just a few outfits—including the strapless dress I'd worn my first night in Paris and something dressier for tomorrow night's party. I hung those in the closet next to Lucas's pants, shirt, and coat, and experienced a strange hitch in my chest at the sight of our clothes hanging side by side. This was so intimate, visiting his family's country home, attending a family engagement party, sharing a bedroom, a bathroom… It felt like we were a couple. A real couple.

I had to steady myself on the closet door.

It was time to face it—I felt something more than physical for Lucas.

Something that warmed my belly and wobbled my knees and made me smile just thinking about him. Did he feel anything like that for me? Or was he totally able to keep his emotions from running away with him? Maybe it was different for guys, or maybe if you were used to mind-blowing sex, it was easier to keep your feelings out of it. Was I mistaking amazement for affection? Biting my lip, I watched him take a few things out of his bag and toss them on the bed.

Oh, did I mention the bed?

It was queen-size, covered in crisp white linen, and topped by a tall headboard made out of a set of iron gates like the ones at the foot of the driveway. When we first entered the room, Lucas came up behind me and said low in my ear, "That headboard is giving me some ideas involving you and a tie I brought. I think I've got a better use for it."

He wants to tie me up.

Bones turned to jelly. Vision went starry.

Now he was taking a tie out of his bag. *Oh my God, is that the one?* I'd never been tied up before but I nearly went sprinting from the closet over to the bed with my hands in the air. Instead I remained where I was, scared to let him to see my face as the full force of my feelings hit me.

I think I'm in love with him. For real.

"Oh, you know what I forgot? Shampoo." Lucas turned toward me, and his brow furrowed. "Mia?"

Move. Get out of the fucking closet. Act natural.

"I have some. You'll love it, actually. It's going to spoil you for any other hair products." On legs as unsteady as my voice, I went over to my bag and pulled out my makeup cases. "Use whatever you need."

In the bathroom, I set my things on the vanity, glancing in the mirror at my flushed cheeks. *Get a grip, Mia. It's totally obvious something is up with you.*

I shut the door and splashed some cold water on my face.

You're not in love with him. You're just happy to be here.

Really supremely fucking happy.

And all hopped up on the fresh air and orgasms.

I dried my face and hands on a towel and made a new list.

5 Appropriate (And Yet Also Wildly Inappropriate) Thoughts You Are Allowed To Have About Lucas

1) You are allowed to imagine him whispering all manner of dirty words in your ear.
2) You are allowed to imagine him screwing you in every room in this house. Even the closets.
3) You are allowed to imagine going down on him at any given moment, including while he's driving, at mealtimes, and in the pool. (You are not allowed to actually do this, however. Well, maybe the driving one.)

4) You are allowed to imagine what it would be like to be tied to the bed by him, helpless and at his mercy.

5) You are even allowed to imagine tying him to a chair and bossing him around a little. Whatever turns you on. But no matter what, you are not allowed to think or—God forbid—utter the L word. Got it?

I gave the girl in the mirror the fiercest look I had, and she seemed to understand.

When I came out of the bathroom, I noticed Lucas had changed from jeans into red swim trunks, and the sight of his bare chest did whirlpool things to my insides. "I thought maybe we'd sit by the pool a little after our walk. If you're up for that, I mean. We have some time before dinner."

"Sounds heavenly. I'll get my suit on." I rummaged through my clothing without seeing any of it, still feeling out of sorts. "So…do you get to visit here often?

"About once a year." Lucas pulled a gray t-shirt over his head. "Usually every summer."

My hands fumbled through my suitcase as I watched his abs disappear. When he caught me staring, I looked down. *Damn. What am I looking for again?*

"My mother guilts me about only visiting her only once a year," he went on, "but planes *do* fly the other way across the Atlantic. Sometimes I think she forgets that." Lucas pulled a pair of flip-flops from his bag and tossed them on the floor.

I smiled half-heartedly, but an insidious thought had invaded my brain. Had he ever brought his girlfriend here? Before I could decide if I really wanted the answer, the question was out. "Have you ever brought anyone here with you before?"

"Once."

Jealousy gripped me hard by the throat as I closed my fist around my bikini top. "Jessica?"

"Yeah. We came for my oldest brother's wedding a few years ago."

"How nice." I took my bathing suit out of my bag. *I hate you, Jessica.* "What a perfect spot for a wedding." I could envision the entire thing—the white linen tablecloths, wooden dining chairs, candles in white frosted glasses, centerpieces made with lavender or maybe olive branches.

For a moment, I pictured myself in a beautiful wedding gown, not the formal beaded one I'd chosen before, but something softer and simpler. Arm in arm with my dad, I was floating down a gravel path lined with candles toward…

I swallowed hard.

That is not on the Appropriate list.

"I guess so," Lucas said, running a hand through his hair. "Um, I'll give you a minute to get your suit on, and then we'll go down."

I couldn't help smiling. "Lucas. You've seen every inch of my body up close and personal. I don't mind if you watch me change into my bathing suit."

"In that case…" He flopped onto the bed and set his head in his hand. "Start the show."

Chapter Seventeen

Although I was nervous, meeting Lucas's family was not as uncomfortable as I'd feared. His mother, Mireille, was a striking dark-haired woman with luminous skin and a petite frame. After welcoming both Lucas and me with kisses on each cheek, she insisted that we sit with her for a chat.

We sat at a table and chairs beneath a huge umbrella, where she asked me about where I lived and how I was enjoying my trip. She also asked how we'd met, and when Lucas told her the truth—omitting the bit about the canceled wedding—she didn't seem to think it strange we'd only made each other's acquaintance a few days before.

"How nice," she said. "Lucas is a perfect tour guide for Paris."

"He is," I agreed. "I really got lucky."

Frenched

Lucas pinched my leg under the table.

#

"Your mom is so beautiful." I leaned over to inhale the fragrant white flowers along the path Lucas and I were following through the garden. "No wonder she had all those men falling for her."

"Well, lots of men are fools for beauty." He nudged my arm. "Myself included."

Straightening up, I blushed and smiled sideways at him. "Thanks." We ambled slowly through the private little paradise. Even the bees seemed content here, buzzing about the blossoms without bothering us. "Your brother seems nice."

Lucas rolled his eyes. "Another fool."

"Oh, come on. He's in love."

I'd met Lucas's older brother Gilles and his fiancée Lisette by the pool too, as well as several of their friends staying at the villa for the party. Gilles fawned over Lisette to the point of absurdity, fetching her towels and sunscreen and water and magazines, all the while gazing at her adoringly. He resembled Lucas in a way, but was taller, lankier, and not quite as handsome.

At least in my opinion.

Lucas's oldest brother, Nicolas, had been playing tennis with Mireille's husband Sebastien, but I was introduced to his wife Carine and their little girl, Gisele, a little fair-haired sprite in a bubble-gum pink bathing suit.

"And Gisele's adorable. How old is she?"

He cocked his head. "She's two, I think? I really wish I saw her more often."

I grinned at him. "She adores you. Her face lights up every time you talk to her."

"She just likes it when I swing her around by the arms like that. Makes her dizzy."

"It made me dizzy just watching you two." Or maybe it was my feelings making my head spin. There was something about seeing Lucas indulge the little girl that had me warm all over. I wondered if he wanted children of his own someday and if he'd bring them here in the summertime. I even entertained a brief fantasy of myself in the role of Madame Fournier in such a scenario before I gave myself a figurative slap on the wrist. *Have you lost your mind? Knock that shit off!*

"My dad used to spin me around like that, in our front yard when I was little." Suddenly Lucas stopped to pick a pink bloom off a long stem. He studied it for a moment and held it out to me. "Here. You were wearing something in this color that day at the cemetery."

My heart skittered. "That's right, I was." I took the flower from him and lifted it to my nose. Looking at him over the petals, I breathed in its sweet scent. *Christ, this is getting ridiculous. I want to keep my thoughts from straying into Inappropriate territory, but I need a little help here.*

"Lucas." I twirled the flower around by the stem. "I'm going to have to ask you to tell me something about yourself that isn't sexy, sweet, or charming."

He raised his eyebrows. "What?"

"Seriously. I'm starting to think none of this is real." It was a lie—I was afraid it was all too real.

"Hmmmm." His face took on a look of mock concentration as we started walking again. "Oh, here's one. I'm a huge Rangers fan and I get very animated when watching games. I scream and swear and jump around."

"No good. I'm from Detroit. We get hockey." I shook my head. "In fact, I think you just made it worse."

"Oh. OK, ummmm…" He looked skyward for a moment, then snapped his fingers. "Aha! You'll hate this: I cut my own hair."

I stared at him, mouth agape. "What? That's ridiculous. You can't cut your own hair!"

He laughed. "Sure I can."

"How can you even see?"

"I turn around and use the mirror. It's not that hard. And it's not like my hair is that difficult." He shrugged. "If I fuck it up or it gets really uneven, eventually I'll wander into a barber shop."

I sighed. "Well, I'll grant you that is odd, but I still need something worse. Something that will make me say, 'Boy I'm glad I don't live in New York. I'd hate to run into that asshole again.'"

He elbowed me and scrunched up his face. "OK, how about this: I rarely make reservations at restaurants. I just like to get there when I get there."

I winced, but I nodded. "Now we're getting somewhere. That would drive me crazy." Moving ahead, I stepped in front of him to walk backward. "OK, one more thing. Something I'll totally hate."

He stopped walking and thought a moment. "I don't ever want to get married."

I blinked. "You don't want to get married to anyone, ever?"

"Nope."

"Why not? Because of your parents?" Despite the warmth of the sun on my skin, I sort of felt like someone had just thrown ice water in my face. I'd been teasing Lucas, but this felt serious, like he was telling me something significant. *Oh God, he knows what I've been thinking. He's trying to tell me not to get carried away.*

He shrugged. "Probably that's there in the back of my mind. I was there when their marriage fell apart. I saw what it did to my dad. But it's not just them; *most* marriages don't last. And also, I've just never wanted to get married."

224

I turned around and took a couple steps forward, struggling to make my voice sound casual. "What do you see yourself doing in the future?"

"Well, I want to finish my research, write about it, maybe teach a few different places. I like to travel a lot, and I might like to open up my own bar sometime, either in Paris or New York, I'm not sure."

My heart ticked faster than it had a right to, agitation itching under my skin. *What the hell are you getting upset about? Jesus, probably a couple should exchange phone numbers before they exchange rings. You haven't even known him a week.*

Plus, it wasn't like I thought everyone my age wanted to get married. Even Coco said she wasn't sure about it. But I'd always known I would. In fact, I remembered asking Tucker about it once we'd been dating a few months and thinking that if he'd said he didn't ever want to get married, then I'd move on. He'd said it was part of his plan eventually, just not any time soon, and I'd been OK with that.

Suddenly I had a thought, and as usual I couldn't let it go. I took a deep breath. "Is that why you and Jessica broke up?"

Lucas took a moment before answering, his eyes glued to the gravel. "It wasn't the only reason, but yes," he admitted. "She wanted to get married. I didn't." Then he stopped walking and put a hand on my arm. "But if you're thinking I did to her what your ex did to you, I promise you, I didn't. I'd always made my views on marriage perfectly clear. It wasn't like it was a surprise or anything."

"No. No, of course not." I told myself to ask about something else, but the subject of Lucas's ex was like that stupid breakup song you can't stop listening to even though it makes you feel horrible. I had a twisted fascination with her.

"You said marriage was just one reason. Can I ask about the others?" It was a personal question, too personal, and he had every right to tell me to mind my own business, but he didn't.

"Well…" He appeared to struggle with words. "For one thing, we had different appetites."

Appetites? "What do you mean?"

He glanced at me, and I saw the red in his cheeks. It was more than color from the sun. "Remember how I told you I was nervous about scaring you with…things I wanted to do to you?"

"Nothing you do scares me."

"Well, some things I liked used to scare her. Or at least, she wasn't into them."

That was amazing to me. How could any girl be with Lucas and not want to submit to his every whim? Maybe I was a little sex starved, or at least good-sex starved, but Lucas was perfection in that regard. He made me feel like an angel, a devil, beauty and desire incarnate. He let me do anything I wanted to him and did things to me I'd never even dreamed of. *How will anyone else live up?*

I cleared my throat. "Was the breakup bad?"

"Pretty bad. She said I didn't love her enough to change, or to make a promise that she was ready to make to me."

"Wow. That's rough." I actually felt sorry for both of them—yes, even goddamn Jessica. Because they were both right, in a way. I could see both sides. "So when was that?"

"Last Christmas."

Six months ago. Lifting the soft petals of the pink flower he'd given me to my nose once more, I inhaled and exhaled. "Do you still love her?"

He shook his head. "No. I mean, I still *care* about her. I want her to be happy, but I knew that it ultimately wasn't going to be with me. I guess I'd known it for a while and should have ended things sooner, but I didn't want to hurt her."

I nodded, wondering if that's what Tucker had felt like. Had he wanted to end things sooner too? Had he stifled the impulse to tell me he didn't want to get married because I was so obsessed with the wedding? God, I could hardly recall a conversation between us in the last year about anything non wedding-related. *What a fucking circus it was going to be.* For the first time, I felt an iota of sympathy for Tucker. *One* iota.

"It must have been hard after such a long time," I said.

"It was. I felt horrible. But she wanted something I couldn't give her. I didn't want to lie about it, make a promise I knew I couldn't keep."

I nodded, thinking he'd done exactly as I'd asked—told me something about himself that made me realize he wasn't perfect for me, at least not in the long run.

So why did it feel so shitty?

We reached the edge of the garden where it bordered on the olive grove. Lucas stopped walking and took me into his arms. "Come here." He kissed me warm and soft. "Let's not talk about the past. Or the future. Where we came from and where we'll end up don't matter to me as much as being here right now with you."

I melted into his kiss, telling myself he was right. OK, maybe I did have some feelings for him, and maybe it was more than a fuck fling, but it wasn't love, not the kind that would last. Because as shitty as it felt to have my wedding called off, I still wanted to get married someday. I still wanted a home and a family. I was sure of it.

Lucas didn't. And he was sure of it.

So even if some secret piece of my heart had been hoping for a different outcome, my head knew for certain now—this was all temporary.

Just a dream.

Frenched

#

We went back to the pool and spent the rest of the afternoon swimming and hanging out with his family and dozing next to each other on a cushioned double chaise lounge. And the more I analyzed the conversation we had in the garden, the more I was certain this was a rebound thing, for both of us.

I liked that Lucas was the opposite of Tucker, and Lucas liked the necessary short and sweet nature of our fling. It had an expiration date that wouldn't be his fault—he wouldn't have to break my heart to end things.

And the sex? Well, we both liked that.

As the tension drained from my shoulders and my mind wandered to the episode in the back seat, my entire body rippled with gooseflesh. My nipples got hard.

It didn't go unnoticed.

Lucas put a hand on my thigh and tipped his mouth to my ear. "Are you doing that on purpose? You know, your bathing suit top is white."

I smiled without opening my eyes.

"You are a very bad girl, Mia Devine," he whispered. "I think you need to be punished tonight."

My toes curled.

#

For dinner that night, one of the patios was transformed into an outdoor dining space with a long picnic-style table covered with soft, cream-colored cloth, benches lined with colorful pillows, and various lanterns hanging from the ribbed pergola roof. All twenty-four guests were seated at the table while the meal was served by waiters supervised by a critical-eyed Jean-Paul at one end of the table. He was seated across from Henri, whom I couldn't help think of as The Count and picture in a black cape. He was tall and lanky like his sons, silver-haired like Jean-Paul, although not quite as handsome, and had welcomed me warmly.

Music played on hidden speakers, accompanied by the low hum of conversation and the clinks of forks and glasses. The food was delicious, platters laden with local produce and poultry, flavored with herbs grown in Jean-Paul's gardens. The wine was delectable, almost as delectable as Lucas, who sat beside me wearing charcoal slacks and a white shirt that set off the color in his cheeks from the sun today. But it was the tie around his neck that really made my insides clench.

Is that the one he mentioned before?

As if that wasn't enough, he'd let me fuss with his hair after he got out of the shower. I'd put some product in and sort of neatened the curls while he stood there with a towel around his hips.

It was too tempting. I'd yanked it off and dropped to my knees.

We were late for dinner.

I only hoped Lucas found me as enticing as I found him tonight.

I was finally wearing my new shoes, which he'd watched me put on with an incredulous look on his face. "God, Mia. Your legs in that dress…and those shoes…" He swallowed. "I know we're late already, but damn. Let me just look at you."

I'd stood in from of him, blushing like crazy. My hair was pinned up in a twist to complement the flirty strapless dress I'd worn my first night in Paris. I was happy to give it a much nicer memory than wandering the streets of the Latin Quarter alone. Had that really been just four nights ago? It didn't seem possible.

Not when Lucas would slip his hand onto my lap and gently rub my leg. Not when he'd lean over and brush his lips across my bare shoulder. Not when he'd put his mouth to my ear and say, "You look so beautiful tonight, princess. Too beautiful. It's making me so crazy, I can hardly sit still. My dick has been hard for hours. You'll have to pay for that."

Once, I leaned over to him and whispered back, "If I was wearing panties, they'd be soaked right now."

The look he gave me could have seared flesh.

God, what a relief it was to fall back into this easy pattern of sex and teasing. As long as the vibe between us crackled with this kind of sexual energy, I couldn't think about anything other than our physical attraction.

After dessert, the younger crowd went to the pool deck for more music and drinks, but Lucas shook his head when I asked if we'd join them. "I have other plans for us," he said, taking my hand.

I was a little tipsy from the wine and pastis, but I said nothing when Lucas took me into the living room and grabbed a bottle of scotch off a bar cart. From there he led me into the kitchen and asked one of the waiters for a bucket of ice. While we waited for it, he kept one hand pressed to my upper back, fingers spread. It was possessive in a way that ratcheted the tension between us one notch higher. The word *appetites* kept running through my mind.

Upstairs in our room, Lucas shut the door behind us and locked it without turning on the light. I drifted toward the open window, stopping just short of where moonlight pooled on the floor, and stood listening to the sounds from the party below.

"We can hear them. They could hear us." Lucas set the bucket down and came up behind me, standing so close my entire body was on edge. I could feel his breath on my neck, his chest on my back, his erection on my ass. "So you can't make any noise."

I nodded, unable to find my voice.

Frenched

He kissed the back of my neck. "If you want me to stop at any time tonight, just tell me. OK?"

My belly flipped—what was he planning to do to me?

A moment later, I gasped when I felt an ice cube sweep across my shoulder blades.

A hand covered my mouth. "Shhhh. I said quiet."

My heart started to pound.

He unzipped my dress and it fell to the floor. Chills swept down my arms and legs, doubling when I felt the ice cube at the back of my neck. Slowly, he dragged the ice down my spine, over each vertebra, beyond my tailbone and lightly between my buttocks. I shivered.

Ohmygod ohmygod ohmygod.

Reaching between my thighs, he brushed the ice against my tingling folds, slipping the tip of the crescent shape inside me. I whimpered against the hand clamped over my mouth.

Fuck, this is hot.

I couldn't even believe the cube was still solid—my body was on fire.

"Don't move."

He released me, and a few seconds later I heard the clink of an ice cube hitting the bottom of a glass, and then the sounds of him pouring the scotch.

"I want to taste you all the time, Mia. I want the flavor of you on my tongue every fucking minute of the day. And you know it. You shouldn't tease me by telling me you're not wearing panties when I can't have my mouth on you." It was a tone I'd never heard from him before—hot and angry.

I liked it.

He came up behind me again, pressing his lips to the back of one shoulder and dragging them up the arc of my neck. My legs trembled with apprehension, with excitement, with need.

God, I'm so wet.

I didn't dare say it.

He slid a hand around to my stomach and down between my thighs. I sucked in my breath at the easy glide of his finger inside me, and fought the moan trapped in my throat. But when his other hand stole up to one breast, I couldn't help the sound of pleasure that escaped my lips.

He pinched my nipple. Hard.

I gasped at the zing of pain, but at the same time, I delighted in his nimble fingers sliding in and out of me, his palm pressing on my clit. I was dying to turn around, shove him down on the bed, tear off his pants, and ride his cock until he begged for mercy.

But I knew he wouldn't let me.

Instead I moved my hips, rocking against his hand, hoping to get him so worked up he'd have to fuck me.

"You want something from me?"

I nodded.

"Good girl. You have to stay quiet if you want it." He shoved his fingers deeper into me. "Can you do that?"

"Yes," I whispered, aching to scream but terrified he wouldn't give me what I wanted if I did.

"Good." He took his hands off me, and I nearly wept with frustration. "Now turn around."

I turned around to see him backing up to the bed, fully dressed, his white shirt glowing in the shadows. "God, you're so fucking beautiful." He sat on the side of the bed, picked up his scotch from the table and took a drink. "Here are the rules. You speak only when I tell you to. You only do as I say. Understand?"

My Jimmy Choos teetered as I nodded.

"Good. Come here."

I stepped out of my dress and stood in front of him, naked but for my skyscraper heels.

"Take your hair down."

With trembling hands, I pulled out my hairpins, letting them fall to the floor. My hair fell to my shoulders.

"Now lie across my lap. On your stomach."

Moving to the foot of the bed, I crawled up the length of it and over his thighs. On my knees and elbows, I looked over my shoulder to see him removing his tie. I nearly climaxed at the sight of it.

Oh, God. He's really going to do it.

"Put your hands up here."

Holding my breath, I reached out and took hold of a bar on the headboard slightly above my head, one hand on top of the other.

And he tied me to the bed.

He fucking tied. Me. Up.

And as he wrapped and knotted and pulled the silk tight around my wrists, he spoke to me in a low, even tone. "This is what happens when you tease me, Mia. When you make me feel helpless to resist you. I have to make you feel helpless too."

I do! I do! I wanted to scream. But I bit my tongue, frightened to do anything that would make him deny me. I had no fucking idea how much being treated this way would turn me on—I was feverish and panting and shaking. And Lucas—I'd never seen him this way. Far from the lighthearted, generous lover he'd been in Paris, this Lucas was demanding and unapologetic and slightly frightening.

God*damn* it was hot. I wanted him more than I'd ever wanted anyone or anything, ever.

Do it now, I begged him silently. *Fuck me now.*

But he wasn't finished with me.

Chapter Eighteen

First, he ran his hands all over my body, avoiding every spot I wanted him to touch. I bit my lip and hung my head beneath my bound hands, desperately wanting him to make me come and unashamed to act like it.

But he stayed away from any body part he knew would set me off, although that list was shrinking rapidly. He slid one palm from my shoulder down my back; the other, from my ankle up my calf. He touched my tailbone, my belly, my neck, the back of my knees. My skin rippled with gooseflesh, puckering my nipples, and I tried to arch my back and drop lower so they'd rub against the pillow. But my hands were tied to the headboard in a way that prevented me from being able to move them up or down.

A tiny, strangled sound escaped my throat, although I wanted to scream and curse and thrash.

"Frustrated, princess? I know just how you feel." He put a hand on my ass and rubbed in slow circles. "But you were a bad girl today. And bad girls need to be punished a little."

For a second I was nervous—what did he mean by punished? Was he actually going to—

The sound of Lucas's hand smacking my bare ass was as much a shock as the sting, and I threw my head back. Immediately he held his palm over the tender spot, giving me a few seconds to adjust to the idea and feel of being spanked.

Fucking *spanked*.

Like a naughty little girl.

Was it wrong to love it?

He did it on the other cheek, again holding his hand over my burning skin while pleasure and pain zipped along my nerve endings like Fourth of July sparklers.

I wasn't sure what turned me on more—the physical sensation of his hand smacking my skin or the idea of Lucas punishing me for being too beautiful, for tempting him too much. My mouth hung wide open, my breaths coming so fast and hard I thought he might scold me for being noisy again.

Frenched

The third spank was harder, hard enough to make me cry out involuntarily, and I slammed my eyes shut, biting my lip. "Sorry," I whimpered as he held his palm over my blistering hot skin.

"Shhhhh. I think you've been spanked enough." He dropped a kiss on my tailbone before somehow maneuvering beneath me so that my knees rested on either side of his head. "And I've been wanting to lick your pussy all day. I'm done waiting."

Looping his hands around my thighs, he pulled me down so I was straddling his face.

Straddling. His. Face.

Oh my God and I can't even scream are you kidding me...

"You don't move. Understand?" he said, his breath nearly causing me to explode.

I nodded, wanting to scream every curse I knew out loud. In French and English, and maybe some other languages too.

It was the worst punishment and also the most sublime pleasure I'd ever felt.

He teased me with his tongue like he was tying a knot in a cherry stem.

A double knot.

He licked me like a double scoop of French vanilla on a hot summer day.

At the equator.

He savored me like I could melt in his mouth but he didn't want me to.

That was a losing battle.

I didn't last longer than a minute, maybe not even thirty seconds—hell, maybe not even ten. I had no sense of time anymore. The moment he touched me with his tongue, it was like he threw gasoline onto a fire that was already burning. I fought every instinct my body had, which was to rock and writhe and smother his mouth with my pussy. I wanted to ride his tongue. I leaned forward and banged my head against my wrists, dying to cry out, to combust, to collapse.

I knew he was trying to prolong it because every time I neared the edge and stiffened up, he'd back off my clit and bite my thigh or just breathe warm air on my skin. When I'd relax slightly, he'd flutter his tongue over me again, taking me back to the brink, until finally I thought I'd go insane.

"Lucas," I begged, on the verge of tears. "Please."

Finally, he pulled me tighter to his mouth with one hand, shoved his fingers inside me with the other, and devoured me hard and fast.

I fucking *detonated*.

I have no idea how long it actually lasted, how Lucas managed to breathe, or how I didn't break the skin on my upper arm, because I bit myself *hard*. My entire body was paralyzed by the force of this orgasm, which turned the world white and set off a siren in my head, racking my body with undulating surges of ecstasy so powerful I couldn't even breathe. By the time it subsided, I was gasping for air and my left shoulder bore the indentations of my teeth.

Top and bottom.

Before I had regained the ability to form a sentence, Lucas slid out from between my legs and knelt behind me. "I'm not done with you yet, princess. Don't even think about moving."

He needn't have worried about my thinking *anything* except wanting to feel his cock inside me. I heard him tear open a condom packet, and I was tempted to tell him not to wear it, but more than anything I just wanted him to fuck me and he might make me wait longer if I disobeyed the no-talking rule.

A moment later I felt his erection rubbing my ass, hard and thick. He reached up and took my hair in one fist, pulling my head back hard enough to make my scalp sting.

"What do you want?" he asked. "Tell me."

"I want you to fuck me," I whispered without hesitation. "Hard. Now."

"Yeah? You want to get fucked hard?" He pulled my hair tighter, and I winced.

"*Yes*," I said through clenched teeth. God, if my hands were free I'd force him to do it, grab him, pull him into me.

But Lucas had all the control, and *holy hell*, did he have patience.

He teased me with the head of his cock between my legs, rubbing it on my wet, swollen folds

241

and slipping it in just an inch before pulling back out. He slid it between my buttocks, murmuring words of praise for my hot, tight ass. He held onto my hair with one hand and reached around to one breast with the other, pinching my nipple and rolling it between his fingers. He whispered dirty things to me, telling me what a good girl I was being, how hard I made his cock, how he could still taste my pussy on his lips, how badly he'd wanted to fuck me like this all day.

When I was near tears again, he finally pushed inside me, and the relief was so magnificent I actually looked to heaven and thanked God.

"Talk to me." Lucas breathed hard, moving one hand to my hip and keeping the other wrapped around my hair. "Tell me what you like."

"Oh, God." I wasn't sure I could talk—my body was spiraling out of control again.

He yanked my hair. "God's not here."

"*Lucas*." I licked my lips and arched my back, my arms stretched over my head. "Yes, yes, yes, like that. I love your cock inside me. I love the way you fill me and stretch me and pound me. You're so big and hard and fucking perfect."

He groaned, thrusting into me deeper and faster.

"I love the way you move," I went on, struggling to keep my voice to a whisper. "It makes me so wet. I love the sound your body makes against mine when you fuck me like that. It makes me want to scream."

He dropped my hair and took me by both hips, digging his fingers into my flesh and jerking me back onto him with a ferocious, savage rhythm. I couldn't see him but I imagined what we looked like—Lucas still dressed, his white shirt undone at the neck, pants around his knees; me tied to the headboard, naked but for my high heels. It was so hot and he was fucking me so hard and I was so wet and everything inside me began to tighten and pull and as Lucas's fervor reached its breaking point, I widened my knees and dropped as far forward as I could to take him even deeper.

It pushed him over the edge and he held himself deep inside me as he came, gasping and growling as he throbbed. My mouth hung open in disbelief as he reached around me with one hand and rubbed hard, fast circles on my clit, making my insides clench and spasm around him.

Un. Fucking. Believable.

Lucas, breathing as heavy as I was, tipped forward and dropped his forehead to my back. His hair tickled my skin and I shivered.

"Uh." His voice was weak.

"Yeah. That's about all I've got too."

He kissed my spine. "You're amazing."

"Hey, that was all you. I was tied up the whole time."

And loving every minute of it.

Laughing, he pulled out of me and stood up. "And as tempting as it is to leave you there because you look so fucking good, give me one second and I'll untie you."

He went into the bathroom for a moment, then appeared at my side with his pants fastened and his shirt off. After untying me, he rubbed my wrists before bringing them to his lips and closing his eyes. The gesture was so sweet, it made my throat squeeze up.

"They don't hurt." I didn't want him to think it was anything less than incredible for me.

Jessica. You silly bitch.

He opened his eyes but didn't take his lips off my skin.

I smiled. "Promise."

Just then we heard a squeal and a huge splash out the window.

"Someone get thrown in the pool?" I guessed.

"Sounds like it. Do you want to go down and join them?" Never had a question been asked with less enthusiasm.

"Are you kidding?" I reached up and played with a lock of curly hair that had overpowered my product and sprung forward. "There's nowhere I'd rather be than in here with you." I glanced over my shoulder at my feet. "Although I would like to take these shoes off."

He smiled. "Take them off. Punishment's over."

I got off the bed and slipped my heels from my feet. "Lucas, can you still call it punishment if the person enjoys it? Because I did."

His eyebrows went up. "Oh yeah? Maybe I'll have to get the whip out next time."

I froze. "You don't really have a whip, do you?" Although frankly, I'd let Lucas do just about anything he wanted to me. I trusted him.

He grinned and picked up his scotch. "No. But I'd get one if you wanted me to. Maybe you'd like to whip *me*. You'd look awesome in one of those dominatrix getups."

I smiled slyly. "I'll add that to the outfit calendar."

#

We spent the next morning visiting with Lucas's family and the afternoon by the pool again. Later, when we'd had enough sun and chorine, he found a blanket and we took a little picnic of fruit, bread, and cheese into the olive grove. After we ate, we drank wine and I read the love letters of Abelard and Heloise aloud to Lucas, who lay with his head in my lap while I leaned back against an olive tree.

245

It was pretty fucking perfect.

So perfect that I began to feel uneasy about the peace I'd made with the fact that this thing with Lucas, whatever it was, had to end soon. So perfect that every time he opened his mouth to speak I held my breath, hoping he'd mention something about seeing me again. So perfect that when I noticed Lucas had drifted off to sleep, I set the book down and studied his face, feeling the need to memorize every feature. The way one eyebrow arced higher than the other. The way his scruff covered the dimples that appeared when he smiled. The plump lips and square jaw. The dark lashes fanning down toward chiseled cheekbones.

Oh shit.

Five Inappropriate Thoughts I Had In The Olive Grove

1) His face is so goddamn beautiful, and I fucking straddled it last night!
2) Wonder when I can do that again.
3) Would it be rude to wake him up for sex?
4) What the hell am I going to do when I have to go home to my real life?
5) I'm going to miss him so fucking much.

A warm breeze blew his curls over his forehead, and I brushed them back again and again, finally admitting to myself what I'd been trying so hard to deny.

I'm going to miss him because I'm in love with him. It's crazy and stupid and not practical and totally too fast and bound to end badly—but it's real.

It didn't matter what I called it—friends-with-benefits, fuck fling, rebound thing... What mattered was the way I felt when I was with him. The way he made me feel like I could do anything, say anything in my head, have anything I wanted. He was teaching me things about my body and desires I'd never known. He was teaching me about the beauty of living for the moment. He was teaching me not to worry so much about what things looked like, what other people thought, what *I* thought I should be.

I loved who I was when I was with him. And I loved him.

An ache rooted in my chest began to grow, and I imagined it like a seed from which black vines sprouted in every direction, constricting my stomach, suffocating my heart, squeezing my throat. The ache spread throughout my entire body, making my limbs heavy with its weight. Before I could stop it, a tear escaped and slid down my cheek, followed by several more, one of which plopped onto Lucas's forehead.

I sniffed, and Lucas stirred.

He opened his eyes and looked up at me. "Sorry, I fell asleep. Your voice is so soothing. Did you get to a sad part?"

I nodded. Wiping at my eyes, I forced myself to brighten up. "Sorry, I'm just a little emotional."

He sat up and moved next to me, leaning against the tree and placing his arm around my shoulders. "You don't have to apologize to me." We sat like that for a moment before he spoke again. "Listen, I didn't even think about an engagement party being kind of difficult for you, and I should have. I will totally understand if you don't want to go."

"What? No." His voice was so worried, and I put a hand on his leg. "That's not it, Lucas. I'm not…I don't have a problem with the engagement party. I want to go. Really."

"OK." He didn't sound convinced, but he didn't argue.

I settled into the crook of his arm, closed my eyes, and took a few deep breaths, embarrassed that I'd been caught crying and praying I could fight back against the rest of the tears waiting to fall.

"Is it me then?" he asked.

My eyes flew open. *Don't tell him.* "What do you mean?"

Against my back I felt his chest expand. "You're upset. Did I do something?"

"No, of course not." I blinked, too nervous to look at him. He'd know I was lying if he saw my face.

"I hope last night wasn't too much for you. You're just so beautiful and I got carried away—"

Frenched

"No. Lucas." I turned to face him and pulled my legs beneath me, sitting on my heels. He'd see the sadness on my face but I couldn't let him think it was because of what we'd done last night. We'd stayed up half the night doing all kinds of fun stuff, including naked checkers, licking scotch off each other's bodies, and taking a bath in the clawfoot tub—then he let me tie him to a chair and do all sorts of things to his body, anything I wanted.

And he'd obeyed my every command.

"Last night was amazing," I said. "I promise you, I loved every minute of it."

He looked relieved. "OK, good. I did too." He shifted his position and adjusted his pants. "Just thinking about it is making me hard."

Glancing down, I smiled. "I can see that."

"So you're not going to tell me what's wrong?"

I love you. That's what's wrong.

I shook my head. "Nope. Because it doesn't matter. What matters is enjoying this moment here with you."

He tackled me, throwing me onto my back and lying above me. "I *am* enjoying this moment. But I'd enjoy it even more with my pants off."

I smiled at his insatiable desire. "You're a fiend, you know. And I think we're visible from the house."

"Totally visible." But he lowered his lips and kissed me, opening his mouth over mine and meeting my tongue with his.

I wrapped my arms around him, kissing him back with a desperation he must have sensed but didn't question out loud. God, how could he be so nonchalant about this whole thing? I felt like my world was going to split apart in four days, and nothing seemed to bother him about goodbye. I was envious of his ability to be so fulfilled by the present that the future, even the near future, didn't affect him.

Because he knows, Mia. He knows what this is and he's never pretended it was anything else. Get that into your head and keep it there.

Lucas picked up his head and traced my mouth with one finger. "I love your lips, have I told you that? But before I decide my family won't care if they see a show out here, we better go in and start getting ready for the party."

"OK."

That's it. Agreeable. Game for anything. Just here for a good time.

As we walked back to the house, I carried the picnic basket with both hands—maybe it was silly, but I didn't want Lucas to hold one. Those were the kinds of things that had to stop. And when we returned to Paris, I had to stay in my own hotel room at night. Hell, maybe I should even spend the days on my own too. I had to get used to being without him.

Because even though he wasn't the type to worry about the future, I was. That hadn't changed. As much fun as I was having with Lucas, I was still the same person underneath—and just like Jessica, I wanted things in my life that he couldn't give. Comparing myself to her sucked, but I knew where she was coming from. I was twenty-seven already. I'd be twenty-eight in the fall. Maybe it was dumb to put a timeline on my life, but that's the way I was. And if he hadn't been willing to change for a woman he'd loved for three years, he wasn't going to change for me. I wasn't that stupid.

I just hoped I could find someone else I had such great chemistry with, someone who wanted to make that promise to me. *And* let me tie him up and suck him off before kneeling over his face.

I felt like laughing and crying at the same time. My eyes started to fill again and I had to look at the ground and blink furiously to get the tears to go away.

Lucas opened the back door for me and smiled as I passed through it, but his face still wore a worried expression. I'd have to do a better acting job if I wanted to convince him that everything was fine.

Upstairs in the shower, I made myself a list.

Instructions For the Night

1) No affectionate gestures that say "relationship potential." This includes hand-holding, hair touching, forehead kissing.

2) No fantasizing about a future with him, especially anything related to engagements or weddings.
3) No tears, frowny faces, or admitting what's wrong. If he asks, you continue to say nothing or, if necessary, lie and say it's the wedding thing after all.
4) DO NOT make any plans for when you get back to Paris. If he tries, you grit your teeth, summon your willpower, and suggest maybe spending some time on your own. List some attractions at super-high heights you want to see.
5) No more sex.

Actually, I didn't really put that one on there. Ain't nobody got that kind of willpower.

Chapter Nineteen

Gilles and Lisette's engagement party was the kind of event I wish I'd planned. In fact, I took a ton of photographs during the evening and got excited when I thought about showing them to Coco. In my head, I made a list of the possible venues where an outdoor Provençal-style wedding might be possible, although recreating the look and feel of this place would be a challenge. The colors, the light, the scents, the textures, the tastes…they were all so particular to this part of the world. But there were things I could imitate—the tables for four with wide easy chairs, the antique lace tablecloths, the lavender and wildflowers on the tables.

It occupied me for much of the night, which was good. I needed something to take my mind off Lucas, whose appearance in a wheat-colored summer suit, light blue shirt and THE TIE rivaled the scenery.

253

His shave was clean tonight, and I fought the urge to rub my cheek against his jaw many times. And the urge to lick it. Yeah, I had that one too.

I kept up a stream of bubbly chatter about my job to avoid breaking down, and he listened with interest, never complaining when I wandered off with my camera. But the I'm Totally Fine, Really I Am act was taking everything out of me—I was exhausted by the time everyone sat down for dinner, unsure of how long I could keep up the pretense.

We sat with the family at a long head table, and the meal looked lovely, but I wasn't hungry. I picked at my food, mostly just moving it around on my plate.

During dessert, Lucas asked me if I was OK.

"Of course." Picking up my wine glass, I took a hefty sip.

"You seem quiet," he said, running a finger over the halter strap of my bright pink dress.

I set the glass down. "Just thoughtful."

"What are you thinking about?"

Don't you dare, Mia Devine. Don't you fucking dare.

"Uh…" I took another swallow of wine, which gave me time to think up an allowable answer. "What's left on the Paris list, actually. I'll only have three days once I get back from here, really only two and a half, depending on what time the train gets in." My voice sounded terribly unnatural to me.

"That's right. You're leaving Tuesday, huh."

"Yep. Back to reality." Bright, toothpaste-commercial smile.

His lips tipped up, but it wasn't his usual grin. "I guess so. I have to work at The Beaver Saturday night, so—"

"That's OK," I chirped. *Come on, Mia. More enthusiasm, you can do it.* "Now that you've showed me how to get around, I'll be fine on my own. No worries."

"I was only going to say that we can take an early train tomorrow." Eyes troubled, Lucas studied me carefully. "But…do you mean that you don't want to hang out anymore when we get back to Paris?"

More wine. That's it. Drain the last drop. "Uh, no, not exactly." I fussed with the stem of my empty glass. "I just meant that you don't have to play tour guide anymore. I can do things by myself."

Silence. "Is that what you want?"

Of course not, you dummy.

I opened my mouth to continue with the night's slightly-less-than-Oscar-worthy performance but Lucas ruined the whole thing by answering his own question.

"Because I'll be really sad if it is."

Oh no. Oh, Jesus. Tears were coming.

Desperate, I looked around the table. Where the hell was the wine bottle? The rest of the family was engaged in chatter and didn't notice the quiet drama unfolding between us, but I knew if I didn't get up and leave, the dam inside me was going to burst.

"Mia?" Lucas reached for my hand.

"I'm sorry." Pushing my chair back, I jumped up and flew past the other tables, across the pool deck and around to the other side of the house. Into the dark I ran, working my legs as fast as I could in my heels, grateful that I ran track in high school and had kept up the habit for exercise. Through the garden—ever tried to run on gravel? It sucks, and that's in running shoes—beyond the fountain, all the way to the back of the olive grove. I ran so hard I couldn't even cry, lungs threatening to split wide open, a painful stitch in my side. When I reached the edge of the vineyard, I collapsed against the side of an old stone outbuilding.

Laying my cheek on the cold, rough surface, I pounded the heel of my hand into the stone and sobbed. I cried just as hard as I had when Tucker had called off our wedding, and the crazy thing was, I felt even sadder. Unlike the tears I cried then, these were fueled only by a broken heart, without anger or regret or shame to dilute them.

"Mia!" Lucas's voice echoed through the grove. Could he see me? I stifled my sobs, but a moment later, I heard his fast footfalls and then felt his hand on my back. "Mia, oh my God. Are you OK? Come here, please."

Maybe it was a mistake, but I let him turn me into his arms and continued to cry silently on his shoulder for a minute. He held me tight, rubbing my back, saying nothing. When my shuddering slowed, he swayed me gently and kissed my head. I lifted my tear-stained face from his chest, and he kissed each of my wet cheeks. Then my forehead.

Stop doing these sweet things. I'm already in love with you and you're making it worse.

But I couldn't say anything then because his mouth was on mine, and his arms were around me, and our bodies were pressed together in a way that turned my hopelessness into desperation, making me greedy for what he could give. I wanted it. I wanted it now, and I didn't care about the price.

Jumping up, I wrapped my legs around his waist and kissed him with ferocious desire, fisting my hands in his hair, biting his lip, gasping for air. His hands groped my ass and moved me against him, and I could feel his cock pushing against me through his clothing. *It's not enough. It's not enough.*

He backed me into the stone wall, and I knew I'd go out of my mind if I couldn't have him inside my body. "Lucas. I want you to fuck me. Now," I demanded against his lips.

He didn't fight it. Letting my legs drop to the ground, he undid his pants while I kicked off my underwear. In two seconds he'd lifted my dress and had me right back where I was against the wall, only this time his bare cock was driving into me.

Our mouths hovered inches apart, teeth bared, breath hot. My passion for him was so immense I felt like my skin couldn't contain it, like I might burst wide open with it. Every time we were together was incredible, but this was something different. It was frantic and panicked, driven by anguish as much as arousal.

It feels like the last time. It feels like fucking goodbye.

What if it is? What if it is?

I clung to him and he pumped into me hard and fast, then he pulled me tight to his body, grinding me against him. "Oh, God, Lucas," I panted frantically. "I'm gonna come..."

"I want you to," he growled. "I want you to come on my cock. I want to feel it. Then I'm going to come inside you *so hard*."

My head thumped back hard against the stone as my climax hit, and with every contraction of my body around his, words pulsed through my head... *fuck, yes, oh, my, God, right, there, you're, fucking, amazing, I, can't, get, enough...*

He groaned and pinned me harder against the wall, dropping his face to my neck and filling me completely. I felt him—I felt the pulsing of his orgasm as if it were my own, and I gripped him with my legs and held his head in my hands, my heart drumming in my chest. I opened my eyes and looked at the sky.

I saw stars that haven't even been born yet.

God, I love you.

And then it happened. It was in my head one second and on my lips the next. It was kind of like a movie, where you know the heroine is going to do something stupid and you reach for the screen in slow motion, yelling *nooooooooo!*

"God, I love you."

As soon as the words were out, I froze.

Lucas picked up his head. "What?"

"Oh my God." Embarrassment flooded me, my cheeks hot with shame. "Oh my God, I didn't mean that."

"Wait." He closed his eyes a second. "You didn't mean it? Or you didn't mean to *say* it?"

"I—I—" I whimpered in hideous, humiliating agony. "I'm just a little overwhelmed right now." I glanced down to where our bodies were joined. "I can't think at all. Maybe we can have this conversation, um…"

Lowering my feet to the ground, he pulled out of me, and immediately I felt the warm stream run down my inner thigh.

"Oh, crap." I held my dress away from my legs.

"Sorry about that. Uh, want me to get you a towel or something?"

I shook my head. "No, that's OK. But do you think I can make it into the house without being seen? I need to change my dress and I should probably mop up my face too." I didn't even want to think about what my eye makeup looked like.

"Yes, I think we can get you into the house unseen. But Mia…" He ran a hand though his hair. "We need to talk."

I looked over his shoulder beyond the vineyard, as if maybe hurtling the wall and taking off in the direction of Paris on foot was an option. "Yes."

Oh, God. How the hell was I going to explain myself?

#

Up in our room, I hung the soiled dress in the closet and changed into the one I'd worn last night. I also took off my heels in favor of going barefoot. In the bathroom, I scrubbed my face and splashed it with cold water, but my eyes still looked a little puffy. I covered up with makeup as well as I could, neatened my hair, and reapplied my lip pencil and balm.

OK, think. How am I going to spin this?

I had two options, best I could tell. I could be honest and say that I had strong feelings for him that were confusing and overwhelming, or I could pretend it was just an emotional reaction to the sex and try to laugh it off. Maybe I could try to read him first. He hadn't seemed all that freaked out. Maybe my dignity could be salvaged, although Jesus, it had taken a beating lately.

Lucas met me at the bottom of the stairs and handed me a glass of red wine. "Here. It's one of ours."

"Thank you." If he was going to break my heart, at least he would do it over good wine.

"So I thought maybe we'd sit by the pool? It's not too noisy over there." Lucas held the door for me and took my elbow as we walked toward the pool. On the patio, he chose a double chaise with a view of the party, where the Gilles and Lisette's friends still lingered over dessert and drinks. Music played over the outdoor speakers, "Dark Paradise" by Lana Del Rey, a song I'd liked in the past but now seemed a bad omen.

I settled back and crossed my legs at the ankle, holding my wine glass on my belly. Lucas sat at my side and stared at my legs for a minute without saying anything.

Oh God. Oh, fuck. It was too much. I scared him and this is where he realizes I'm a lunatic on the rebound and drops me like a hot croissant.

I took a deep breath and pasted on a smile. "So here's where I tell you to pay no attention to anything I say after sex like that."

He looked at me with furrowed brows. "Why not?"

"Because I open my mouth and bat-shit crazy things fly out." I swooped a hand through the air. "It's totally embarrassing."

He shook his head. "You shouldn't be embarrassed about what you said."

"Well, it's a little late for that, but anyway, I don't want you to think anything of it, OK? I was just, um, happy." Holy crap, could I make this any more awkward?

"Mia, come on." He hooked a hand under one calf and squeezed. "These last few days with you have my head spinning too…I don't know what to make of it. This has never happened to me before."

"Me either." I took a drink of wine. "But then again, I've never been on the rebound before."

Lucas frowned. "What do you mean by that?"

"Well, you know…we're both just coming off bad breakups. I mean, I was supposed to get married last week, and you recently broke up with someone you dated for three years. I think we were both due for a fun little fling." Gulp. Gulp.

"This isn't a rebound thing, Mia. At least not for me." He looked so hurt I nearly dropped the charade.

"OK, maybe not rebound exactly, but whatever it is, I know it's just for fun. I mean, it's not real." I went to lift my wine to my lips again, but he grabbed the glass, set it on the ground next to his, and took my hands.

"I feel something real for you, Mia."

I winced. "Please don't say that just because I tripped and 'I love you' fell out. You don't have to."

"I'm not just saying that. Look, I keep telling myself that I shouldn't be taking advantage of you, that you're vulnerable and not in any state to make good decisions. But...I can't stop the way I feel. I want to be with you." He was serious. I could see it. Hear it. Feel it.

I sighed, dropping the pretense. "Lucas, you're not taking advantage of me. I've known what I was doing every step of the way." I swallowed, finding my throat tight. "And I know it has to end when I leave, so it's hard."

"Why does it have to end when you leave?" Lucas squeezed my hands. "I live in New York. Detroit's not that far. Are you saying you never want to see me again?"

"Of course I want to see you again. But what good would it do?"

He shook his head. "You lost me."

"We want different things, Lucas. I know you'll think I'm crazy to think so far ahead, but I want to get married someday. I want a family. I want a home, in one place, wherever that place may be. You don't want those things."

"But you're talking about a 'someday' in the far future. You don't even know when that will be."

I shook my head. "It's not that far in the future to me. I'll be twenty-eight this year, Lucas. I'd like to start a family by the time I'm thirty. That's in two years."

"Why are you putting deadlines on your life that way?" Anger and frustration colored his words. "Why can't you just enjoy life as it comes?"

"It's not a deadline, Lucas, it's a dream. And it's my life, OK? Just because you don't want those things doesn't make it wrong for me to want them."

"I never said it was wrong to want them, I just—" Lucas let go of one hand and rubbed the back of his neck. "God, I don't understand why you have to obsess over the future like that. You don't know what that will be—no one does. Life could end tomorrow. We can enjoy what we have now without having to take out a mortgage or name our kids or buy a dog."

I knew what he meant, but I couldn't live that way. "I understand what you're saying. But for me, what we have now needs space to grow into something else, something bigger." I put a hand to my chest. "I know it's hard for you to understand, but making that kind of commitment to someone is important to me. It doesn't have to be today or tomorrow, but it has to be possible."

Lucas sighed and shut his eyes briefly. "I just want to spend more time with you, Mia. I've never felt this knocked out by anyone."

"Really?" I took a time-out from Strong and let Flattered have a moment.

"Yes. You're amazing. I mean, aside from your insane drive to plan out every minute detail of your life from birth to death, you're the most fun person I've ever been with. And you're beautiful and smart and funny and *Christ*, you're hot in bed."

Oh yeah. Flattered was killing it. "And in the kitchen?"

He smiled sideways at me. "And in the kitchen. And the living room. And the shower, the villa, and the orchard."

The orchard. Fuck. My body shivered involuntarily.

He took my hand again. "Mia, I can be my real self with you like I never have with anyone else. In every way."

I knew exactly what he meant because I felt it too, but I wasn't hearing what I needed to hear. To avoid pressing a hopeless point or dissolving into tears again, I made a joke. "You're just happy I let you tie me up."

"No, I'm not. Well, yes I am, but that's not all I meant." He tipped his head from side to side. "I guess I'd be lying if I said the sex had *nothing* to do with it—I love that you're not scared of anything."

"I'm not with you," I said honestly. "Not for one minute."

"And I love that you're so passionate and willing and vocal about sex—I've never been with anyone like you who knows just what she wants and isn't afraid to ask for it. Or take it." He ran a hand up my leg. "Being with you is…" He shook his head. "I can't describe it. But oh my God."

I smiled ruefully. "Don't worry, the sex has a lot to do with it for me, too. I think you've spoiled me for life."

He squeezed my thigh. "Good."

I lay back again, crossing my arms over my chest. Talking about sex wasn't going to help us—we both liked it too much. The chemistry was too spectacular. "No, Lucas, it's not good. I'm all caught up in the way I feel about you, but we want different things—maybe not sexually—but ultimately. In life. And neither of us is willing to change." I dug my nails into my upper arms.

Tell me I'm wrong. Deny it. Please.

Lucas spoke softly. "I just don't see why we can't try to make this work without knowing what the end result will be. I think I could make you happy."

My insides crumbled. God, he made this so fucking hard. "I know you could, Lucas. But I'm done with casual dating. I'm not interested in just fooling around—I need to know that we're moving toward something. And maybe that makes me crazy, considering what I just went through, but that's me."

266

My lower lip quivered and my stomach churned. "And it isn't you."

Say you'll change. Say I'm worth it.

But he said nothing. A full minute ticked by with Lucas staring at his hand on my leg in silence.

"Am I wrong?" I asked softly.

He shook his head. "I don't want to make any promises to you that I can't keep. It wouldn't be fair, especially after what you've been through."

"Then this is what we'll have." I swung my legs off the chair. The deluge was coming, and I wanted to leave him so I could go cry it out alone, but he caught my arm.

"Please, Mia." His voice cracked, and it nearly shattered me. "Don't go."

"I have to, Lucas. I came here to get stronger, to start enjoying life on my own again. Instead I fell for you, and knowing that I have to walk away is enough to break me. Let me go, please."

Don't let me go. Please.

But he did.

Chapter Twenty

I went upstairs, undressed, and got ready for bed. I'd like to say that I remained strong and sure of my decision, but the truth is I blubbered like a baby for the next three hours straight. Had I made a huge mistake? How could he have let me go without fighting for me? Where was he now, back at the party? My stomach heaved. I could hear the music perfectly from here through the open window. Was he dancing with some other girl? Speaking French in her ear? Would he not sleep in this bed tonight, the one I thought of as *ours*? Jumping up, I shut the window, closed the curtain and buried myself under the covers. I tugged at my hair and hunched up my knees, soaking the pillow with tears.

Eventually I fell asleep, because I woke up when the bedroom door creaked open. I opened one eye and watched Lucas undress, my thighs clenching tight at the sight of him removing his suit and tie. I loved his body, the sinew and lean muscle, the smooth skin, the easy way he moved. He draped his clothing over a chair, and went into the bathroom. My heart was thudding fast but I tried to feign sleep. I couldn't handle any more talking.

The bathroom door opened and Lucas got into bed. I kept my breathing deep and even, and I lay facing away from him, my hands beneath my cheek. *How is he lying? Facing me? Away from me? On his back? Is he looking at me? Will he touch me?* I couldn't even decide if I wanted him to or not.

Actually, that's a big lie. I wanted him to touch me. I wanted to be with him one more time and know for certain it was the last time. It might not do me any good—in fact, it would probably do me harm—but if he reached for me, I'd go to him.

After a few minutes of silence ticked by, I figured he'd gone to sleep and a shuddering sigh escaped me. *That's it, then. It's over.*

A moment later, the mattress shifted and I felt soft lips on my shoulder. Resting there, sending chills down my spine. A hand crept onto my stomach. A warm body cradled mine from behind, and I closed my eyes in bliss.

A hand brushed the hair from my neck and the lips swept up and pressed kisses below my ear. The hand on my belly slid under my tank top and closed over one breast. My nipple responded to his touch, and he caressed it lightly. Then the other. I felt his erection stiffen and swell on my lower back, and my hand moved to it automatically, stroking it through his boxers. When his breathing grew ragged, I rolled onto my back and looked up at him.

The room was so dark I couldn't read his eyes, but I sensed his sadness as well as his desire, and I knew exactly how he felt, how one could feed the other. "Lucas. What are we doing?"

"I don't know," he whispered, brushing the hair off my forehead. "I told myself not to touch you, I know it isn't fair. But I'm lying over there and I can smell your skin. And just like that I could taste you."

"I want you to touch me." I reached for the hem of my tank top and drew it over my head, and he put his mouth on my breasts. Flinging my arms over my head, I arched beneath him, wanting to offer him every inch of my skin to taste.

He kissed his way down my belly and pulled my underwear off. "Should I get a condom?"

"No." I reached for him and pulled him up on top of me. "I want to feel you. Closer."

We went slow this time, savoring every kiss, every touch, every hushed word and breath. We ran our hands and mouths over each other's bodies, committing to memory the curve of a shoulder or hip. The arc of a back or neck. The lines of muscle and bone.

Frenched

Finally, with our eyes locked on each other, our hands clasped above my shoulders, he slid inside me and moved in deep, unhurried strokes until I was breathless and trembling, torn between trying to make it last and telling him to fuck me hard and fast, to make me come, to fill me up. My mind wanted to slow time down while my body longed to race toward release.

Not really a bad problem to have.

Eventually, my body won out and I begged shamelessly for what I wanted.

He gave me everything.

By the time we exhausted ourselves, soft pink light was glowing through the filmy curtains. I fell asleep on a pillow damp with tears, begging the sun not to rise.

#

Lucas and I spoke very little on the way back to Paris. I fell asleep on the train, waking up only once or twice to see Lucas staring out the window, a grave expression on his face. I knew he didn't want to say goodbye today, but I think he understood why I had to. In fact, I was debating putting in a call to Erin and seeing if her mom would help me change my ticket so I could go home tomorrow. Staying here three more days knowing that Lucas was nearby would be too difficult—I didn't trust myself to stay away from him.

Several times I had to squeeze my eyes shut to combat the tears that were constantly threatening to undo me. *Just wait until you get to your room. You can hole up, drink wine, and eat pain au chocolat until it's time to go. Or until you burst, whatever comes first.*

When the train pulled into the Paris station, I congratulated myself on making it back to the city without breaking down. *See? You got this. Now you just have to stay strong for twenty more minutes.*

If only that twenty minutes didn't include saying goodbye.

"You don't have to see me back to the Plaza," I told Lucas once we got off the TGV at the Gare de Lyon. "I know which Metro to take and I can find my way." I pulled up the handle on my suitcase and looked around for a sign to the line I needed, but really I was just trying to avoid looking at him, and he knew it.

"Mia, please. Look at me."

Reluctantly I met his eyes, and felt my resolve weaken. I looked away. "I can't, Lucas. It's too hard."

He sighed. "So this is it? I can't even see you again before you leave?"

I shook my head, not trusting my voice.

"I want to tell you what you want to hear so badly."

"But you can't." It was a dare.

272

"I just don't want to lie to you. Goddammit, will you please just look at me?" He put his hand under my chin and forced me to meet his eyes. They were angry and sad. "You can walk away. I won't stop you. But I'm telling you now that I have feelings for you and I don't want you to go. I know a relationship wouldn't be easy, I know we're different, and I know long distance isn't much fun. But Jesus, Mia." His dark eyes glittered. "Can't we at least try?"

My throat was so tight, I thought my voice would come out in a squeak. "I want to say yes, Lucas. But I'm scared. I pinned all my hopes on one person before, and he let me down. I'm not saying you're anything like him," I said when I saw his eyes flash in outrage, "I'm just telling the truth. And you know what?" I took a deep breath. "You are too, and I'm grateful for that. I have no desire to make you say anything that you don't want to, or make any promise you can't keep. And maybe I still have some healing to do." My eyes finally filled, and a few tears spilled over.

His beautiful mouth was set in a straight line as he wiped them away with his thumbs. "I know you do. I'm sure this is too much for you, and I'm sorry." He took his hands from my cheeks and ran them down over his face. "I really wish I'd have met you under different circumstances, Mia Devine. But I'm not sorry about anything we've done. Only that this is hurting you."

"I'm not sorry, either," I whispered. People rushed by us and maybe they even looked at us with pity—what's sadder than a train station farewell?—but I didn't care. I threw my arms around Lucas and held him tight, breathing in the scent of lavender and the olive grove, which still clung to his clothing and skin. My stomach was churning. Was I making the right decision?

"You know my number." His voice was shaky but his arms around my back were firm. "I won't bother you, but if you want me for anything…"

I nodded, and he released me, took my face in his hands and kissed me full on my trembling lips.

"You go first," he whispered.

"OK." I sniffed and offered a small, watery smile before walking off in what I really, really hoped was the right direction. I never did see a sign.

No luck.

"Mia?"

I turned to see him unable to hide that grin I adored.

"You're going the wrong way." He pointed in the opposite direction, where I finally saw the fucking sign.

"Oh." With all the dignity I could muster (not much), I wheeled my suitcase around and passed him again. "Thank you. For everything."

"It was my pleasure," he said, watching me. "Every moment."

Frenched

I forced myself to keep going.
It was the hardest thing I've ever done.

#

I rode the train to my stop with one arm over my aching stomach and the other hand cradling my forehead. I was glad there was an open seat because my legs felt too shaky to stand. Staring at my suitcase between my knees, I reminded myself to breathe and tried not to think about Lucas sitting alone on a different train, going back to that little apartment I loved.

I'd never see it again.

My lower lip quivered. I closed my eyes and begged God to get me back to my hotel room without another tidal wave of tears. It was one thing to cry alone in your room or even in front of a friend, but crying alone in a crowd was not something I needed to cross off a list. Jeez, hadn't my pride suffered enough?

Barely holding myself together, I kept an eye out for the stop I wanted, got off when I was supposed to, and dragged my suitcase into the Plaza.

Inside the elevator, a few heaving gasps escaped, and then a wrenching sob. Squeezing my eyes shut, I tried holding my breath, which just caused my shoulders to jerk. When the doors opened on my floor,

I bolted through them and tore down the hallway, weeping openly.

I dug through my purse for the key card and shoved it in and out. When the green light flashed, I pushed the door open and burst into the room, prepared to throw myself onto the bed and wail for hours.

Imagine my surprise when I found that I was not alone.

Chapter Twenty-One

I gasped. "Tucker, what the hell are you doing here? You scared me half to death!" The door slammed behind me and I moved deeper into the room, one hand over my knocking heart.

Shirtless, Tucker rose from where he was sitting at the desk, and I panicked for a second, wondering if there was any evidence of my fling with Lucas in the room.

For *one* second. Then I remembered that I didn't have to care. *Fuck him. What the hell is this?*

"Hello to you too." Tucker came toward me, and took my suitcase from my hand, moving it to the side before giving me a hug. "It's nice to see you. Are you all right?"

I was so stunned, I let myself be hugged and half-hugged him back before I could stop myself. *I forgot how tall he is.* His embrace pulled me up on tiptoe. His bare, muscular chest should have turned me on, but it didn't.

I backed out of his arms. "Nice to see me? Are you kidding? What the hell is this, Tucker?" Stepping around him, I went to the desk and set down my purse. My heart was knocking hard on my ribs, and not in a good way. Something caught my eye to my left, and I noticed for the first time the huge bouquet of red roses on the coffee table. Those hadn't been there when I left. I spun around and looked at him. "What's going on?"

Tucker went over to a black garment bag on the bed, unzipped it and pulled out a white dress shirt, which he slipped on but didn't button. "I know you're surprised to see me," he said, "and probably not all that happy, but I can explain."

"I hope so." I went into the bathroom for some tissue, dried my eyes and blew my nose. Ugh, I was a mess. In the mirror, I saw Tucker appear in the bathroom doorway.

"What's wrong? Why the tears?"

I scowled. "As if you care."

"I do, Mia. Come here, please." He took my arm and led me out of the bathroom and over to the couch, where he gestured for me to sit. In addition to the flowers on the table were chocolates and a black box with a white ribbon. The box said Chanel. *Holy shit. What the fuck is going on?* Tucker sat next to me, but I commandeered my arm back and stuck both hands between my knees.

"Hear me out, Mia. I know you're mad, and you have every right to be, but please give me a chance to speak." I'd never heard this kind of pleading tone from Tucker before, but it only made me angrier.

"Why should I? I don't want anything from you, Tucker. Not these flowers, not gifts, not an apology." But I kept my eyes on the Chanel box. Damn if I wasn't curious what was inside.

"I know you don't want anything, and I don't blame you. What I did was unforgivable. Mia, can you at least look at me?"

I refused. In fact, I crossed my arms and swiveled away from him. He sighed and got off the couch, walked around the table, and dropped to his knees at my feet. To the best of my recollection, he hadn't been on his knees in front of me since his proposal. *And there's not even an audience here.*

"I panicked." He closed his eyes and held up his hands. "I know that's no excuse, but it's the truth. I panicked at the thought of such a permanent commitment, and I didn't think I was mature enough to handle it."

"And how long had you known you couldn't handle it? The doubt must have been lurking there for a while, yet you waited until we had one week to go before jetting off to Vegas and leaving me, alone and humiliated, to tell everyone!" I gestured wildly in the

279

air between us. "We could have come to this decision together, you know! I had doubts too!"

He blinked, surprise evident on his handsome face. "You did?"

"Yes, I did. But I was too caught up in planning the wedding to stop and think about them."

"We should have just eloped. Got married on the beach in Tahiti or something." Tucker reached out and rubbed my knee.

"What? No!" I jumped off the couch and skirted around him. "It wasn't the wedding that was the problem. It was *us*—you and me. We weren't right together, Tucker. I can see that now. And as much as it pains me to say this, you were right to call off the wedding. The way you did it sucked, but it was the right decision."

"What if it wasn't?" Tucker got to his feet, brushing off his charcoal pants. They looked very wrinkled for him—had he just gotten off the plane? "What if I was wrong to call it off?"

"You weren't. God, Tucker, we weren't even that in love! I mean, maybe we were once, but if you're going to marry someone, you should feel like—" I stopped. I knew how a person should feel, because I was head over heels in love with Lucas.

"Like what?" Tucker asked.

"Like you can't breathe when that person's in the room. Like you can't get close enough to them, no matter how hard you try. Like you're going to burst if you can't show that person how much you feel for them, and then you do burst—together."

"Burst?" Tucker arched a well-groomed brow.

"Burst," I confirmed. "It's called an orgasm. It happens to women too, you know, and sometimes it even happens to men and women at the same time."

"We burst." Tucker stuck his hands on his hips and looked indignant. "We burst every time."

"No. *You* burst." I pointed at his chest. "I was lucky to get an occasional rupture, but it never happened together. It didn't even feel like you cared."

Tucker's jaw protruded. "That's not fair, Mia. I had no idea you weren't being satisfied. You never said anything about it."

"How could I? As soon as you were done, you went running for the bathroom to clean up!"

"Why didn't you bring it up when we weren't actually in bed?" Tucker's face was actually going a little red.

Good, he should feel shame. "God, I don't know! It just seemed like we had a routine and you were happy with it. I didn't want to rock the boat." I put my hands on my head. "Ugh, it doesn't matter anyway, Tucker. It's over."

He reached for me, but I backed up. "Don't say that, Mia. Let me try again. I love you, and I can do better."

I threw my hands up and moaned to the ceiling. "No! This is so frustrating! We could have had this conversation two weeks ago, Tucker. But *you left*."

"I'm sorry about that, I really am. And I came all the way here to beg you for another chance." He even clasped his hands together. I wanted to slap him.

"When did you get here, anyway? Today?"

"Yes, about ten AM. Where were you?"

I looked him right in the eye. "I took a short trip to the country."

He dropped his hands. "Oh. Alone?"

I lifted my chin. That was none of his business. "Yes."

"That wasn't on your itinerary, was it?"

I almost laughed. "No. I made some...*adjustments* to the itinerary once I realized I'd be here by myself."

"Well, now I'm here." He came toward me as if he might embrace me again, and I put my hands up.

"No. If you want to stay here, that's fine. I'll go somewhere else. Or I'll go home. But we're not on this trip together, Tucker." I moved my hands back and forth between us. "Because we're not together anymore."

"Please. Please give me one more chance, Mia." He dropped to his knees again, right in front of me, and took my hips in his hands. "I'll do anything you want. You want to go to counseling? Fine, I'll go. I'll be more adventurous with you in bed. I only treated you

282

carefully because I knew I wanted you to be my wife—I thought you'd like that. I put you on a pedestal, where you belong. I see the way guys treat their women in porn, and I don't want to be that way."

I rolled my eyes. "There's a big middle ground between pedestal and porn."

"We'll figure it out, Mia. Just say we can try again, please. I want you to be my wife. I want to marry you. I want the family we talked about."

I crossed my arms. "And why will this time be different, huh? What's happened that makes now so different from two weeks ago?"

"I realized what life would be like without you. And I hated it." He looked up at me with wide blue eyes and I almost felt my foundation cracking. Then he tipped his forehead to my stomach. "I'm so sorry, baby. Please give me one more chance."

The pounding on the door startled us both.

Tucker picked his head up and looked at me funny. "Are you expecting someone?"

"No."

"Mia?" shouted a male voice through the door. My breath hitched. It sounded like Lucas, but what would he be doing here? And holy fuck, how awkward! I knew I better go answer it before Tucker did. "Just give me a second. Stay here."

I hurried over to the door, my nerves rattling. When I pulled it open, there was Lucas, looking anxious and adorable. Before I had a chance to say anything, he started in.

"OK, here's the thing. I'm not letting you go."

My heart stopped beating for a second. "What?"

He grabbed my hand. "I'm not letting you go. I'm not letting you walk out of my life without giving me a chance to make you happy."

"Lucas, I—"

"Just listen. I got all the way to my apartment on the most miserable train ride ever. I just kept thinking how you should have been beside me. The flea market's open today, and I thought, Oh, I should take her. Or I'd think, she wanted to see a castle, I need to take her to Versailles before she leaves. But then I'd realize I can't, because you won't let me. And I felt it like a punch in the gut. I couldn't breathe."

I glanced over my shoulder. "Lucas," I whispered. Actually it was more like a whimper.

"I'm not done. Because then I got home to my apartment, and it sucked. There's nothing in there that doesn't remind me of you—not my kitchen, not my couch, not my bed, not my shower. Nothing. And I realized something else—I can't let you go. I don't want to. And—"

"Mia, what's going on? Who's at the door?"

It was another one of those moments where things seemed to happen in slow motion—I knew Tucker was walking up behind me, and I bet that peacock hadn't even bothered to button his shirt—because I watched Lucas's eyes go from warm and earnest to wide and shocked. He dropped my hand, and a second later I felt another one on my shoulder.

"Babe? Who's this?"

"Uh…" Fuck! What should I say? I couldn't tear my eyes away from the trainwreck that was Lucas realizing who was in my hotel room and piecing together why. He was jumping to all the wrong conclusions, but my tongue was stuck in the same sludge my brain was. I couldn't think, couldn't speak.

"I'm nobody," Lucas answered, his eyes sweeping back to me. "Just a friend. Mia, I thought you might like to have coffee but I can see you're busy. This must be Tucker?"

Jesus, he was covering for me. The sludge thickened with shame.

"Yes, I am. Tucker Branch. And you are?" Tucker, a note of reservation in his voice, held out a hand toward Lucas.

"Lucas Fournier. Mia has talked a lot about you."

Gulp.

"Well." I could hear the pleasure in Tucker's tone. "Good things, I hope. Although I can't imagine why. I haven't done much to be proud of lately. But I'm going to remedy that." And the bastard put an arm around me. "How did you meet her?"

285

Get out! Get out of his arms! You're giving Lucas the wrong impression! But I was stuck inside Tucker's iron grasp, and all I could do was plead with Lucas with my eyes to go away and let me explain later.

"Uh, I'm a bartender. Mia came into my bar the first night she was here and I recommended some sights to her." Lucas's voice was wooden and hollow.

"Nice. Which sights?"

"Père LaChaise cemetery. Notre-Dame." He looked at me as he said it, and all the flirty, romantic tension that had simmered while we spent that first day together hit me full force. My stomach muscles clenched, and I wanted nothing more than to throw Tucker's arms off me and hurl myself into Lucas's arms. "The Rodin museum."

The Rodin Museum.

The memory of the afternoon we spent there was enough to snap me into action. I lifted Tucker's arm off me. "Yes, and I loved all of them."

"Oh, you went already? Good, that means I won't have to go to a museum with her." Tucker laughed and ruffled my hair. "She loves that moldy old stuff, but I don't. Well, thanks for being kind to her. Mia, do you want to open your gift now? It's from Chanel," Tucker singsonged.

I'd never been more annoyed with him. My face was burning with indignation. "No. Tucker, just wait, please. Lucas—"

But he was already backing away from the door. "No problem, Mia. I can see you're fine now. I'll let you go." And he turned away from me and stormed down the hall toward the elevators.

Chapter Twenty-Two

No! Don't go!

I put my hands to my head and breathed deeply, furious at myself, at Tucker, at the universe for the poor timing of everything that just happened—Tucker's fucking apology, Lucas showing up at my door, Tucker deciding to play the role of concerned fiancé all of a sudden. I slammed the door and whirled on him.

"You can't just come in here and expect to have me back!" I yelled. "You don't deserve a second chance!"

"Everyone deserves a second chance, Mia." His face darkened. "Who was that, anyway? Did something happen between you two?"

"He's just a friend," I said miserably. "He was here for me when you weren't." And he'd come back for me. He said he couldn't breathe without me, and he wasn't going to let me go.

But he had.

Because he thought you were back with Tucker! screamed the inner voice, which suddenly seemed to be on Lucas's side.

"Well, I'm here now." Tucker came to me and put his hands on my shoulders. "And I promise I'm going to make up for all the time I wasn't." He put his lips on mine, and it kind of repulsed me. I turned my cheek.

"Don't."

Tucker sighed. "How about opening your gift?" He went over to the table and picked up the Chanel box. "I went straight to the store, didn't even come to the hotel first. I thought you'd be here, and I wanted to have it to surprise you with." He brought the box to me. "I know it can't make up for what I put you through, but I just wanted to show you that I'm thinking of you and I'm going to work hard to win you back."

I sighed. Backing up, I sat on the bench at the foot of the bed. He set the box on my lap and I opened it to find a darling rectangular handbag in pale pink with darker pink metallic cross-stitching and Chanel's signature interlocking C's on the flap and gold chain strap. It was beautiful.

But I didn't want it.

"Tucker, it's very pretty, and it's a nice gift. But I can't accept it."

"Why not?"

"Because we're not getting back together."

"Don't say that, Mia. Please." He dropped down in front of me again. "We had so many things planned. I still want them all. It was just cold feet, I swear. I was a fool, and I'll never take you for granted again. I can make you happy, Mia."

I looked into his face, the one that only weeks ago had still set my heart aflutter. The one I thought I'd want to look at every morning, every night, because it was so handsome. But the blue eyes just looked cool to me, and the neatly trimmed hair was all wrong. The perfect symmetry of his face seemed uninteresting, and even the tall, muscular body held no allure. I glanced down at his bare chest and felt only sadness—for Lucas, for myself, and even for Tucker, with this misguided attempt at winning me back.

He was doing it the best way he knew how, with flowers and money and expensive gifts, but it wasn't what I wanted. I wanted him to say, Of course I'll go to a museum with you, of course I'll take you to the flea market, and here's that book I was telling you about…

I wanted Lucas.

"Tucker, the answer is still no. You were right to call off the wedding. We won't make each other happy."

"You're not even giving me a chance," he whined. "I came all the way here for you."

"I'm sorry about that, but the answer is still no." Now that I'd found my voice, it was firm. "You can stay here if you want, but I'll find another room to stay in."

"How will you afford that?" he snapped, popping to his feet.

"I'll stay somewhere else, then." Suddenly I was scared he'd stick me with the bill for this suite so far. How the hell would I pay for it?

"Fine." Tucker finally began buttoning his shirt. "But I think you'll change your mind. You'll realize that no one can treat you better than I can, Mia. You'll miss everything that my money can buy. You could have a great life, an easy life."

God, had I really given him that crass an impression of me? That I cared so much about wealth?

"I don't want an easy life. I want a happy life. And it's not with you." Rising, I glanced around the suite. "I need some time to pack."

He dropped his arms from the buttons. "Don't go," he said, his approach changing again. "Take some time. Think it over."

"I'll be doing plenty of thinking, Tucker. You can bet on that."

He looked pleased, probably because he figured no woman would actually turn a life with him down once she pondered it some more. "Good."

"Can I ask you to leave me alone while I pack?"

"Oh, uh…I guess so. I'll go down to the restaurant. How will I know if—I mean when—you've changed you mind?" He flashed his Millionaire Heartbreaker smile at me.

Give it a rest, Tucker. I'm not that girl anymore.

"If I don't come back here tonight, then I'll get in touch back in Detroit."

He paled for a moment. "You're going home?"

"I don't know yet, Tucker. I don't know what I'm doing." Damn, that was the truth. Once I packed my bags, I had no clue where to go. Try to find Lucas? Just fly home? Find a new (cheaper) hotel?

While I took my big suitcase from the closet, Tucker used the bathroom and finished dressing. Before he left, he kissed my hand and said, "Everyone deserves a second chance, Mia. Even me."

Was that true? As I folded clothes and repacked shoes and toiletries, I wondered if I was being too hard on Tucker. After all, he seemed earnest. He'd called me last week, then he flew all the way here, he was saying all the right things—well, most of the right things. He was young and handsome and successful, and he said he loved me. He was sorry for what he had done. He even wanted the same things that I did. Was I crazy to turn down a second chance?

As quickly as I had the thought, it dissipated. Because even if it was true that he deserved one—and the jury was still out there—I didn't want a life with Tucker anymore. I didn't love him.

I loved Lucas.

Flopping back onto the bed, I stared at the ceiling and felt that ache in my chest, the one that threatened to undo me every time I thought about never seeing Lucas again. But what should I do? I needed to talk to someone. Rolling onto my side, I picked up the phone and dialed Coco's cell.

"Hello?"

"Hi." I barely got the word out before the sobs began.

"Hi! Oh my God, what's wrong?"

"Everything. Everything's so fucked up, Coco. I don't know what to do." I lay back and felt hot tears leak from the corners of my eyes.

"Tell me everything, sweetie."

I took a breath and launched into the entire story from Paris to Vaucluse and back again, ending with finding a repentant Tucker in my suite.

She gasped. "You've gotta be fucking kidding me!"

"No. He was here, shirtless and sorry and bearing gifts," I said glumly.

"Shirtless?"

"He was changing. And then right in the middle of his big I'm Sorry For Being Such An Asshole speech, Lucas knocks on the door and tells me he can't let me go."

"Oh my God, Mia. This is like a soap opera!"

"I know. And before he has a chance to finish what he was saying, Tucker comes over—with his shirt unbuttoned, mind you—and starts acting like we're back together. And I didn't know what to do!" Fresh tears spilled. "Now Lucas probably thinks I took Tucker back, but I didn't! I want Lucas, but I can't have him!" I was crying so hard, I couldn't even see, and my nose was running like a four-year-old's.

"OK, shhhhhh, let's talk this out," Coco soothed. "Everything's going to be OK."

"How?" I wailed.

"We'll figure it out, honey. God, I wish Erin was here. She's better at thinking this stuff through than I am, but I'll try to think of what she would say. All right. First, do you want Tucker back?"

"No." I was positive about that.

"Are you sure? Even if he really is serious about wanting to change his ways and try again?"

"Even then. I don't love him anymore. And you know what?" I sniffed as the realization hit me. "I forgive him completely. I'm not angry anymore, and I know he did the right thing. Maybe the way he did it was shitty, but even so. I wouldn't have had the strength to call it off, and I'm glad he did."

"OK, that's good. No anger, plus forgiveness, is progress. Now what about Lucas?"

I sighed. "I think I'm in love with him. For real."

"You do?"

I smiled through my tears. "Yes. I do, I love him."

"How do you think he feels?"

"I'm not sure. I mean, he didn't say he loved me or anything, but he sort of got interrupted right in the middle of what sounded like a promising speech. But Coco, he doesn't want to get married. He doesn't want a family."

"How do you know that?"

"Because he told me. Even before we admitted having feelings for each other, he said he never wants to get married. And even afterward, when we talked about the way we felt, he said he couldn't promise anything."

"Well, what the hell would he have to promise?"

I blinked. "What do you mean?"

"I mean, you just met this guy, like, six days ago."

"Five."

"Right, five. And you fell for each other right away, so fast you probably didn't even have time to breathe."

I exhaled. "Yes. Breathing here has been difficult."

"And he's telling you he has feelings for you, feelings he's never had for anyone before, even though he dated someone for years. And he's willing to try to make it work between you, even though it would be long distance and he knows you hate to fly, which means he would be coming to see you a lot."

"Well, yes, I guess so, but—"

"And you're expecting him to process all those feelings, tell you where you guys will be a year from now, or even six months from now, and also make a promise to you that he'll consider marriage before you guys have even tried dating?"

When she said it that way, I felt foolish and demanding. But weren't my feelings valid? "I wasn't asking him to propose or anything. I was just asking if he'd reconsider his viewpoint on marriage. That's fair, isn't it?"

"I don't know, Mia. I mean, I love you, you know I do. And I want you to have everything you've ever wanted. But your demands here sound a little extreme."

"They're not demands, they're dreams!" Coco sounded like Lucas, and it was making me angry. "I'm allowed to have dreams."

"Calm down, Mia. Yes, you're allowed to have dreams. But if all that mattered about your dream was getting married and having a nice house and family, frankly you could just marry Tucker and be done with it. But I know you—you want more."

She was right. I did want more. Chewing my bottom lip, I tried to find words to defend my point of view and couldn't.

"Look," she went on, "remember when we first had the crazy scheme to start our own business? We had all those ridiculous plans and imagined ourselves in a luxury penthouse office designing gala after gala for hoity-toity people with deep pockets. But it didn't go that way, did it?"

"Not at first," I admitted. "But what does that have to do with this?"

"Because our dream had to adjust to real life. We took any gig we could get, and we worked from your apartment, and we didn't make any real money for a year and a half. And frankly, we didn't know for sure if we'd ever make money—we had faith in our talent and the willingness to put in the work, but that was it. There was no promise of success."

"But we had it all thought out," I said, even though I was beginning to understand the connection. "We mapped out a business plan in minute detail. We had projections. I had lists! I have nothing to go on with Lucas. Nothing! That terrifies me."

"You have everything you need to go on, Mia." The edge was gone from her voice now. "You have your feelings, you have his willingness to try, you have fanfuckingtastic sex."

"We do." Just thinking about it made my blood warm.

"Well, then stop it with the projections and the fucking lists. I think he deserves a little more faith. I think you should give him a chance. After all, maybe you won't even want to marry him after dating for a while. How can you know for certain how you'll feel in the future?"

"God, Coco. Are you really taking his side?" I was half teasing, but she answered me seriously.

"I'm on your side, and you know it. I would never tell you to do this if I thought it wasn't what you really wanted. But I can hear it in your voice, Mia. You want him. And there's no reason you can't have him. If this thing between you two turns out to be as amazing as it sounds, then you'll find a way to make it work between you. Forget about marriage and family and just get to know each other better. Fall in love completely. Let fate take over."

Fate again. "You really believe in that?"

"I do. Everything happens for a reason, Mia. You know I have a sense about these things, and I've always felt you were supposed to be in Paris this week. I just didn't know why until now. Go find him."

My stomach flipped. Could I really do this? I was scared, but the thought of embarking on an unknown journey with Lucas was exciting too. Anything was possible. "OK. I will."

She squealed in my ear. "Good girl! Call me when you can, OK? Erin's still planning on picking you up Tuesday, so let me know if anything changes."

"Like if I decide to move to Paris?"

"Don't even kid about that," she said seriously. "We have a business here to run and I'm lost without you. Get your derrière back here on Tuesday."

We hung up, and I sat on the bed for a moment. My heart was beating way too fast. I put one hand over it and breathed in and out. A million thoughts raced through my head—I needed a plan, a list. Yes, that was it. I could still hear Coco admonishing me to stop it with the fucking lists, but they comforted me, and I needed something that felt familiar right now.

To Do List For Turning Life Upside Down

1) Accept Tucker's apology. Say goodbye.
2) Find Lucas. Declare love.
3) Find a place to stay. (If all goes well with #1, perhaps this will take care of itself.)
4) Have sex with Lucas.
5) Do it again. Many times. For three days straight.

Locking myself in the bathroom in case Tucker decided to show up again, I showered and changed, throwing the pink sweater Lucas remembered from the cemetery over my shoulders. As my hair dried, I finished packing and went over my list again and again. Item one made me a little queasy, but items two through five put a grin on my face every time.

God, I loved lists. I'd never fucking stop.

With one last look around the suite to make sure I hadn't forgotten anything, I pulled the door open and charged out with no regrets.

Well, maybe one.

That Chanel bag was adorable.

Chapter Twenty-Three

"You're making a mistake." Tucker set down his coffee cup and looked me dead in the eye.

"That may be," I said, exhaling, "but it's my mistake to make."

He stared at his hand on the cup handle. "Tell me what you want to hear. I'll say it."

"That you respect my decision and you'll leave me alone. That you'll find someone else and treat her better from the start." I put my hand on his wrist. "That you'll love someone more than you loved me. And you'll show her that."

Tucker looked up at me, and I took my hand away. "I still love you. And I'm sorry."

"I accept your apology. And I'm not angry."

Nodding slowly, he looked so miserable I almost felt bad. Almost.

"A word of advice, Tucker. Don't post shit about your bad behavior on social media. It's tacky."

His fair complexion flushed. "God. My friends are such assholes."

"I'd say they share the blame. Goodbye, Tucker."

He said nothing, just kept staring at his coffee, likely in shock that he'd been rejected. Poor guy had probably never had that happen before.

First time for everything.

#

I contemplated leaving my luggage in storage at the Plaza, but in the end decided to drag it with me to The Beaver. If things went badly with Lucas, I could go straight to the airport, and if they went well…stomach clench…maybe I could go straight to his apartment.

It was raining again, so instead of traipsing through the rain to the Metro with all my stuff, I took a cab to The Beaver. It was only five o'clock, and I had no idea what time his shift started, but if he wasn't there, I'd build a fucking campfire and wait. I'd wait all night long for him.

Despite my confidence in the decision, my anxiety returned as soon as I saw the familiar awning and sign out front. I remembered standing in front of it the first night I was here and how much I dreaded walking in to find a whole lot of couples in love inside. And now here I was about to go in and declare my love and throw myself in Lucas's arms. *Maybe years from now we'll be telling this story to our children.*

Gah! Stop it! No children!

I paid the driver and he helped unload my bags onto the curb, then left me standing there in the rain with dripping hair and live wire nerves. Was Lucas inside? I couldn't see through the glass.

Come on, Mia. Be brave.

But I needed a minute. Filling my lungs with damp air, I inhaled and exhaled, composing myself. And for the first time, I saw there was another bar right next to The Beaver called Bar Petite. It looked more upscale, prettier, more French than Lucas's bar. In fact, if I were choosing between the two of them based on looks alone, I would have chosen the other. But I hadn't even noticed it Monday night. I hadn't even looked around, really. I'd stopped in front of The Beaver, read the sign, and barged in.

Maybe Coco is right about fate. I reached for the door.

Now, in a movie, this is a great scene. The heroine pulls open the door, rushes in looking windswept and breathless and hopelessly beautiful, and the hero strides forward and takes her in his arms. Kissing ensues.

My entrance into The Beaver? Not so much.

For one thing, the fucking door to The Beaver is heavy and I was trying to prop it open and drag two suitcases through, but my one leg wasn't strong enough to hold it. I struggled awkwardly for several minutes, feeling like every eye in the place was on me. Shit, why had I thought bringing my luggage was a good idea? My hair was dripping in my eyes and I had no free hand to wipe my face, so by the time I managed to squeeze myself and my stupid baggage through the door, I looked like a soggy mess, I couldn't even see, and one of my heavy-ass suitcases tipped over, blocking the entrance.

I reached for it, stumbling over the other bag, but managed to pull it upright and drag myself and my luggage further into the bar. *Oh my God, please don't let him be watching this.*

But he was. Of course he was, everyone was.

Once I'd wiped the rain off my face, I looked across the bar, and my heart blew up in my chest at the sight of him. His eyes were wide with surprise but I also saw a hint of amusement.

"Hi," I said.

"Hi." He stayed where he was, filling a glass at the tap.

"I'm looking for someone." I walked toward him, leaving my bags where they were.

He set the beer down in front of a customer who was watching the scene with interest. "You are?"

"Yes. And I found him. It's you."

"You sure about that?" Lucas grabbed a clean towel from under the bar and tossed it to me.

I wiped my face and nodded. "I'm positive, Lucas."

His eyes softened. "Give me one minute." He disappeared through a door at the end of the bar, and I tried to pull my bags more out of the way. In a moment, he appeared at my side. "Mia."

I had planned to apologize, explain what Tucker was doing in my room, tell Lucas I loved him and I wanted to try to make it work, but when he stood there in front of me and said my name that way, like he was afraid I wasn't real, all words failed me.

"Nothing to say? That's not like you." He smiled at me before reaching for my luggage, and shoving it out of the way underneath the bar.

"Sorry." I flapped my hands. "I'm all...flustered." *Jeez, Mia, pull yourself together.* "And wet."

He grinned. "You love the rain now, remember?"

At the memory of kissing him in the rain, my lips stretched wide. "I love it when I'm with you. And I want to be with you all the time."

"Yeah?"

I nodded, my heart swelling inside my chest. "Yeah. I'm sorry I sent you away before. Tucker showed up, and I was right in the middle of turning him down when you—"

"He wants you back?" Lucas's eyes went hard.

"He does. But I'm not interested." I took a deep breath. "I want you, Lucas. I want to try to make it work. Because I'm in love with you."

Instead of saying anything, Lucas grabbed my head in his hands and crushed his mouth to mine. He held me there for a moment, during which some random Beaver patrons applauded and whooped.

"Yeah, Lucas!" hollered a loud male voice.

I couldn't help laughing, and Lucas broke the kiss. "We have a bit of an audience," I said.

He rolled his eyes. "It's a few friends of mine."

"Introduce me?"

"Of course. Come sit down. Are you—where are you staying now?" He looked at me with concern.

I shrugged. "Not sure. Maybe you can recommend a hotel a little less expensive than the Plaza? I have three more nights here." Behind my back I crossed my fingers.

"As if I'd let you stay anywhere else but with me. You've only got three days, and I want to spend every moment possible with you. If you want me to."

I beamed, my entire body tingling. "I want you to."

He pulled me into a hug, burying his face in my wet hair. "God, I love the way you smell," he said softly. "I can't wait to get you alone."

Frenched

My thoughts exactly.

#

After a burger and fries and several glasses of wine, I got in a cab with Lucas's keys in my pocket. He'd meet me at his apartment after his shift.

Letting myself into Lucas's apartment without him felt strange but thrilling. If I hadn't been so exhausted, I might have been tempted to snoop around a bit, try to get to know him better, but the moment I was inside, I went straight for the bed and collapsed, face planted into a pillow.

I woke up two hours later, and Lucas's bedroom clock told me it was nearly eleven. His shift ended at midnight, so I jumped out of bed and got into the shower. I wanted to be ready and waiting for him when he got home.

The moment I stepped naked under the spray, I was struck with memories so vivid my body's reaction was visceral. I had to close my eyes and lean against the wall while my head swam with sensory perceptions. Steam rising. Wet bodies sliding against one another. Hot back on cool tile. Lucas buried deep inside me.

Oh, fuck.

I was so turned on I nearly lost myself to it. Only the thought of Lucas coming home soon propelled me to grab the shampoo, wash my hair, soap up and rinse off as quickly as I could.

When I was dry, I rubbed my entire body with lotion and blow dried my hair. Praying he wouldn't get home early, I set it in some large Velcro rollers for a little lift and went into the bedroom to dress.

Not that I'd be wearing much to answer his knock.

From my suitcase, which I'd set on the bench under the window, I pulled my Aubade lingerie. I slid the panties up my legs and checked my reflection in the mirror. Black and lacy, they sat like tight boy shorts on my hips but were actually a thong in the back. I turned around to check out my ass and grinned when I thought about Lucas's reaction to it. Then I slipped my arms into the bra and reached behind me to clasp it. Cups trimmed with white lace tied together between my breasts, and I imagined Lucas unraveling the little black satin bow.

With his teeth.

In the bathroom, I put on the barest of makeup—a little concealer, some eyeliner, and mascara. Skipping the lip liner altogether, I filled in my lips with coconut lip balm and rubbed them together. After pulling the rollers from my hair, I tipped my head forward and messed it up. I wanted to look a little like I'd just come from bed, even though that's exactly where I hoped I was headed. I lit the candles on the coffee table and found a few extra ones in a kitchen cupboard, which I placed on the nightstands in the bedroom.

There. Mood set.

I was just pulling on my black heels when I heard the knock. With one last look in the mirror, I turned off all the lights and headed for the door.

"Yes?" I called before opening it. Best to make sure it was really him before opening the door in lingerie and heels.

"It's me."

It's you.

I turned the lock and opened the door. "Hi, you."

His jaw dropped. "Oh my God."

After a moment of stunned silence, he came at me, kicking the door shut behind him. I laughed as he swept me off my feet and carried me like a baby straight for the couch, where he lay me down on my back and stood up. "Jesus Christ. Let me look at you."

I propped myself on my elbows and bent my knees, widening them a little, enjoying the way his chest heaved inside his shirt as his eyes traveled slowly down my body and back up again.

"Fuck," he breathed. "I have never seen anything like you in all my life. I could look at you all night."

I grinned. "No, you couldn't."

He groaned. "You're right. I couldn't."

I reached out and stroked him through his pants. He was already hard. "And I wouldn't want you to."

"Ah." He grabbed my wrist. "That feels so fucking good, but I want to talk for a minute."

I sat up, swinging my feet to the floor and bringing my other hand to his zipper. "Let's talk later."

He groaned again. "You're killing me. Just wait one minute." He took both my hands in his and pulled me to my feet. "I want to tell you something."

"Lucas, it's OK." I slipped my hands around his waist. "I'm not asking you to say anything, to make any promises. I just want to be with you." I tipped my chin up and kissed his lips.

"Mia. I want to make you a promise right now. Listen." He put one hand to my face. "I realized a lot of things this afternoon when I thought I might never see you again."

"Like what?" I asked, resting my cheek in the palm of his hand.

"Like I'm in love with you. And I can't let you get away. And I'm a fool to tell you I'll never do something when I have no idea what the future holds. I changed my mind. Anything is possible for us."

My entire body vibrated with happy energy at his words. I nodded. "Anything is possible."

Our lips came together and I welcomed his tongue into my mouth, slipping my hands beneath his shirt. His skin was hot, and I couldn't wait feel it everywhere on me.

"Mmmm, wait," he said when I tried to lift his shirt off. "I'm not done looking at you."

He walked me backward until my legs hit the couch and I sat down, looking up at him through my lashes. "What is it you'd like to see?"

"All kinds of things." His eyes raked over me again. "Fuck, you're hot. Do you really have to leave in three days? How am I going to get enough of you before then?"

I sat up and bracketed his legs with my knees, moving to the edge of the couch. This time he let me undo his pants. "I don't know. But I'm looking forward to watching you try. Want to watch me?"

"You know I do." He sucked in his breath as I took his cock into my mouth, an inch at a time. I used my hands and lips and tongue just the way he liked, and gasped when he put his hands in my hair.

"Yes, pull it," I whispered, licking him from base to tip, then spiraling my tongue over his smooth pink head. He grasped two fistfuls of my hair and pulled tight, and I dug my fingers into his hips and yanked him into me, deep, right to the back of my throat.

He groaned and held my head where he wanted it, thrusting into my mouth, and I loved the way he took control. I could feel myself getting hotter and wetter and more turned on with every push between my lips.

Suddenly he pulled all the way out and shoved my shoulders back. "I have to taste you. Now." He dropped to his knees on the floor in front of me and yanked me toward him so my ass hung off the edge of the couch. I reached behind me to grab the back of it, crying out at the first stroke of his tongue against the lace panties.

"Don't you want to take them off?" I asked between pants.

"No." His fingers gripped my thighs as his mouth worked me through the lace until I could feel how soaked they were. Then he pulled them aside and flattened his tongue on my clit, pressing hard before sliding it in a slow circle. My eyes nearly popped out of my head watching him devour me in the candlelight.

"Oh my God," I moaned, reaching down to slide one hand into his hair.

He looked at me, but I could only hold his gaze for about five seconds until my head dropped back and my eyes closed in utter ecstasy.

"Yes," he breathed. "Come for me. I want to watch you." He reached up and untied the bow between my breasts, and the bra fell open. "Touch yourself."

Frenched

I moved my hand to one breast, squeezing it before twisting the hard, tingling nipple between my fingers.

Moaning, Lucas slid two fingers into me and flicked my clit with the tip of his tongue before sucking on it hungrily. My body moved of its own accord, my hips rocking against his fingers and my hand pulling his mouth into my core. I opened my eyes again, desperately wanting to see myself come undone at his mouth.

"You want to watch me?" I whispered, the fire rising inside me. "Watch me now. Watch me come. Lucas, oh my God!" I cried as the climax rocketed through me. My feet came off the ground, knees toward my chest, toes pointed in my high heels.

The moment the pulsing bliss subsided Lucas pulled me to my feet and dragged me over to the wall between the windows. My legs were so weak I could barely stand, and I fell forward, bracing myself with both elbows. He stood behind me, and in my heels I was the perfect height.

"Spread your pretty legs." His breath was hot on my shoulder.

I did as he asked, and he moved my thong aside, teasing me with the tip of his cock at my entrance. I arched my back, desperate for him to plunge into me, but he loved to make me beg.

"You want my cock?" he asked, giving me one more inch.

"Yes," I panted. "I want it."

"Say please." Another agonizing inch.

"Please. Fuck me, I want it now." I looked over my shoulder, and maybe it was seeing my face that finally made him give in, but he gave up his teasing and shoved into me, deep and hard.

I almost laughed it felt so fucking good. My mouth fell wide open as he gripped my hips and pulled me back against his thrusts. "Yes, like that," I said. "I love the way you fuck me."

"Oh my God, I can't even last," Lucas moaned.

"Good." I arched my back even more, sticking my ass out and bringing my feet together to make myself even tighter and wetter for him.

He must have liked it because two seconds later he cursed and squeezed my hips harder with his fingers, yanking me back as he throbbed inside me. I pushed against the wall and closed my eyes, reveling in the feel of his release inside me.

When it was over, he reached up and pulled my upper body to his, an arm across my chest. "I love you." His lips rested on my shoulder. "Oh my God, I love you. I never expected this to happen."

I hugged his arm to me and smiled. "Me neither. But someone once told me Paris was magical. I guess she was right."

Frenched

Dear Mia,

Unless you cheated and peeked, you're reading this on the airplane. I know you're nervous about the flight, but don't worry. Everything is going to be fine. (God, my handwriting is really bad. Sorry. If I'd known how bad it would be, I might have typed this or something. But anyway.)

I wanted to tell you how much this entire week with you has meant to me. No seven days have ever felt so short, and yet they made me feel as if I've known you for much longer. Time is a strange thing when you're in love.

And I love you. So much.

I promise I will be back in the US within a month or so. As soon as I'm in New York, we will make plans to see each other—if you don't want to fly to see me, I will be on the first plane to Detroit. I cannot wait to hold you again. Please call me as soon as you're home to let me know you've arrived safely.

And now, since I know how much you love lists and you're feeling a little tense right now, I thought I'd write my own list for you. I hope it makes you smile.

5 Things I Will Never Forget About This Week

1) The moment you burst into the bar the night we met, looking gorgeous and insane in equal measure. I think I loved you then.

2) The way your eyes lit up when I told you the story of Abelard and Heloise, and the sweet sound of your voice when you read the letters out loud at the villa. I keep hearing this in my head: "God knows I never sought anything in you except yourself; I wanted simply you, nothing of yours."

3) The first time I kissed you, standing on the street corner on Quatre Vents—I'll walk by that spot every day and think of you.

4) The shower... I knew I loved you then.

5) Watching you sleep next to me the first night you stayed over and thinking how happy I would be waking up to you every morning.

You know what? I can't do this in five things. Because every moment with you was unforgettable, and everything about you is burned in my brain—your face, your hair, your skin, your laugh, your smile, your eyes, your hands, your lips, your legs, your smell, your taste—oh God, your taste. I'll think about all of it every single day.

Frenched

Sometimes I think about how you almost didn't come to Paris. Thank you so much for taking a chance.

All my love,
Lucas

A note from the author...

Thank you so much for reading Frenched. I'm truly grateful for your purchase, as I know there are many amazing books and authors out there.

If you enjoyed the book, please consider leaving a review on a retail site, such as Amazon, or Goodreads. Reviews are a fantastic (and free!) way to support indie authors, and they are much appreciated.

Visit **www.melanieharlow.com** to sign up for my monthly newsletter—you'll get exclusive content and the chance to win sexy books and swag from me and author friends!

Cheers,
Melanie

Frenched

ACKNOWLEDGMENTS

This book would not have been possible without the love and support of my husband. Merci, merci, merci. You endured many frozen meals, nervous meltdowns, and nights with me driven to distraction. I'm so lucky to have you. Let's go to Paris again!

Thank you to Tom Barnes for providing me with a cover I adore and tolerating my anxiety. You're awesome. Thanks to Cait Greer for formatting.

A million thanks to Angie Owens for her eagle eye and speed reading—I am beyond grateful.

To Team Harlow—I adore you! Thanks for being a part of my journey. To the ladies at AtoMR and all the bloggers who do so much to help authors, thank you so much for everything. You are amazing.

To the Wrahm Society, thanks for always being there to make me laugh, cry, think, and swoon. I want to hug every single one of you. So glad we found each other! (Estes Park, look out...)

To M. Pierce, for the kindness you've shown me. I'm so glad we are friends.

To Laurelin Paige, for helping me make Frenched so much better in every way. I have feelings, I swear.

To Gennifer Albin, for inspiring me from day one. Thanks for the hard words.

To Bethany Hagen, whose brain I would like to eat and body I'd like to inhabit. At least for a day.

To Tamara, for editing, table-flipping, and unwavering confidence. You're so beautiful.

To Kayti, for endless enthusiasm, Snow selfies, and a million laughs. You get me, sister. That's no small thing.

I love you all.

Praise for Speak Easy

"Hot gangsters, illegal nightclubs, a foul-mouthed daughter of a bootlegger, and scorching sex scenes...This book captured me from page one." -- Laurelin Paige, bestselling author of Fixed on You

"This was an incredible story packed with excitement, laced with prohibition-era ambience, a strong female heroine and swoon worthy gangsters. I could not put it down. You will not regret picking up this impeccably written book." -- Seeking Book Boyfriends Blog

Praise for Speak Low

"I thought there was NO WAY Harlow could write scenes hotter than she did in Speak Easy. I WAS WRONG!" -- Tamara Mataya, author of The Best Laid Plans

I will never pass up Historical Romance novels again. Because if half of them are as difficult to put down as these, I'm hooked. Melanie Harlow is on her way to becoming one of my absolute favorite authors. she can make me forget that I'm even reading a book. –Biblio Belles Book Blog

About the Author

Melanie Harlow likes her martinis dry, her lipstick red, and her history with the naughty bits left in. She's the author of the Speak Easy historical series as well as Frenched, the first novel in a sexy contemporary romance series. Find her sipping cocktails at posh places in Detroit or online…

Website: www.melanieharlow.com

Facebook: www.facebook.com/AuthorMelanieHarlow

Twitter: @MelanieHarlow2

Email: melanieharlowwrites@gmail.com

Pinterest: www.pinterest.com/melanieharlow2/

Tumblr: http://melanieharlow.tumblr.com/

Goodreads: www.goodreads.com/melanieharlow

Amazon: www.amazon.com/Melanie-Harlow

Made in the USA
Las Vegas, NV
28 August 2022

54228911R00184